THE RACE OF FIRE
Awakening Sand

ALSO BY THIS AUTHOR

Ella Mortimer

The Race of Fire

Awakening Sand

MY THANKS TO

My father, who was immensely proud and supportive of all his children and never had a bad word to say. He was always there and is dearly missed.

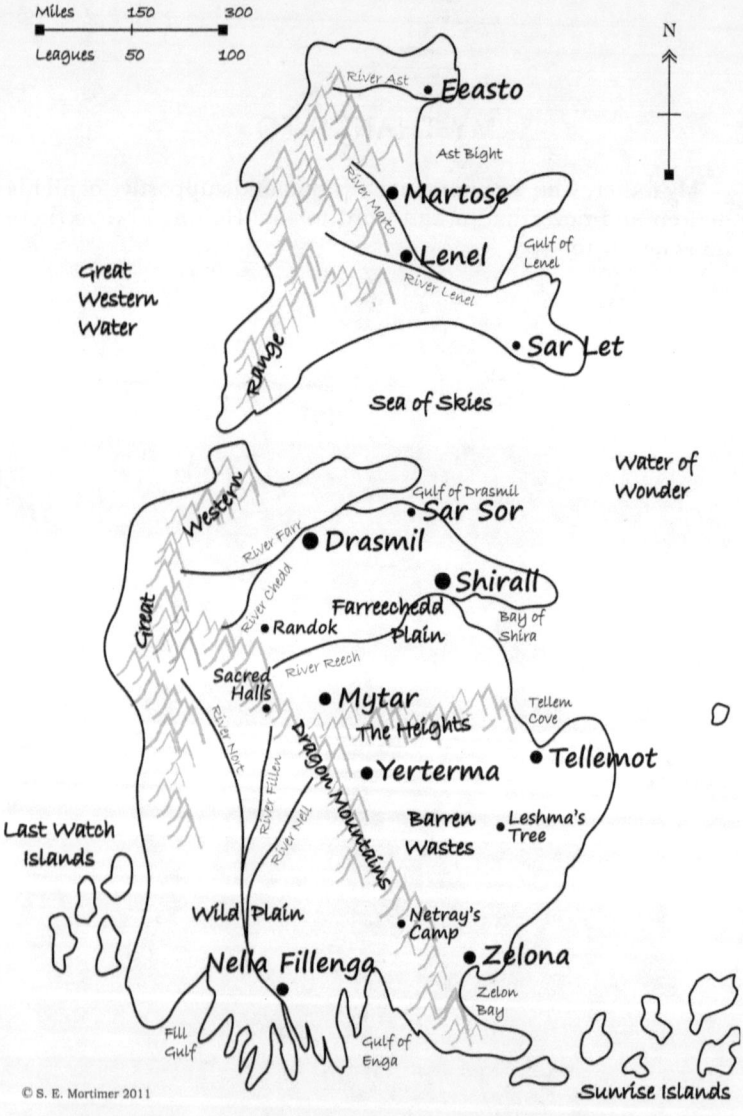

Miles 150 300
Leagues 50 100

N

River Ast • Eeasto

Ast Bight

• Martose

Great
Western
Water

River Marto

• Lenel

River Lenel

Gulf of
Lenel

• Sar Let

Sea of Skies

Water of
Wonder

Gulf of Drasmil

Western

River Farr

• Sar Sor

• Drasmil

Great

River Chedd

• Shirall

Farreechedd
Plain

Bay of
Shira

• Randok

River Reech

Sacred
Halls

Tellem
Cove

Range

• Mytar

The Heights

• Tellemot

River Nell

Dragon Mountains

River Fillen

• Yerterma

Last Watch
Islands

Barren
Wastes

• Leshma's
Tree

River Nell

Wild Plain

Netray's
• Camp

• Zelona

Nella Fillenga

Zelon
Bay

Fill
Gulf

Gulf of
Enga

Sunrise Islands

© S. E. Mortimer 2011

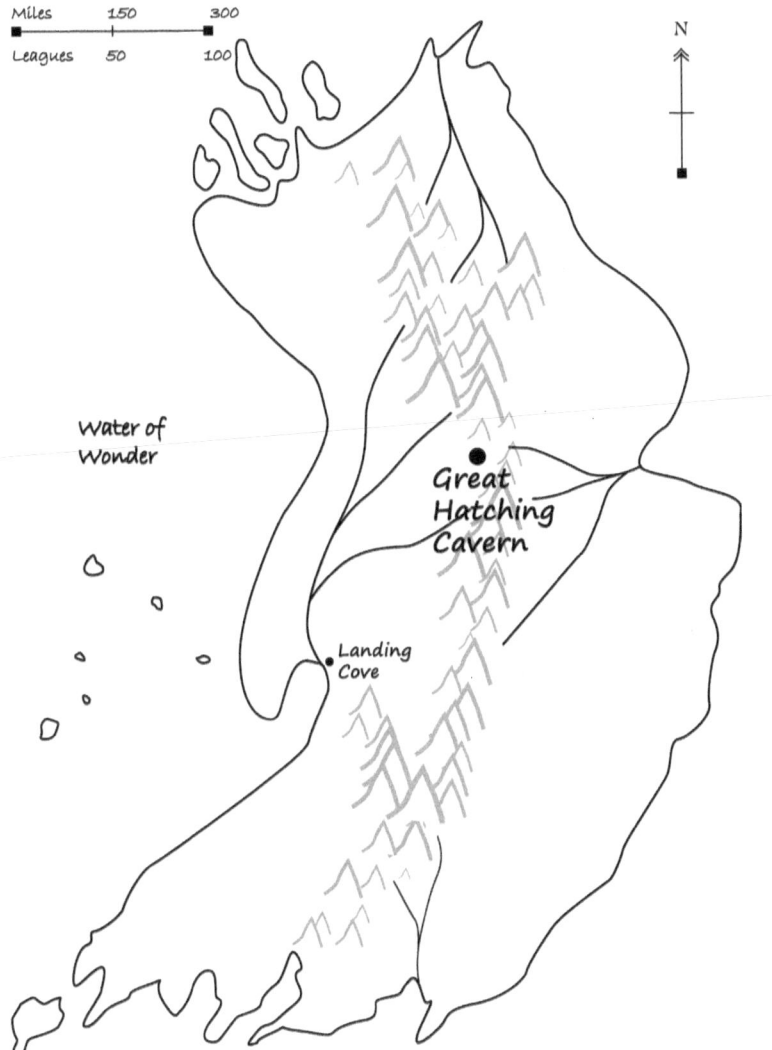

Miles   150   300

Leagues   50   100

N

Water of
Wonder

Great
Hatching
Cavern

Landing
Cove

AUTHOR'S NOTE

I was born and raised on the Central Coast of New South Wales on the east coast of Australia. This book has been with me for most of my life. The first tentative scenes were written down as a young teenager. I graduated from University as Bachelor of Arts with Honours in 1994. Then I picked up the book again. The first draft was complete by the end of 1996. The novel went through several edits until the fourth draft was complete at the end of 1999. Then life took over and the book was put on a shelf.

Ten years later, I stumbled across the Amazon Breakthrough Novel Award via a post on Facebook. There is a certain satisfaction in coming back to a book after such a long time. I was able to improve on the lives and loves of my characters in ways that I would never have been courageous enough to do when I was younger. So, I sat down to undertake this final edit. I discovered that I had in fact written two novels. So the book was split and I began work developing both halves separately. This volume is the second.

The first edition of Awakening Sand was published in 2011 under the pen name Ella Stradling. It was the name I invented as a teenager, and I never considered using my real name. The name Ella was given me by my father in honour of his favourite singer, Ella Fitzgerald and the name Stradling was used in memory of my 4th Great Grandmother, who was the last of her line. Now, I am reclaiming my books under my legal surname.

PROLOGUE
THE PROPHECY OF THE AWAKENER

In strife reborn, he will come:
The Awakener brings the truth.
His coming will be heralded,
By signs writ here forsooth.

Born in a tent of the keepers of knowledge,
Who live in the sandy places.
Proudly rekindling times once forgot,
The first to remember their faces.

Honed in the world of the keepers of power,
Trained in secret and stealth.
Treading down the forgotten path,
Of truth and spiritual wealth.

The first shall be clairvoyance, trace
The memory of a presence.
He takes the echo in the rock,
And tracks its living essence.

The second will be telepathy,
Of kind ne'er seen before.
The mind of a beast speaks open with him,
The wild unheard no more.

Divination is the third,
To seek by echo alone.
The message in the wood will guide,
And find what once was gone.

Fourth shall be a channel of stone,
To double the power he holds.
A crystal of sand captures the sun,
To free the King of old.

The one who gives him power and life,
A distant linking of minds.
A place of peace when all is in flame,
This, the fifth of the signs.

His strength will come to give him hope,
In sorrow lachrymose.
Translocation, rarely seen,
Brings a treasure close.

To take a path away from his task,
The seed of rebellion is pain.
To put him outside the unwritten law,
'Till justice and reason remain.

Imparting knowledge when needed most,
The spirits await the eighth sign.
From old their voices now have been heard,
Coming to touch his mind.

At last revelation, he knows the truth,
The Awakener knows his name.
His destiny writ in the stars above,
His fate now his to claim.

ONE

Princess Kandina huddled in the stall, her beloved horse snuffling at her hair. She loved coming here and sitting in the quiet with only Swiftly for company. She loved smelling the hay and that horsey smell. Just sitting here was enough to calm her when she thought too long on her shattered life.

This stall was the only place she could wallow in self pity without interruption. Swiftly never judged, never told her she was a silly girl, and never assumed that she would get over it. Every time she thought about it, the tears came unbidden. The pain was as strong now as the day her prince had married another.

How could she have read the signs so poorly? She knew she had made a mistake and that she had wronged her only friend, but a part of her still hoped the Prince would one day realise she was the one he really loved. She knew it had not been his fault, and she even admitted that Netta was probably no more guilty than he. It did not make it any easier to accept.

Curled up in her corner, listening to the quiet noises of the stable, she suddenly held her breath. There was a faint scraping of feet on the dirt floor and she carefully moved over to the stall door to peek over the top. Netta! She ducked down again and listened.

"Hey my little Glimma," Netta was saying. She was talking to her new horse, Kandi realised, the beautiful white mare that had been a joining gift from the King of far off Nella Fillenga.

"Shall we go for a ride, girl?" Netta murmured.

There was a jingle of tack as the Princess prepared to saddle the horse. Then Kandi jumped as she heard a gasp and a heavy smack and a thud. Her blood went cold as Atwin's wild stallion screamed, and she cowered down in Swiftly's stall, terrified.

Something had happened, and she knew she should run for help, but what if someone else was there, someone who had hurt Netta and would hurt her too? Trembling in fear, Kandi peeked over the stall door again. The stable was empty but for the horses. Kandi could hear the wild horse crashing about, screaming his rage.

She carefully opened the door and slipped out of the stall, creeping to look in on Glimma. She sidled past the angry stallion, keeping her distance as he glared balefully from his stall, nostrils flaring. The white horse was still there, sniffing at something on the ground. Moving closer, Kandi saw it was the saddle, dropped carelessly in the straw.

Kandi ran from the stable, hoping to get help, but stopped with a gasp. There, across the courtyard, was a cloaked figure on a grey horse, with a limp form slung across the saddle in front, hooves clattering as he galloped away.

"No!" Kandi cried. "Not this! This is not what I meant!"

Desperate to catch them now she ran, but the rider had already passed unchallenged through the outer gate. By the time she reached the gatehouse the kidnapper was down the hill and rapidly disappearing down the road. She cried out for the guard but there was no answer. Only then did she see the poor man, killed by a blow to the head.

* * *

Domyn had only been five years old when his mother died. Almost his first living memory was the day he and his sister Miyam had been forced to leave their home, to live with a father they hardly knew.

He had not been told why, he had been too young to understand. It was a trauma that would haunt him for the rest of his life. But he had learned to forget and had grown to love his father, becoming used to his new life. Then, last year, it had all changed again.

Domyn's father was gone, killed by an irate customer annoyed by substandard goods passed off as quality. Miyam had told him everything, the illegal deals his father excelled in, a corrupt business the only thing they would inherit. Then she had told him about his mother and the home they had left so long ago.

"Wake up there, young Domyn," said the scullery master with a frown.

"Sorry, Sir," said Domyn.

He hurried to continue washing the hundreds of dishes that sat heaped on the scullery table from breakfast. But his mind would not stay on task. He remembered the amazing story he had heard for the first time only a year ago.

Mist was a revealer of the highest calibre, a talented fighter, skilled in the use of the mind to sniff out information. Not only greatly skilled, she was admired and respected, a role model for girl novices and an inspiration to everyone. She was made artisan two years early and was dead a year later.

His mother's story had inspired Domyn to come to the College, to return to the home of his infancy. At ten years old he had been just the right age to seek admission as a novice. Once there, he had learned more. The stories he heard in the College filled him with pride and gave him something to strive for.

The masters talked about his mother in their lessons. The amazing story of Mist and her student Sand, heading out on a dangerous mission, collecting sensitive information about the growing threat of invasion and her glorious death in battle.

They told of the young journeyer, Sand, bringing her body back to the College, reporting the information and ensuring the success of the mission. Losing his grip on the next pile of plates, Domyn was shaken from his daze by the shattering sound of ten breakfast plates falling with an almighty smash on the slate floor.

"Domyn!" the Master yelled. "Get your head out of the clouds. Now you'll need to sweep up that mess. You'll be late for your lessons at this rate!"

"Sorry, Sir," he said again.

He grabbed the broom and began sweeping the broken pieces into a pile. He tried to keep his mind focused, but he was soon daydreaming again. Yesterday, Domyn's world had exploded with the most exciting event of his young life.

Sand had returned to the College, and he had brought Miyam with him. Domyn felt somehow close to the famous man who had been with his mother when she died. Sand had become the hero of every young boy at the College. In five short years he had gone from journeyer to artisan, gaining three levels in the time most people would achieve only one.

Domyn's boast was now much grander than before. Not only was he Mist's son, but he had finally met Sand! More amazingly, the time Domyn had spent with his sister and the Artisan had led him to a startling conclusion. Their close intimacy suggested a lot more than friendship. Sand and Miyam were a couple! He could not wait to tell his friends.

At lunch, Domyn watched eagerly for their entrance, and when they finally appeared he stared in surprise. His sister was wearing the brown bordered cloak of an apprentice. Miyam wasn't a member of the College! She had been once, but that was before their mother died and their father had removed them both. Domyn couldn't believe it.

Nobody ever came back. Not even a child born in the College was allowed to stay if they did not choose to become a novice. He pointed them out, telling his friends how he had met Sand.

"See, there he is, sitting with my sister."

"Yeah, right."

"It really is Sand. I met him last night."

"Sure, Dom, pull the other one."

"What's the most amazing thing about Sand?" said Domyn. "He was made artisan ten years early. Look at that man with Mym. No way he's thirty-five years old!"

The boys peered dubiously at the man at the Maestro's table.

"I'll settle this," said one boy.

Boldly, he stood up. Novices were forbidden to rise from their seats at meal times. One of the masters stopped him.

"Who's that man with the Maestro?" said the boy courageously.

"You mean Sand?" said the Master.

The boy sat down again, dumbfounded. Domyn grinned at his friends, who stared awestruck at the man in the red bordered cloak sitting at the Maestro's table.

"Gee, Dom," said one. "I wish I could meet Sand."

"Maybe you can."

"How?"

"I'll see what I can do," he replied magnanimously. "After all, he *is* in love with my sister!"

"Sure, Dom, whatever you reckon."

"It's true. All I have to do is find Mym and he'll be there."

"Bet you he won't."

"So, if he's not, Mym will know where he is and take us to him."

"I'll believe it when I see it."

When the couple in question arrived at the Maestro's office, concerned by an urgent summons, they found him pacing in agitation. He looked very worried.

"I'm sorry, Sand," he said, "but I'm afraid you are going to have to go out again."

Miyam shook her head and slipped her arms about Sand's waist. "But you said he could stay here while I study for the testing."

"I know what I said," the Maestro stated as he paced the floor. "But I can trust no other with this case."

"What is afoot?" asked Sand.

"I have just received a message from Shirall. I really am sorry, my boy, but I need you there."

"Has something happened?"

The Maestro took a deep breath. "Princess Nettayna has been kidnapped."

Miyam sat in a daze, staring at the Maestro as he told her the preparations he had been making on her behalf. The fact that she was back in the College, as a registered member, was a shock that coursed through her mind, filling her with renewed wonder every time it was mentioned. But how was she going to succeed in the testing? The Maestro expected her to somehow learn five years' worth of lessons in a few weeks. It just wasn't possible.

"I have faith in you," was all he would say.

"But Sir, how can I learn enough to pass even one test? It's five years' work, Maestro!"

"I believe in you," he said. "And so do the masters. Besides, most of the testing will be in mental and physical skills, which you will have no trouble with."

She shivered. "But what if I fail?" she cried. If she failed she would be expelled, no second chances. "What will I do if I have to leave again?"

"You won't fail," he said. "To that end, I've had the masters prepare this." He held out a thick notebook, bound in brown leather.

"What is it?" she asked, reaching a trembling hand to take it from him.

"Notes," he replied. "A study guide, with a section from each of the masters, containing all you will need to prepare for each test. You will have private lessons, an hour with each of the masters every day, working from this book. Every one of the masters is delighted to have you back and determined to help you succeed."

She shook her head. "Why? Why would they do this?"

He smiled benignly. "You were a brilliant student, and you are remembered. It's not often a person gets the chance to come back. We all want you to stay."

She felt the tears falling on her cheeks and tried to blink them away. It seemed like all she did lately was cry. She swallowed hard on the lump that filled her throat.

"I've found a spare bunk in the apprentice quarters, so you can start assimilating."

She shook her head. "But I..."

"Is that really necessary, Sir?" said Sand from by the hearth. "I thought Mym would stay in my apartment while I'm gone."

"She's welcome to spend her free time there, certainly, and even sleep there, but she needs to get to know her peers. The two girls I've placed her with are both testing too, so she'll have study partners. Besides, I don't want to be seen showing favouritism."

The Maestro rounded on Sand then with a frown. "Why

are you still here? You have a mission. You need to get to Shirall and find my... the Princess."

Sand shrugged, face a mask. "I have some things to prepare. I'll head off in the morning."

"The longer you tarry, the further away her captors take her. What could you possibly need to prepare?"

"I... need supplies, my horse needs attention from the farrier, my saddle needs repair, not to mention new boots for me..." he rattled off the excuses without even blinking.

The Maestro chuckled. "So go do it, then! Miyam will be fine," he said and gave a knowing wink. "You can join her later."

Sand sighed and nodded. "Yes, Sir," he said reluctantly, and moved toward the door. His hand brushed Miyam's shoulder as he passed and she covered it with her own, gazing up at him with tears in her eyes. He brushed them gently away and bent to kiss her, but stopped at a knock on the door. He stiffened and made to slide back into the shadows.

"Stop that," said the Maestro. "Since you're here, you can add your endorsement to mine in front of the apprentices." He raised his voice. "Come!"

The two girls who entered were giggling and whispering, insensible to the dignified atmosphere of the room.

"Apprentices!" Sand barked. "Show some respect in front of the Maestro!"

The two girls stiffened and sobered. "Sorry, Maestro," said one.

"Sorry, Sir Artisan," said the other and her eyes rested on the name badge at his neck. "Sand!" she said, wide eyed, and snapped to attention. "Sorry, Sir!"

The Maestro chuckled, and Miyam hid her smile behind her hand, but her eyes twinkled with the bubbles of laughter that threatened to surface as she shared a look with the

Artisan.

'Promise me you won't turn into one of them,' he said in her mind.

'Never,' she whispered silently in return.

"Now, girls," said the Maestro. "I have a new room mate for you." He gestured for Miyam to rise. "This is Miyam. She will join you in the testing. I would like you to take the time to help her settle in."

"Yes, Maestro," they chorused.

They turned their eyes on her in curiosity and one smiled.

"I know you," she said. "You were a year above me as a novice. But I thought you left?"

Miyam smiled uncertainly. "Yes, I've been away."

"I'm Jepsa," she said with a smile.

"I thought you couldn't come back once you resigned from the College," said the other girl with a frown.

"It does happen on occasion," said the Maestro. "When circumstances are right."

"What circumstances?" said the frowning one.

"That is not for you to know, Pallia," the Maestro admonished. "Nor is it your place to question."

The girl grumbled but said no more.

"Now, I'd like you girls to show Miyam to your room and introduce her to the other testing apprentices. The sooner we all accept her and make friends the better."

"Yes, Maestro," they chorused again.

Jepsa took Miyam's hand to lead her away. Miyam followed with a worried glance at the Maestro, who winked with a smile. she sent a long look at Sand, who whispered reassurance in her mind. She allowed the girl to guide her out of the Maestro's office, with Pallia scowling as she trailed behind.

*

Domyn and the other boys found Miyam alone in the apprentice common room reading from a large brown book.

"Where's Sand?" said Domyn eagerly.

"Why, Dom, I'm crushed," she said. "I thought you might have come to see me!"

The boy looked crest-fallen, and Miyam laughed.

"He's busy at the moment, preparing to head out again tomorrow, but he'll come here when he's free. You can wait if you like."

The boys crowded into the room and looked about.

"Why aren't you in Sand's quarters?" asked Domyn.

"Isn't that a rather direct question for a lad your age?"

Domyn looked at her witheringly and Miyam smiled.

"They're being cleaned. Sand has been away for a long time, you know. Why aren't you boys in class?"

"We're free, silly. 'Till later this afternoon."

"What's this afternoon?"

Domyn grinned. "Theology."

"Ah. And what have you been studying in theology lately?"

He grinned again. "We've been reading about the Awakener."

Miyam looked up sharply. "I'd forgotten about him!"

"He's supposed to come and teach the world about the truth."

"Yes, I know. Aren't there a series of signs that will point to his coming?"

Domyn nodded. "Everything he does is really big. He's supposed to be the best revealer ever."

"What are the signs?"

He rattled them off. "Clairvoyance, telepathy, divination, channelling, mind linkage, translocation, rebellion, divine contact and revelation. But they have to happen in that order and they have to be really unusual."

"I see," she mused. "Interesting."

"Mym?"

"It's nothing, Dom. I had a strange idea, that's all." Then she smiled. "I have something for you."

The boy's eyes lit up and he followed her as she went to collect a metal box that sat on the table. She returned to her seat and sat down to open it.

"These are some things of Mother's that I thought you might like to see."

The other boys gathered around, eager to see the things that had belonged to Mist. She drew out a knife and belt and handed them to Domyn.

"These are for you. Father made them for Mother after she became master. I have my own, which he made for me when I took a place with the novices. He never had a chance to make yours. Would you like these?"

The boy nodded wordlessly, and threw himself into his sister's arms.

"There, Dom," she said, hugging him tight. "Let's see how they look."

Both were a little teary-eyed as Miyam fastened the belt about his waist and secured the knife in place, but when it was done they grinned at each other, and Domyn paraded for his friends. Then Domyn looked in the box and picked up a silvery arm band.

"What's this?"

"Be very careful with that. Here, let me show you." Miyam slipped the band onto her arm and showed the boys the mysterious panelling on the top side.

"The wristband helps focus the mind to control the weapon. Stand back, boys."

With an upward flick of the wrist, a tiny knife hidden in her hair leapt into the air. The boys gasped and watched the deadly thing as she played with it for them. She sent it darting to and fro and made it hover and dance in front of their astonished faces.

"Can you aim it?" said Domyn in a hushed whisper.

Miyam grinned and sent it zooming across the room toward the back of the door. At that moment the door opened. With a strangled gasp, Miyam stopped the blade in mid-air, right where Sand's head would have been if he had not ducked.

From his crouch, Sand looked up to see the knife hovering above him. He stood slowly, avoiding the deadly thing, his eyes fixed on the instrument that could have ended his life. He held out his hand and looked at Miyam. Sheepishly she dropped the knife into his waiting palm and switched off the arm band. He looked at the knife and back to her.

Then he grinned. "Are you sick of me already?"

She simply shrugged her shoulders and he chuckled. He came toward her and returned the little knife to its sheath in her hair. Then, as he bent to kiss the top of her head, a movement caught his eye. The boys had huddled together in a corner, trying to be inconspicuous.

"You have visitors," she said.

"So I see," he replied.

The boys spent the afternoon throwing eager questions in Sand's general direction. The story Miyam told filled them with wonder. Her and Sand had been on a great adventure together, a grand quest in search of the King's amulet, Naali and they had succeeded. Now the Queen's amulet, Leena, had been reunited with her long lost partner and finally, for the first time in eight hundred years, the troubled queendom of Shirall would have a king!

"But how did you know where to find him?" said Targit eagerly.

"We conducted a clairvoyant search," Sand replied.

"We followed his trail through the Dragon Mountains, all the way to the southern pass," said Miyam.

The boys gasped. "But that's... that's forever!" cried Targit. "Nobody can search that far, it's heaps further than Master Drab said."

Sand shrugged. "We did it."

"But how?"

"I want to know how you talked to a horse?" Winsom interrupted.

Again Sand shrugged. "It's just an extension of the mind speak we use in the College."

"But how can that be?" Winsom said. "I don't think anybody has ever talked to a horse before."

"How would you know?" said Domyn, coming to his hero's defence.

"Master Fort said we can't use telepathy on animals because their brains are too different!"

"Maybe Master Fort was wrong," said Domyn stubbornly.

"Dom!" said Miyam then. "You don't question your masters."

"So how did he do it, then?" said Winsom.

"He just did!" said Domyn.

"And how did he find Naali by drawing on a table, that's what I'd like to know," Targit piped in.

"Basic divination," Sand explained. "I found the echo in the wood and read the message it left behind."

"Basic?" said Targit. "It was awesome!"

"I love the bit with the diamond," said another lad, Crispin. "Now that was awesome. How did you make a diamond out of sand anyway?"

"I honestly don't know," Sand admitted. "I just knew what to do."

"And then you used it to break the crystal and free Naali. That was really cool!" said Crispin.

"That was channelling," said Miyam.

"No ordinary channelling, I'd say," said Crispin.

"None of those things are too hard for Sand though," said Domyn.

"What do you mean?" said the Artisan cautiously.

"Well, Sir, you're already the best revealer ever. Why wouldn't you be able to do big powerful things?"

Sand sputtered. "I don't think it was like that..."

Miyam laughed. "I think it might be time to get back to class, boys."

As they left, Sand sank gratefully into an armchair, pulling a weary Miyam down with him. The effusive exuberance of several eleven year old boys in the presence of their hero can be enough to wear out the most energetic of people. They huddled together in silence for a long moment, listening to the utter quiet the boys had left behind.

Finally, Sand stirred. "The cleaning is finished," he said.

Miyam sat up. "Why didn't you say so earlier?"

"And send the boys away?" he replied. "That would hardly have been fair."

She looked at him knowingly. "How does it feel to be a hero?"

He looked at her in confusion, just a bit panicked, but then he shrugged wryly. "It's quite an experience."

"Don't let the attention go to your head," she laughed.

"Would I do that?"

She sobered. "Come to think of it, you wouldn't." She smiled tenderly. "And you were going to give it all up after Mother died."

She touched the side of his face with her free hand.

"All of that self-torture and guilt you put yourself through," she murmured. "See how unnecessary it was? You should give yourself more credit."

* * *

TWO

On the battlements of the ruined palace at Shirall, Prince Atwin of Drasmil stared south over the city and the river beyond. He knew she had gone south. Naali, the King's amulet, could tell him at least that much. He itched to follow the trail but Averil, the Princess Regent of Shirall, wanted him to wait for the revealer.

When he closed his eyes he could see through the link with the Queen's amulet. He could see the tribesmen about her, feel the ropes that bound her and it made him crazy being stuck here while they got further and further away.

They were headed for the Heights. He could feel it in his bones. Once they started into the mountains they would be impossible to track. He slammed his fist down on the stone parapet in frustration.

A small hand was placed gently on his and the amulet at his neck gave a little jolt.

"How do you expect to wield a sword with a broken hand?" said Kandi in an admonitory tone.

Now why had Naali reacted to her in that way? He pulled his hand away and massaged it.

"I am not stupid enough to damage myself, Kandi. There is too much at stake."

"Come downstairs," she said. "You are doing yourself no good up here."

"Just leave me alone Kandi, please."

He closed his eyes and saw the hand that reached out

to pull Netta off the horse by her hair. He made to punch the wall again, but stopped himself, fist hovering tensely in the air.

* * *

Sand coughed uncomfortably as the door opened and the quiet was broken by the entrance of a group of apprentices returning from classes. Miyam quickly slipped off his lap as the Artisan's face closed, his habitual mask hiding his vibrant personality.

The crowd grew silent as they noticed the Artisan and they whispered to each other in surprise. One girl broke away from the group and came toward them. It was Jepsa, smiling at Miyam.

"I'm glad you're here," she said. "You can meet everyone."

Miyam glanced at Sand uncertainly and he murmured in her mind. *'I'm not going anywhere.'*

"What's he doing here?" Jepsa whispered.

"Waiting," said Miyam enigmatically.

"For what?"

Miyam just smiled. With a questioning look, Jepsa took her hand and led her over to the milling group. Gesturing to each in turn, she introduced three young men and a girl.

"Miyam, this is Malus, Grobe, Fardle and Sylvan. You know Pallia."

Miyam smiled shyly as they took her hand in turn.

"You've caused quite a stir, Miyam," said Grobe with a mischievous grin.

"You must have really impressed the council to get reinstated," said Malus, tall and dark with piercing eyes.

Miyam ducked her head. "I'm just very lucky," she said quietly.

"I'll say," said the blonde girl, Sylvan. "I don't think I've ever heard of anyone being allowed to return after retiring from the College."

"I'd like to know how she managed it," said Pallia.

"I..."

"I want to know, too," said Fardle from where he stood with Pallia, an arm about her shoulders.

"Leave her alone," said Jepsa, with a glance at the Artisan still seated in the arm chair, watching with an inscrutable expression. "It's not our place to question the council."

"Actually, it wasn't the council who allowed it," said Sylvan. "I heard the masters talking about her. It was the Maestro."

"Is that true?" said Fardle.

"I..."

"Yes, it's true," said a calm, lightly accented voice.

Sand unfolded from his chair, rising to his full height and striding across the room.

"Miyam was removed from the College against her will. In cases like these it is College policy to keep the membership open to allow the person to return in better circumstances." It wasn't exactly a lie. "Technically, Miyam never left."

Malus whistled. "I've never heard of that rule."

"I'm not surprised," Sand replied. "It's little used and not generally made public."

"A lucky rule for you, Miyam," said Grobe with another grin.

Miyam smiled uncertainly.

"It's alright," said Jepsa. "You'll fit in just fine once everyone gets used to the idea."

"Come and sit," said Sylvan then. "We can all get to know each other."

"I'm sorry, I need to steal Miyam for a while," said Sand carefully. "We have some business to attend to before she can be fully reinstated," he lied.

Miyam almost laughed at that.

'Let's head out to the Artisan wing, where it's more private,' he said in her mind. *'I've asked for supper to be brought for us, so we don't have to eat in the hall.'*

'What a nice idea.'

Hand-in-hand, Miyam and Sand walked slowly down the corridor on their way back to the Artisan wing of the College complex. They said nothing, savouring what little time they had before Sand had to leave.

"Evelar?" a female voice called from some distance behind.

Sand froze. There was only one person who ever used his real name while in the College. He looked behind and Miyam followed his gaze. An adept approached, smiling broadly.

"Opal," said Sand quietly. He kissed Miyam's hand. "Wait here," he said.

Sand strode to meet the woman, who smiled mischievously.

"Who's the Apprentice?" she asked.

"Miyam," he replied and looked back to gaze at her, his eyes smouldering. "With grey mist in her eyes and a walk like a white tiger..." he murmured.

"Excuse me?" Opal stared at him as if he had just sprouted polka dots.

Sand shook himself, reluctantly breaking eye contact with Miyam. "Sorry. I'm a bit distracted at the moment."

"So I can see!"

He lowered his eyes. "I have to leave in the morning."

"How long have you been here?"

"This is only the second night."

"Hmmm. She must be good!"

"Excuse me?" He echoed her so exactly that they must have been twins.

"Two days and she's got you waxing lyrical on me!"

Sand shook his head. "Mym came with me from Shirall," he explained. "She's sort of a special case. The Maestro has reinstated her after six years away."

"How long have you known her?"

"Close to a year now," he said as he looked back at Miyam and was caught again. "I need to ask a favour," he said then.

"Ask away."

"How long will you be here?"

"A few weeks, I suppose. Unless something comes up."

"Could you make yourself available? Mym's going to need a friend. Her peers will have all gained the green at least a year ago and if she's to make it through the written exams she'll need all the help she can get."

"What about physical and mental skills?"

"No problem. Physically she's at least at master level and mentally she's closer to adept. Once she gains the green there'll be no stopping her," he said proudly.

Opal looked at him appraisingly. "She really has caught you, hasn't she?"

Sand grinned and his sister blinked in shock. Then he took hold of her arm and led her to where Miyam waited.

"Mym, this is my sister, Seiliar. Opal, this is Miyam. My wife."

Opal glanced at him in surprise.

"Not officially," said Miyam with a gentle smile.

The two women looked at each other in interest.

"It's a pleasure to meet you at last," said Miyam.

"Why, Sand," said Opal then. "Her eyes are green, not grey."

"You haven't seen them in moonlight," he replied thickly.

Miyam shot him a quizzical look.

"May I congratulate you on the change you have wrought

in my brother," said Opal. "He seems to have become more human somehow, perhaps because he's finally learned how to smile!"

"I have reason to smile now," he said a little defensively.

"Never mind, dear," said Miyam. "I know what she means."

Sand looked from one to the other in utter confusion. Opal laughed delightedly.

"Brother dear, I think I'm going to like her!"

Opal took Miyam's arm and the two walked off down the corridor, laughing like old friends. Sand looked after them in amazement. Then he gathered his shattered wits and hurried to catch up. He laid a hand on Miyam's arm and cleared his throat. They stopped and looked at him innocently.

"Ah... if you don't mind, it's getting rather late," he hinted.

"Diddums!" said Opal with friendly sarcasm.

Sand looked at her witheringly, but his eyes held a plea.

"You're right," she said then. "I should be going. Dock will think I've deserted him," she smiled at Miyam. "Don't keep him up too late," she said suggestively. "Come and see me tomorrow. We'll have lunch."

"I'd like that."

Then Opal was gone. Sand took Miyam's hand and they continued on their way to his quarters.

* * *

Princess Nettayna huddled on the ground where she had been thrown. Leena trembled and pulsated at her neck, but gave her no idea how to escape. When the Princess tried to communicate with the amulet all she heard was a pathetic blubbering. To have lost Naali again after such a short time had thrown Leena into a catatonic fit. The presence within the amulet was lost in the memory of those hundreds of years without her husband's presence.

Netta was aware of a commotion as the tribesmen milled about her, pulling back to give access to a newcomer. The figure that swaggered toward her was tall and stocky, dressed in resplendent velvet with gold trim, a battered crown lopsided on his head.

A rough hand grabbed at her hair again, making the Princess flinch away. Her head was forced up and back and a shadow blocked the sun. She looked up defiantly, straight into the eyes of the mad king.

Prince Atwin paced. He had seen his father's face. He longed to tell someone that he knew who was behind the kidnapping, but he also knew he could be accused of treason or worse if he mentioned it.

He wished Evelar would hurry up, he would know how to deal with it. But the revealer had only received the message yesterday and it would take him three weeks to get to Shirall, even if he pushed the whole way.

He could not wait that long! In three weeks the tribesmen would be high in the mountains, taking Netta out of reach. He groaned.

King Gerard of Drasmil bowed to no-one, riding ahead of his escort stiff in the saddle. His soldiers and the tribesmen eyed each other uneasily as they marched toward Drasmil. Netta had tried to reason with him but the King was lost in the grip of his madness.

"Without you, my traitor son will fail in his empire building. That snake will never become king in Shirall, not if I can help it."

"Your Majesty, Atwin carries the King's Amulet now. I fear you do not understand the true significance of that."

The King snarled. "You are the future queen, you will be

removed, he will never rule in your place."

Netta just shook her head. "He will be king even if I never return. His possession of Naali ensures that."

The King laughed. "We will see about that."

"So do you plan to keep me locked up at Drasmil? Or will you have me killed instead?"

"Not at all," the King sneered. "I have much more interesting plans for you. The deal I have made will take you so far you will never be able to use your influence to escape."

* * *

Miyam woke suddenly and sat up with a start, feeling an empty space beside her. Her mind flashed back to the last time she had awoken alone, when Sand had tried to slip away, leaving her with friends as he travelled back to the College. Then a gentle mental touch reassured her and she sighed with relief. She sank back into the pillows and looked to where Sand had turned from the window to look at her.

"You know I'll never do that again," he said gently.

She smiled. Then she noticed that he was fully dressed. He even wore his cloak, though the hood was down.

"Is it time?" she said in a small voice.

"Not quite," he replied.

He pushed away from the sill and came toward her, his boots sounding uncharacteristically loud on the floor-boards. He sat on the end of the bed and took her hands, pulling her up again.

"I want to try something," he said then.

"Oh?"

"Would you be willing to lower your shield?"

She smiled. "It's already down."

He looked surprised.

"I stopped shielding from you a long time ago," she said.

"Why?"

"I have nothing to hide from you."

"But you hid your mother's identity."

"No," she replied. "If you had wanted to look you would have found it." She smiled again. "Do you still shield from me?"

"Of course not," he said, and then he stopped, realising what he had said. He grinned. "I never realised it before now."

She returned his grin. "What did you want to try?"

"Remember when I controlled your body from within your mind to cure you of that charm?"

She nodded, glancing at the long scar running the length of her right forearm, the only reminder of the wound that had let in a spell which had almost killed her.

"I want to try the link again."

"Why?"

"I think I can make it permanent. Then we will never really be apart."

"What a nice idea," she said.

Miyam closed her eyes and felt Sand enter her mind. He quickly penetrated the outer layers, through the public mind and the surface thought centre. Then he entered that part of the conscious mind usually buried behind a shield. He resisted the temptation to stop and explore.

He by-passed the pathways that led to the short and long term memory centres and continued down into the deeper layers, those places where learned automatic responses are stored, the place where years of training finally rests, the home of those things that have become so ingrained that they are almost unconscious.

Finally he broke through into the true unconscious mind, that place to which even Miyam herself could not gain access. He burrowed deeper until he reached the very centre of her mind. He broke through into that most private of places, that tiny haven wherein rests the very essence of being.

He had been there before. She welcomed him. Then he told her what he wanted her to do. She entered him, echoing his journey. She found his centre of being and entered into the place of his essence. Then, they swapped.

It was easy. They had done it once before. She was him and he was her. She looked out of his eyes and saw herself and he was looking through her eyes. Then she backed out, as he had instructed her and he did the same. They backed out of that private place within each other, leaving open that previously locked door to the unconscious mind.

But the conscious minds that they returned to were their own. Miyam opened her eyes. The world had not changed, but somehow she had. He was watching her curiously. She looked inside herself. All was as it should be. Then she found the open door.

She entered in and burrowed down and found him there. She merged with him and she looked out again through his eyes. Then she backed out, returning to her own mind and looked at him.

"How bizarre," she said.

He grinned.

Miyam walked with Sand to the stables and then out to the gate house. Before Sand left, he gave her the key to his rooms.

"I know the Maestro has assigned you apprentice quarters, but you won't get a lot of privacy down there. You may want to escape."

"I feel like my life was finally getting back on track. Now I have to stay here without you."

He held her close. "It won't be for long," he said, as much to reassure himself as her. "Soon you will be a journeyer, with a name and a badge and nobody will ever take that away."

"I still can't believe it's happening."

"Have you any idea what your Art name will be?"

She smiled. "I'm taking Mother's name. If you approve, I will be Mist."

He grinned. "It's perfect."

She smiled wanly.

"Hey," he said gently and tapped her forehead. "Remember this?"

"I know," she said, slipping her arms about his waist and snuggling against him. "But I can't touch an essence."

"You just get through those exams so you can come and join me."

With that he walked his horse through the gate, opened by Master Worm the gatekeeper, and stopped to look back as the gate slammed shut, a grim reminder that he was now leaving the sheltered world of the College.

He swung up into the saddle and gazed back at his wife, her hands clutching the thick bars of the gate as she stared at him.

'Evelar...' Miyam whispered in his mind, using his real name now that he was outside the gate. *'Please be safe.'*

With a smile and a reassuring thought, he turned Lumen and kicked in with his heels, spurring the stallion away.

* * *

THREE

Prince Atwin sat bolt upright in bed. Naali was burning! His princess was now in the company of the kalkar. He knew the tribesmen of the mountains had made a pact with the enemy, but he had not heard of them actually joining together before. He felt his blood go cold as an overwhelming sense of foreboding filled his heart.

Two days from Shirall, King Gerard took his soldiers and continued toward Drasmil, leaving Netta alone with the tribesmen and their kalkar allies. As they left, one of the soldiers pressed a large pack into her hands.

"The boys gathered some supplies for you, Princess," he murmured as he passed. "We all feel dreadful about this and we want you to know that we'll do everything we can to help Prince Atwin find you."

Netta sobbed in gratitude and mustered a smile for the man. "Thank you," she whispered.

She watched in trepidation as the soldiers marched away, falling in behind their king as he headed toward Drasmil. The rest of her captors veered south toward the mountains.

Netta rode in a daze, her mind numbed by the pain of Leena, burning at her neck. The kalkar pack surrounded her, the heat from their thermo reactive bodies wafting over her and sapping her energy. It was all she could do to just continue putting one foot in front of the other.

Since the kalkar had arrived, her chance of escape seemed gone. They travelled by night now, the tribesmen offering her food and water during the day while the kalkar stood dormant. Leena smouldered, her warning mechanism still in operation despite the amulet's catatonic state.

The days wore on and the pain at the girl's neck ceased to hold any power over her. She ignored it now, almost forgetting what it was like to be free of such pain.What puzzled her was the deference the tribesmen gave to the kalkar.

From what she knew of the alliance, she had assumed that the kalkar were being controlled by humans. But what she saw now suggested the opposite. It would have been so easy to let her escape, but the tribesmen held her captive through the long daylight hours until the kalkar awoke at dusk.

Kalkar menaced her from all sides, but the tribesmen kept her in their midst, allowing some degree of protection from those burning red eyes. The sulphurous smell of the dark ones clung to her. She ignored that too. She no longer even hoped for rescue. If it would come, then so be it.

* * *

Miyam spent a manic first day of lessons rushing from one master to the next, and each had a pile of reading for her to get through. It seemed each one expected her to spend every waking moment on their own particular lesson plan, with no regard for the other classes she had to attend.

After a morning of kill-theory, history, theology and alchemy, Miyam rushed to join the other apprentices in the great hall for lunch.

"Miyam!" Jepsa called. "Come sit with us."

With a shy smile, Miyam hurried to join Jepsa and her friends.

"What happened to you last night?" said the girl. "You never came back to the room."

"Ah... no," Miyam blushed. "I was... busy."

"With Sand? Doing what?"

Miyam had no answer for that, ducking her head to hide her embarrassment. Jepsa gasped.

"No!" she cried. "You and Sand?"

Miyam hushed her. This was the last thing she wanted all the other apprentices to know. In fact her acceptance here depended on them not knowing she was married to Sand. Jepsa dropped her voice to a whisper.

"I knew you two came in together, but I never dreamed..." her eyes narrowed. "But isn't he a lot older than you?"

"He's only a few years older than me."

"My goodness, Miyam, he's an artisan. He's way out of our league."

"What are you talking about, Jepsa? He's the youngest artisan in College history. He would have been testing for journeyer when I was a fourth year novice. He's only twenty-seven."

"Oh!" said Jepsa. "Somehow I never looked at it that way." She leant in again and whispered. "How long have you... you know?"

"Almost a year," Miyam smiled. "But you mustn't say anything to the others. They'd never accept me if they knew."

Jepsa snorted. "Don't you worry about them. Most of them have paired off with someone, and half the rooms are empty most of the time. I was only there because my... friend is out on his first mission as a journeyer."

"What about Pallia?"

"Oh, she was out with Fardle most of the night, she didn't even notice."

*

Miyam's first week of lessons passed in a whirl, the classes jumbling together in her mind and the countless books melding in a confusion of words. Each day, she attended lesson after lesson, the written subjects in the morning and the physical and mental classes in the afternoon. Each night she read into the small hours of the morning, desperate to commit the work to memory.

In the morning, before breakfast, Jepsa quizzed her on the previous day's lessons. Jepsa said she was doing fine, and the masters seemed pleased with her progress, but Miyam suffered in silence as her confidence quickly eroded under the sheer weight of work.

Finally, the first rest day arrived. There were no classes, but each of the masters had given her work to complete.

"We're all getting together in the common room today, are you coming?" said Jepsa before breakfast.

Miyam sighed. "I have so much to do, I can't"

"You need a break."

Miyam shook her head. "I wish I could, Jepsa, but this is too important."

"You're going to burn yourself out."

Jepsa was right, but Miyam said nothing. She had been so busy she hadn't had time to listen for Sand in her mind, and she missed him terribly. She hadn't sought out Opal for that lunch date, and she hadn't even met with her brother Domyn. She rubbed at her eyes, her weariness getting the better of her.

"Thanks for the offer, Jepsa," she said. "Maybe later."

Jepsa shrugged. "Alright, but it's going to get noisy. I doubt you'll get much study done."

"I'll go somewhere quieter then."

"Where will you go?"

"Sand's rooms," she murmured with a glance at Pallia, still sleeping in her bunk.

Gathering her books together, she rummaged in her travel pack and pulled out the key Sand had given her. The noise from the common room was already beginning to waft down the corridor and she knew she could not stay there.

With a pile of books and a smile for Jepsa, Miyam hurried away. Using a mental shield of normality she slipped through the milling crowd unnoticed, and hurried toward the artisan wing. At the entrance to the artisan common room, she hesitated.

She needed to reach the staircase at the end of the corridor and she had to get through the large room first. The occupants sat singly and in small groups on the soft couches that circled a central fireplace. She had not realised there would be so many artisans currently resident in the College. The normality spell would not work there, the Artisans would see through it.

She took a deep breath. She would have to just act normal, and pretend she was supposed to be there. Entering the room, Miyam lifted her chin and strode purposefully toward the far corridor. She made it less than half way.

"You there, Apprentice!"

Miyam stopped. "Yes, Sir Artisan?"

"Where are you going? Are you the duty apprentice today?"

"Ah... I just..."

"Leave her alone, Loss," another stepped in. "That's Miyam, the returned apprentice."

Miyam stared, shocked that she was known and recognised. "Ah... yes, Sir. I was just..."

The Artisan waved dismissively. "On your way, dear."

"What is she doing here?" said Loss in protest. "Only the duty apprentice is allowed access to the Artisan suites."

"Maestro has given her access. She and Sand are... you know..."

Face hot, Miyam hurried through the common room and into the quiet corridor.

"An apprentice?" she heard from Loss as she escaped.

Hurrying up the stairs, Miyam found the door and inserted the key with a trembling hand. Finally she stepped through and shut the door behind her, leaning back on it in relief. Hands shaking, she lost her grip on the pile of books, which tumbled to the floor with a series of heavy thuds.

Miyam shivered in the cold room, but its familiar quiet cosiness washed over her and she began to relax. Letting go of a week of stress, the trembling grew more violent and she found herself on the floor, tears flowing unheeded as she sobbed.

'Don't cry, my love,' said a welcome voice in her head, and Miyam moaned as she remembered how much she missed him. A wave of warmth and love swept over her from far away.

'This is so hard,' she whispered over the leagues that separated them. *'I can't do it, it's too much...'*

'Yes, you can. But you've been pushing yourself too hard.'

She sighed. *'What else can I do?'*

His reassuring presence filled her and she finally calmed. *'Take it one day at a time,'* he murmured. *'I'm always here, my love.'*

'Yes I know, but I'm still alone...'

Miyam sat in Evelar's apartment, pouring over the books she had borrowed from the Master of Religion. A strange idea had been bugging her ever since Domyn had reminded her about the Awakener. If her hunch was right, she had been seeing the signs all along.

She found the reference she had been looking for. Carefully sealing off her conscious thoughts to be sure that

Evelar was not listening in the depths of her mind, she read the passage.

In strife reborn, he will come:
The Awakener brings the truth.
His coming will be heralded
By signs writ here forsooth.

Born in a tent of the keepers of knowledge,
Who live in the sandy places.
Proudly rekindling times once forgot,
The first to remember their faces.

Honed in the world of the keepers of power,
Trained in secret and stealth.
Treading down the forgotten path
Of truth and spiritual wealth.

Miyam checked off the signs one by one, skimming the passages and searching her memory for the evidence she had seen.

The first sign was clairvoyance, the ability to read echoes of a presence and follow it. All those months ago, that exceptional mental search for Naali, following the echo in the rock and tracing the King's amulet in its journey toward its final resting place.

The second sign was telepathy, but no ordinary telepathy. She remembered Evelar's unexpected ability to talk to a horse, the great wild horse of the plains, who had allowed Prince Atwin to tame him by expressing his wish in the mind of the revealer.

Divination was the third sign, the ability to seek out and find something. Evelar had used divination to seek out the final location of Naali by tracing a message in a large oak table, the wood taken from the very tree in which the King's amulet was found.

Next was Channelling, the use of crystal to enhance power. Evelar had created a diamond from sand using the power of his mind. She fingered the diamond at her neck on its chain of beautiful glass beads. He had channelled his power through the diamond to free Naali from the crystal that encased him.

Four signs had already been met, and Miyam was sure this exceptional mind link was number five. But she would have to wait and see if the next sign was forthcoming. She read the rest of the passage and wondered if she would know the signs when they came.

The next was translocation, the ability to transport an object or person instantly, a skill that had not been seen for many generations. Then would come rebellion, the act of declaring himself outside the law. Sign number eight was spiritual contact, the ability to talk to non-living, non-physical beings. Finally revelation, the final sign, was the Awakener realising his own identity.

Miyam sat still for a long moment. That last sign gave her pause. It suggested that the Awakener must be kept ignorant of his identity right to the last moment. How could the best, most talented revealer in the history of the College be kept in the dark? Surely he would be able to read the signs himself.

But then Miyam remembered the intrinsic flaw in Evelar's considerable talent. He was Sand, the greatest revealer ever known, but he tended to miss the obvious.

He had missed the clues that told him her mother's identity. He had missed the clues that pointed to her own past history in the College. It all somehow made sense now. It was the very flaw that would give rise to the final sign and reveal the Awakener.

* * *

Netta stared ahead, her feet dragging. The amulet at her neck seared her flesh, new blisters forming over old ones. The climb into the mountains had sapped what was left of her strength, but they were through the high pass now and heading down toward the Barren Wastes.

The nights were long and cold, but the warmth of the kalkar kept it at bay. At least that was something to be thankful for, she thought ruefully.

As the kalkar slowed for the coming dawn, the tribesmen set up camp. Netta sank to the ground, giving in to the fatigue that threatened to consume her. One young man sat beside her and offered a water skin and some bread.

"I need to warn you, Princess," he murmured, lips barely moving and eyes shifting about uneasily.

Netta paused in her hasty meal. "Warn me?"

He nodded. "Once we get down into the foothills, we will be leaving. The kalkar plan to take you on into the desert."

Netta gasped and shook her head in fear. "What will I do? The kalkar have no idea how to keep a human alive in the desert. They need no water, they mind not the heat... I will die!"

"All I can say is... take as much water as you can. Get that pack restocked before you leave the mountains. I'll do what I can to get extra water skins for you."

"Why are you helping me?"

"Nobody should be made to enter the desert unprepared."

Netta watched in terror as the human contingent disappeared into the night. When she was alone with the kalkar, the one that appeared to be the leader ordered her in a rasping, guttural voice to get down from the horse.

Trembling in fear, she slid down. When she moved too slowly, the kalkar grabbed her hair roughly, dragging her to the ground. She smelled the acrid odour of burning hair as her golden tresses were singed by the heat in the kalkar flesh.

The horror with the burning eyes bent over her. A green, bony hand reached down to grab the amulet at her neck.

Prince Atwin burst into the throne room, where the Queen and her consort were holding audience, with Averil standing by. They looked up in surprise.

"You cannot expect me to wait here any longer," he said angrily.

"The revealer will be here in a few days, Atwin," said the Regent.

"Damn it, Averil," he cried. "They have handed her over to the kalkar!"

Delsi gasped, and Ordel rose explosively from his chair.

Netta screamed and Leena froze, literally. As the kalkar clutched the amulet, Leena cooled and became icy. The kalkar screamed, a horrid sound, as the heat was sucked out of it.

Within seconds, it was frozen solid. Gingerly, Netta shook Leena out of its dead grasp, the frozen hand crumbling away. The Princess looked up, daring any other to try. Then a bony hand sent her reeling.

She touched the side of her face, the skin already blistering. Another hand grabbed her arm and dragged her to her feet. The heat rapidly burned through the fabric, scorching the skin. She held back the tears.

Atwin sank to his knees, feeling her pain. Averil went to him, but he shrank from her touch.

"They are hurting her..." he moaned.

He lurched to his feet and stumbled toward the throne.

He knelt on the step below Queen Delsi and looked up at her pleadingly.

"Your Majesty, please," he said in anguish. "Let me go after her..."

Tears spilled from her blind eyes to slide down her face, and she nodded once. The Prince rose with the force of a coiled spring. He glanced at the Queen's consort, who stood stiffly, fists clenched at his sides, and Ordel nodded. Atwin bowed once and was gone.

In the royal stable, the great wild stallion screamed and reared, front hooves bashing at the stall door. When Atwin entered, the horse settled on all four hooves and snorted, ears flicking back and forth. Atwin approached him without fear.

"My Lord Windfoot," said the Prince. "We are finally on our way."

The stallion tossed his head, allowing his friend to position the saddle and packs. The moment he felt the man's weight on his back the horse bolted from the stable, and the chase began.

FOUR

Evelar strode into the ruined palace at Shirall. He was not questioned by the guard; his revealer's cloak guaranteed instant entry. There was something intrinsically wrong with that system. It made it so easy for a spy who looked like a revealer to gain entry to the most secure of places.

Guards, on the whole, have no way of knowing a true revealer from a spy in a costume, since they cannot read the Art name badge that proves a revealer's identity to another member of the College.

He thought on that as he descended the stairs to the underground palace complex, drawing only a smart salute from the sentries on guard outside the double doors to the audience chamber. The revealer bowed before the Queen and offered himself for duty.

"Thank you for coming, Evelar," said Delsi. "Atwin left a week ago. Certain developments prevented him from waiting for you."

"Developments?"

"Princess Nettayna has been passed into the hands of the kalkar," said Averil.

"Then I must follow at once. Can you give me a direction?"

"South," said Ordel in a tight voice.

Evelar bowed, and strode from the room.

Evelar rode due south at a gallop, determined to catch the Prince before he got himself into trouble. The revealer watched the ground for signs of the Prince's passage.

Atwin had been travelling in haste and he was easy to track, but Evelar's mind was not on his work. His training acted automatically, while his mind wandered the halls of the College with Miyam. She had begun her examinations and he was worried.

He was sure she would pass without any trouble, but still something gnawed at his mind. He was labouring under a premonition. He knew there was a chance she might fail one of the tests, but which one?

He assumed it would be one of the written tests, since her practical skills were so good. She had, after all, been absent from classes for five years. He began to 'listen in'. Whenever she became stuck on a particular question, he would quietly implant the answer in her mind. She protested at first.

'You know you shouldn't do that, dear,' she said.

'Why not?'

'Because it's cheating.'

'Not really. Who's going to know?'

'Maestro will find out.'

'How?'

'I don't know. He just will.'

She began to realise his occasional help was actually a good idea when she almost killed herself and several others in the science laboratory.

She was in the middle of mixing volatile chemicals to make a phosphorescent light and had picked up the wrong bottle by mistake.

'Not that one!' Evelar cried out silently.

'What?'

'Do you want to demolish the whole science wing?'

'What?'

'Take a look at the label on that bottle you have in your

hand.'

She glanced absently at the bottle. *'I don't see...'* She stopped in shock as the word 'sulphur' jumped out at her. *'Oh my! Perhaps you're right, dear.'*

After that she accepted his little hints without comment.

Theology had never been one of Evelar's strong subjects, and after gaining the green he had made it a point to study it more fully. Miyam sat puzzling over the next question:

QUESTION FOUR - Name the twelve forgotten spirits who sit on the guiding council under Zayus, leader of the council, and give their epithets.

Miyam struggled. She named: Pollon, reader of the star trail; Nyzus, giver of festivals; Aphris, joiner of hearts; Erra, helper of women; Estiya, keeper of the hearth; Sidon, tamer of the sea; Aven, slayer of foes; Resh, leader of arms; and Temis, mistress of the hunt. She counted them. Nine. Three more.

She drummed her fingers on the table. They hung there, on the proverbial tip of her tongue. But they refused to jump onto the tip of her quill. Evelar hissed at her.

'The harvest...'

She wrote: Demores, master of the harvest. She thought again. Two more. She could not remember.

'Fire...' Evelar whispered in her mind.

'Who?' she replied.

'The blacksmith...'

"Of course," she cried aloud.

She wrote: Phestus, keeper of the flame. She racked her brain for that elusive last councillor god. She knew she should remember him. Yes, she knew he was male. After a minute or so of frantic thinking, she was tempted to write simply 'a male one'. But then...

> *'Messages...'*
> *'Ummm. I know it...'*
> *'Cunning...'*
> *'Ohh... What's his name again?'*
> *'Alphabet...'*
> *'Ohh... Who is it?'*
> *'I'm not telling,'* he taunted.

She groaned. *'Oh, I don't know,'* she howled.

> *'Yes you do. Good luck...'*

She slammed her hand, palm first, down on the table. "HER..." she cried aloud, stopping herself before she disqualified herself.

She wrote triumphantly: Herm, reader of the signs. Twelve. She breathed a sigh and continued on to the next question.

Evelar began to relax. Miyam was almost through the written exams. The last was the written preliminary to the tests on physical technique.

> *QUESTION TEN - Explain, using diagrams where necessary, the five most humane ways to kill an enemy.*

She had four: Asphyxiation (strangulation/ suffocation); Exsanguination (by severing the jugular); Coronary Violation (knife to the heart); Medullic Impact (blow to base of skull). She could not remember the fifth.

> *'Temple,'* said Evelar quietly.

She clicked her fingers and wrote: Cranial Impact (blow to temple).

> *'Thank you, dear.'*
> *'Think practically nothing of it, my love.'*

*

Miyam had passed her written exams. Relieved, Evelar turned his attention to tracking Prince Atwin, just in time to notice something rather strange. Atwin had continued south at his reckless pace. But the trail of the Princess veered off to the east.

Evelar dismounted and examined the ground more closely. The evidence did not match Leena's signal. When he searched with his mind, he could hear her echo far to the east, even though the physical trail continued south. Something had happened in the desert and she had definitely changed direction.

The revealer sat by the road to think. Should he continue after Atwin, or wait for him to realise his mistake and turn back? He closed his eyes and sent out a search. When he found the Prince, he had already begun to feel his mistake. Evelar spoke, not to Atwin, but to Naali. The amulet began to pull Atwin back.

* * *

As Netta stumbled in the midst of the kalkar pack, she searched her brain for a way to stop them taking her into the desert. Trembling in her growing terror, she dragged her feet, hoping against hope that they would not go out there. Ahead she could see the great expanse of sand coming closer with every step.

She could feel the Prince as, riding like a madman, Atwin followed the trail, he and the wild stallion of one mind. They must find her before it was too late. If the kalkar took her into the desert the Princess was doomed.

In the daylight, when the kalkar froze in the sunlight, Netta used the power of Leena. They stood like a ring of statues and their membranous wings, which hung like a fleshy cloak when they were active, were now wrapped protectively about them as they quietly absorbed sunlight. The ground at their feet was scorched and a light miasma of smoke hung about them.

Reaching a hand toward one of the enemy encircling her, Netta took a breath and called on the amulet's power. Leena began to glow and the blue light grew to envelop the Princess. Then she carefully focused the power, bringing the blue glow to a ball of energy in her hand.

She released a burst of blue light which engulfed the kalkar, drenching it in cold flame and quenching its fire. Pushing the dead kalkar to the ground, Netta broke free of the circle.

Leena could feel Naali following, but he was so far behind. The Princess headed back into the mountains alone, her only thought to reach him before the kalkar caught her again. As night fell, she searched for a cave in which to hide.

Concealing herself the best she could, Netta huddled down to sleep, only to wake to the heat of Leena at her neck as the kalkar closed in once again. She watched as they came, flying in on their fleshy wings, silhouetted against the moon. They seemed to know exactly where to find her.

Netta ran, but it was no good. The enemy swooped in on her, clutching her wrists and feet, burning the flesh as they carried her away. The Princess cried out in agony as her skin blistered at the touch, but they ignored her cries.

Netta sent Leena's blue ice to engulf the clutching talons of the kalkar and it was their turn to scream.Dropping to the ground, Netta huddled, the pain in her feet preventing escape as the leader of the pack stalked toward her. It glared at her and her eyes widened as it finally spoke.

"You have injured us, human. You deserve to die!"

The voice was harsh and rasping, barely understandable, but the words were recognisable.

"You injured me first!" she retorted.

The creature raised a hand to strike, but Leena engulfed

the Princess in blue light and the enemy paused. Netta held up her hands, baring the wrists to show the burns.

"Your flesh burns me," she hissed. "Touch me again and more of your pack will face Leena's ice."

The pack leader hesitated. "You will come willingly. If you resist you will be burned."

"If you burn you will be cooled!"

The creature raised a hand again. Netta glowed blue again. Her eyes narrowed.

"I can control the ice," she said carefully. "Can you control the fire?"

The pack leader hissed. "What you ask causes great pain!"

"More pain than being frozen?"

The creature hissed again. Then he nodded. "We will try, but you will come willingly, and the one who kills will not use her ice on us."

Captive again, Netta trudged once more toward the desert. But she knew that if they continued south she would run out of water in a matter of days. As the sands drew closer she held back, trying to think of a way to avoid the certain death that awaited her there.

Finally, the last of the scrub gave way to rolling dunes. Netta sank to her knees in despair. The pack leader stood over her glaring. He reached down to grab her wrist and pull her along but she shrank away.

"My hand is cooled," he rasped. "I keep my word."

She shook her head. "I cannot go out there, I will not survive!"

The creature looked from her to the sands and back in confusion. "I do not understand."

"There is no water there," she cried. "You may not need it but I do."

The kalkar hesitated, then took her wrist and dragged her to her feet. His hand was uncomfortably warm but did not burn.

"You will come willingly," he said. "As you promised. You carry water."

"The Barren Wastes are huge, it will take weeks to cross. I have enough water for a few days at best. When it runs out I will die."

The pack leader thought about it. Then he pulled on her arm and dragged her struggling out onto the sand.

Two days into the desert, Netta's water bags were empty. She trudged slowly in the midst of the kalkar, the shifting sand dragging at her feet. Travelling at night was a mercy, but the days were tortuous, trapped in a ring of kalkar under the baking sun.

At the end of the third day, with no water and no shelter, the Princess was barely conscious when the kalkar pack came to life at nightfall. The creatures milled around in confusion when she did not rise, and the pack leader approached her with anger in his stance.

"Why do you not walk," he glowered.

Netta could not lift her head and stared blankly, mouth moving but no sound escaping her cracked lips.

"Speak, human!"

"Water..." she whispered.

The pack leader snorted in derision then made a decision. "The great water is not far, we will take you there."

"No!" she cried, voice cracking in her effort to speak. "I can't drink sea water..."

"Water is water."

"No..." she whispered. "Sea water is salty. It will make me even more ill... I need fresh water, from the mountains."

The kalkar muttered in confusion. "I do not understand

you human."

"So let me die then."

He made a noise that might have been a kalkar curse. "No, we need you alive. If you die there will be nothing for Naali to follow."

There was a moment of silence, then Netta felt herself taken by wrist and ankle and lifted off the ground. She felt the rush of air as they flew, back toward the mountains.

By the time the predawn glow had lightened the sky, they had reached the foothills, and she was deposited by the bank of a little stream just as the kalkar settled into dormancy with the coming of the sun.

Princess Netta made no attempt to escape. She was so weakened by the desert that she would never have made it. She spent the day immersed in the stream rehydrating, bathing and drinking in slow regular sips. By the time night fell, she was feeling much stronger, and when the kalkar awoke she was able to walk.

The pack leader had made a choice. They now travelled east along the foothills, close to water for the Princess with the desert sand to their right. She wondered what the new plan was, but they moved quickly, keeping her at a forced jog.

The Princess knew that escape was not an option, not without help. She just could not travel far enough nor protect herself from recapture. At the end of the third night she could see the sunrise glistening on sea water at the horizon.

The next evening the leader sent one of his pack mates winging out over the ocean, and the rest stood staring after him, doing nothing, waiting for news. That day, when the kalkar stopped in their circle about her, she found herself held in place, one creature on each side with a firm grip on her wrists.

She wondered what had changed, this new behaviour a mystery. They were taking no chances that she might try to escape. Unable to even reach for food from her pack, Netta sat, arms held aloft by her captors.

In that awkward position she eventually dozed.As night fell the pack stood for a long moment as the wings that hung loose like a cloak slowly spread and hardened. Netta watched in fascination, seeing up close for the first time the bizarre physiological process that stiffened that membranous skin into powerful wings.

She could see fine lines thickening as acidic blood filled the lacework of veins under the skin, plumping up the flesh. They opened their now full wings and lifted off, carrying her with them, following their pack mate over the sea.

FIVE

The door closed quietly behind her. Miyam stood calmly, awaiting the attack that would surely come. She looked warily about the dimly lit room, unsure where the attacker was hiding. A movement caught her eye and she inched toward it. Then she cursed. The disturbance in the corner was a rat.

"Did my pet startle you?" said a voice from behind. "I'm so sorry."

Miyam spun, just in time to catch the full force of the opening blow with her sword. The blade sang with the impact, and her right arm took the strength of it. The fight was on.

"So, you're the one they hired me to kill?" said the attacker in satisfaction. "This is too easy."

In a flurry of lightning strokes, the man pushed her back.

"My freedom is only moments away," he cackled.

Miyam fought back. She had never given up her training, and she was at least a match for this over-confident spy. She forced him to back across the room. He snarled.

"Now I know who you are," he said stiffly. "I recognise the style."

She ignored him. He was only trying to distract her. She knew better than to return his taunts. He was weakening himself with talking, paying too little attention to the fighting. She drove him slowly about the room.

"You fight like your mother," he said. "That makes it all the more easy for me to read you."

She hesitated at that, a mistake. He grabbed the opportunity and fell savagely to the attack. It was his turn to push her around the room.

"You've grown since I saw you in your father's brokerage all those years ago," he said then. "How old are you now? Twenty, twenty-one?"

Catching a constant barrage of blows against her sword, Miyam felt the strain. With each series of blows, her right arm weakened and, unconsciously, she began to favour that side.

"You're weak on the right," he said gleefully. "What fun."

The blows rained down on her right. Miyam felt her arm tremble. She could not fight back. She could barely swing her sword.

Somewhere far to the south, Evelar groaned. He had known that she might fail one of the tests, but he had never dreamed it would be sword-play. He was terrified for her.

Failure in sword-play came only one way - death. The College hired convicted spies, offering them freedom if they could kill the candidate. Miyam held on, but her right arm was aching terribly under the unmerciful onslaught. The spy cackled again.

"I would love to see your father's face when he finds out who killed his darling daughter. Isn't revenge wonderful?"

"My father is dead," she said between clenched teeth.

He paused, but Miyam was too weak to press the advantage. The spy screamed his frustration and flew at her, swinging wildly. She could not hold off the assault. One powerful stroke sent her sword skittering across the floor, flung at last from her weakened grasp.

In the mountains of northern Tellemot, Evelar drew his sword. Then he realised there was nothing he could do to help her and sheathed it again, cursing under his breath.

Miyam fought on, catching the blows with the knife in her left hand. Then she lost that too, and was forced to her knees. The man laughed delightedly and broke off the assault. Miyam was weaponless. He lifted his sword to her chest.

He stood over her triumphantly and she waited for the stroke that would end her life. It did not come. Something in his eyes chilled her to the bone and she felt a terror she had never dreamed possible. She began to shake her head pleadingly.

Slowly, deliberately, the spy sheathed his sword.

"Now you are mine," he said.

Lightning fast, a hand shot out and grabbed the fabric of her cloak at the back of her neck, forcing her head back. He pulled downward, forcing her back into a painful arch. Unable to prevent it, she found herself on the floor, the spy pinning her down.

"Now you are going to give me what your mother never would."

He pressed his mouth bruisingly to hers. Miles away Evelar clenched a fist, tears streaming down his face. Miyam sobbed. The spy pinned her with one hand and fumbled at his trousers with the other.

He rose to his knees to make it easier and Miyam struck. Her knee connected sharply with his groin. The man cried out in agony and rolled off her.

Miyam pulled off the brown sash that held her hood in place and proceeded to strangle him with it, but her right arm protested painfully. There was no way she could kill him that way. She clenched her teeth, but it was no use. She looked frantically about.

She let go and ran for her knife. As she turned back, the knife in her right hand, the spy began to rise. She took a step, lifted a foot and calmly kicked him in the head.

He landed on his back and it was her turn to pin him to the ground. With her strong left hand she held his sword arm to the floor. The knife in her right, she slashed his left arm above the elbow, severing muscle and nerve. The damaged arm flopped lifeless to the floor. She raised the knife above her head and looked the man straight in the eye.

Miyam brought the knife swiftly down, burying the blade in his chest. The man gasped, his eyes locked on hers. She gave the knife a sharp twist and it pierced the heart. The man's eyes glazed over and she felt his death rattle. Miyam sagged over the body, trembling. She gently massaged the weakened arm.

'*Well done, my love,*' a voice whispered in her head.

She sat still for a long time. Finally, a hand on her shoulder brought her back to reality. She looked up at the examiner and he nodded once. Miyam grasped the knife and pulled it from the dead man's chest. She wiped it clean on the spy's shirt and stood slowly. She looked about for her sword.

Switching the knife to her left hand, she bent to grasp the hilt of the sword in her right. Then she paused. She looked at the weakened right arm and flexed the fingers. She switched the knife back to her right hand and picked up the sword with her left. She hefted it experimentally, feeling its weight. She glanced at the examiner, who nodded approvingly. Then she preceded the examiner from the room.

* * *

Evelar was pulled back to himself by the sound of approaching hoof beats. He leapt to his feet, drawing his sword and springing into the saddle. Then he relaxed. He sheathed his sword and slid down, burying his face in

Lumen's mane. Forcing himself to regain control, he drew himself up to his full height and strode out to meet Atwin.

"Well met, Your Highness," Evelar said cheerfully. "You seem to be travelling in the wrong direction."

Atwin shrugged ruefully. "I missed the change in Leena's direction."

"I thought as much. She went this way," he said, pointing east.

"Yes, so it seems."

The Prince and the revealer crested a hill and looked out over the Sea of Mytar. The wind which swept off the lead grey water was bitter and storm clouds brewing to the south announced a cold, rough night. They rode down to the beach in silence and looked around for a suitable place to make camp. A large pile of driftwood and dried seaweed provided a good wind break. They pitched their tents and made a small fire from what dry wood they could find.

Evelar went out after they had eaten and searched the surrounding area. Kalkar had definitely been here. After a few moments Atwin joined him, pulling his cloak tightly about himself against the bitter wind.

"Where did they go from here?" he asked.

"I'm not sure," replied the revealer. "They did camp here, but the trail just disappears."

Evelar crouched in the sand and peered out across the beach. He could see the signs of kalkar, but there was no indication that they had ever left this spot. It was as if they had simply vanished into thin air. Either that or they had suddenly spread wings and leapt into the clouds.

"Your Highness, does Naali have any idea what direction they went?"

Atwin concentrated. "It sounds absurd, I know," he said. "But Naali insists they continued east." He stared out over the dark sea.

"Not so absurd, my friend. Remember the battle of the sands, when the front rank flew at us."

Atwin nodded. "And the sea attack on the way home. We need a ship."

The revealer and the Prince prepared to send a mental communication to Shirall. Not for the first time, Evelar wished he could teach his friend the finer, more streamlined mindspeak used in the College, but of course the secrecy of the training prevented that. Atwin spoke the words of the ancient spell and soon the Regent's mental voice answered.

MY DEAR ATWIN, she said. *WHAT NEWS?*

WE ARE NOW SOUTH OF THE HEIGHTS, ON THE COAST AT THE NORTHERN FRINGE OF THE BARREN WASTES.

AND?

THE TRAIL STOPS HERE.

OH DEAR! DO YOU HAVE ANY LEADS?

NO, BUT WE HAVE A HUNCH.

THAT SOUNDS... PROMISING... she said dubiously.

FEAR NOT, AVERIL, IT IS A SOLID IDEA. BUT WE NEED A SHIP, WELL STOCKED FOR A LONG VOYAGE. WE HAVE NO IDEA HOW FAR WE WILL NEED TO SAIL.

I WILL DISPATCH MY BEST. BUT IT WILL TAKE A FEW DAYS TO SAIL DOWN THE COAST TO YOUR POSITION. HOW WILL THEY FIND YOU?

WE WILL HEAD SOUTH TO TELLEMOT, WE WILL BE WAITING THERE.

Atwin and the revealer rode south and reached Tellemot before the end of the day. They found an inn near the port and settled down to wait. It was the first chance either had had since leaving Shirall to sit quietly in one spot for more than a few hours.

Since meeting up three days ago they had spoken little, intent on following the trail. Now, with a wait of at least two days ahead of them, they had time to relax and talk. Evelar asked the Prince to tell him how Netta was taken.

"Someone infiltrated the palace and took her right out of the stable. Killed the guardsman to get inside. Naali showed me her captors. They were tribesmen. That was how I knew they had taken her south. I could feel it, too." Atwin hesitated then, a look of consternation on his face.

"What is it?" asked Evelar.

Atwin shook his head, unwilling to tell his secret.

"You know something else."

Atwin looked up and nodded dejectedly. "I know who was behind it."

"Who?"

The Prince hesitated again. He looked around, as if afraid of being overheard.

"It was my father..." he whispered.

"Are you sure?"

"I saw him in one of my visions."

"Have you told anyone else?"

He shook his head. "And be accused of treason?"

"None would accuse you, my friend."

"I could not take the risk. It would be seen as paranoia if I were to denounce him." The Prince shook his head again. "But I know what I saw."

"I believe you. The question is what are we to do about it?"

"I know not. I cannot denounce him. That would destroy all I have worked for all these years."

"But in having the Princess taken, he has himself committed treason."

"Still, he will go unpunished," he said harshly, his frustration getting the better of him. "I cannot understand why he would do such a thing. What hopes he to gain by it?"

"I don't know, my friend."

"It makes me so angry, to think my own father would do such a thing," Atwin paced.

"He is misguided. His illness controls him now."

Atwin growled his anger, fists clenched.

"Come down to the courtyard. You need to work off some of that nervous energy."

"I fear I have neglected my training of late."

"All the more reason to practice, Your Highness. Come, spar with me."

The Prince grinned. "You forget, Averil hired a College sword master. I was besting my trainers in Drasmil by the age of fourteen."

"Prove it!"

As night fell, Evelar slipped away from the inn, riding out of the town. He needed to talk to Miyam. Since the incident with the spy, the premonition of danger had faded and Evelar had ceased 'listening in' on her physical examinations.

He had known that she would pass with no problems and he had needed to keep his mind on the trail. But now, as they embarked on a journey of uncertainty into unknown waters, he needed to fill her in on the events so far. He found a secluded place under the cliff by the harbour and settled down.

'Hello dear,' she said as he entered her mind. *'How goes the search?'*

'We have a direction,' he said cautiously.

'And?'

'We go east.'

'Where are you now?'

'*Tellemot, waiting for a ship from Shirall.*'

There was a long silence. '*Ah,*' she said finally.

'*I trust the testing is progressing well?*' he said quickly.

'*Mental Technique begins tomorrow and continues for the next two weeks. The week after, stealth begins. So in about a month, if all goes well, the ceremony will be performed and the oath will be taken.*'

'*You will join us then?*'

She hesitated. '*East? Where am I going to find a sea captain willing to take me out there? And if I did, how would I find you?*'

He sighed. '*You're right, of course. I suppose you'll have to wait there, my love.*'

She groaned. '*How long?*'

'*I have no idea.*'

* * *

SIX

Netta hung from the grip of her captors, the heat in their talons barely stifled, the flesh at her wrists and ankles scalded painfully. Her skin did not burn enough to blister, but the kalkar were making no effort to cool their touch more than strictly necessary.

Gritting her teeth as her muscles protested the ungainly mode of travel, Netta stared down at the endless expanse of ocean reflecting the moonlight and prayed that they did not drop her.

As the first signs of dawn appeared on the horizon she could finally see the small island ahead. It was a race against time. If the kalkar did not reach the island before the sun peeked over the waves they would freeze mid flight and plummet.

Every moment brought a lightening of the sky, but the island seemed to hover in the distance, barely coming closer. Half the pack flew on ahead to safety, leaving Netta and her captors to struggle on as the red blaze of dawn threatened in the eastern sky.

She could see light sparkling on the water now, as the first flush of daylight tinged the horizon. Netta felt her legs drop as the two holding her ankles let go and fled toward the safety of the island, now looming in shadow against the predawn light.

The two remaining kalkar flew on, radiating their fear as the light increased. They were not going to make it and terror lent speed to their flight.

The island came closer, but not close enough. The two kalkar above her grunted in effort between whimpers of panic. Netta could do nothing but watch. From the little island a high pitched ululating keening reached her as the rest of the kalkar mourned the imminent passing of their pack mates.

Then, with a last whimper of fear, the two spread their membranous wings wide and with a crackle of static charge froze midair as the first ray of sun shot out across the waves, bathing them in light. At the same moment the keening was silenced as the pack on the beach also froze.

Netta struggled, but her hands were trapped. They had not thought to let go before they went dormant. For a moment, the outspread wings held them aloft, gliding on the dawn breeze, bringing them precious yards closer to the island. Not close enough.

Riding on the currents of the air, the two kalkar and the human woman slowly descended, covering a little more distance as the ocean rose up to meet them. Netta felt her feet brush the water and the forward momentum slowed further as her legs dragged through the waves.

The two kalkar, still as stone and oblivious to their fate, pitched forward and fell, pulling the Princess with them. With a hiss of steam they hit the water, fire extinguished and bodies melting and dissolving.

Netta found her hands free as her captors' talons bubbled away in a pool of foam. Fighting to stay afloat in the now hot foaming water, the Princess struck out for the beach, determined to save herself.

Finally, she managed to catch a wave and tumbled into shore, pitched unceremoniously onto the sand. Coughing and retching, Netta fought the undertow and crawled up the beach to finally collapse in the dry sand past the reach of the breakers.

Netta had lost track of the days and had lost count of the islands where they had stopped. On waking each evening they wasted no time taking hold of her wrists and ankles and taking wing once more.

Most nights passed without incident, the island found by the advance scout exactly where he had reported through the pack mind of her captors. After one such night they arrived at the next island before sunrise and the pack stood on the beach, silently listening to the progress of the scout looking for the next landfall. But something was wrong.

Netta could see the agitation in their bodies. As the sun lightened the sky they began their high pitched keening and she knew then what was wrong. The scout had not found land and the sun was about to rise.

They stayed on that island for another night, as another scout flew out looking for the next landfall. But that scout failed too. Finally, the third scout found land. Netta prayed this island would be the last.

She was ill from eating fermented fruit, the only sustenance on these tiny islands. Her arms ached from hanging in the grip of her captors for hours at a time, and her shoulders felt like they had been ripped from their sockets.

The next night, the scout found the next stop easily, and the last island was already far distant. They flew through the night, and Netta allowed herself to doze. She had found this the only way to block out the pain in her arms. She was woken by the sound of gulls fishing, and it became clear that land was close.

As the Princess watched the land approach, she knew the crossing was finally over. The shoreline ahead was long and straight, no mere island this time. Without even a dramatic race to the finish, they landed with time to spare on the top of a cliff, the few remaining members of the pack as glad as she to be on solid ground.

* * *

Instead of waiting for a berth in the crowded port, the ship cast anchor off shore and sent a boat over the side. Expecting to be simply picked up, Evelar and Atwin were surprised to see a group of people climb down into the little boat. They watched in silence, waiting patiently for them to reach the sand. As they came closer, the Prince and the revealer looked at each other in surprise.

As the boat pulled up onto the beach, Ordel jumped out and raised a hand to help Delsi alight. Averil stood slowly in the stern and waited for Ordel to return to help her. A young woman in a flowing blue coat clambered out without aid and waded through the ankle deep water. She walked up to Atwin and stood before him. Then she threw back her hood and tossed her head defiantly. It was Kandina. Atwin's face sank and Naali leapt against his chest.

"What are you doing here, Kandi?" he said with a weary sigh.

"I am concerned about my cousin's fate. Besides, I came with Mother. What did you think I was doing here?"

"To tell you the truth, I really am not sure," he frowned, confused by the signals Naali was sending.

"What is that supposed to mean?"

"Come now, Kandina. Your motives are never purely... conciliatory."

"Your point being?"

"Only that you are becoming known as quite the little schemer. I do not wish to be the object of such insincerity."

Kandi's jaw dropped. "How dare you say such things to me! You know..."

"Play not the innocent with me, Princess. I know you

harbour certain... designs... in my direction and I cannot believe that you do not feel a certain satisfaction that my wife has been removed from your line of fire."

Kandi spluttered, hands clenching and unclenching at her sides. She searched frantically for some cutting retort. Finally, she let out a strangled "Oh," spun on her heel and stalked away.

Evelar stepped up behind the Prince. "Are you sure that was wise, Your Highness?"

Atwin sighed. "I know not what came over me. Naali has been reacting so strangely whenever Kandi appears. It threw me off guard."

"How long has this been happening?"

"Since Netta disappeared. I wonder if there is some connection?"

Delsi and her husband made their way to where the two stood, followed by Averil, looking concerned by her daughter's behaviour.

"Greetings, Your Majesty," said Evelar.

"Averil," said Atwin. "What is going on here?"

Averil shrugged. "We thought we might join you."

"But we have no idea where this voyage may lead."

"No matter," said Delsi. "My daughter will be needing me when we eventually find her."

"But who will look after things in Shirall?" said Atwin.

"Worry not," Averil replied. "I will remain behind with Kandina. We have another ship a few hours behind."

"So tell us," said Ordel quietly, "where are we bound?"

"East," said Atwin tensely.

"What did you say?" said Delsi in surprise.

Atwin looked out over the tossing waves. "That way," he said to no-one in particular.

"Excuse me, Yer Worshipfulnesses," a weathered seaman butted in. "But did ye say east?"

"I did," said Atwin.

"I don't think so. I won't be takin' me ship out there fer nobody. Beggin' yer pardons, but I'm no' stupid. There ain't nothin' out there but waves 'n' salt. I won't be takin' me ship over the edge o' the world, thank ye very much."

"Now, Captain," said Evelar calmly. "Our researchers have proved conclusively that there is no 'edge of the world'. You needn't worry."

"Well I won't be takin' yer word fer it, effn ye don't mind. Besides, effn the monsters don't get us first we'll be dyin' o' starvation afore we reach land. There ain't none to be reachin'."

"How much stores do you have aboard, Captain?"

"Enough fer 'bout a month or so, two effn we ration a bit."

"Then I'll make a deal with you. If we have not struck land by the time half the food and water have been used, we will turn back."

"Half?"

"That's what I said."

"All right then, I'll talk it over with me first mate. But effn he don't agree, we won't be movin' nowheres."

"You must be insane!" Kandina interrupted. "How can you seriously consider a voyage east? It is suicide. If Netta really did go that way you will never find her."

Atwin stared at her. "Are you suggesting we give up?"

"Of course not," she said a little too quickly. "I am just saying that you should not be so eager to chase after so vague a trail."

"I will not leave her to be killed or worse at the hands of the kalkar. Wherever they have taken her, I will follow and I will not rest until I have brought her safely home."

"But what if you are wrong and you find her not?"

"Then I will die trying."

* * *

In the underground palace at Shirall, Kandi sat in her chamber in front of her mirror thinking hard. Somehow, the horrible scene with Atwin had finally made her realise how much she had hurt him. The pain in his eyes at mention of Netta, the sheer determination to find her no matter what the cost, gave her pause.

She had never intended for Netta to be kidnapped, and she shivered when she thought about how it had come about. She had been stupid enough to say the wrong thing at the wrong time to the wrong person. She knew now that her own unkind words to King Gerard at the joining feast had caused it all. The mad king had taken her words and put them into action.

She was sure Prince Atwin did not know it was her doing, but he had nevertheless drawn away from her. Kandi knew it was her own silly crush that had pushed him away. She had to come to terms with his marriage to Netta, her best and only friend. She had to push the hurt of her unrequited crush down and be happy for them.

She wiped away tears as she stared at herself in the mirror. Now Netta was gone and Atwin had gone after her into who knew what danger, because he loved her and could not live without her. Kandi sobbed, wishing it was her that he loved, but she forced it down and wiped her eyes.

She had to fix this and there was only one man who could do it. Kandi rushed about, gathering supplies into a small pack. She had no idea what she would need, considering every item several times before finally including it. A blanket, a change of clothes for when she got there, a warm cloak, a purse full of coins. She would get a loaf of bread and some cooked meat or cheese from the kitchen.

She looked at her fine clothing and sighed. A lone noblewoman would be an immediate target for thugs, she realised. She would have to find something more suitable, perhaps a page boy's doublet and hose from the laundry. And she must remember a knife of some sort from the kitchen.

She penned a quick note to her mother and left it on the dresser. Glancing hastily about the room, she squared her shoulders and took a deep breath. She headed to the kitchen and the laundry for the rest of her supplies, then out to the stables for her beloved gelding, Swiftly. The guard at the gatehouse gave her a nod and opened the heavy iron gate, showing no surprise at the departure of a young page on an errand to the town for his master.

When Kandi's maid rushed into the dining hall at breakfast, flustered and worried because the Princess was not in her room, Averil had waved it off as just another silly escapade. But when Kandi did not appear for lunch, Averil grew increasingly worried.

Now she feared for her daughter's safety. When the chamber maid had gone to make the Princess's bed she found it had not been slept in, and it was the chamber maid who found the note and brought it to the audience room. It was a most unhelpful and cryptic message.

Mother,
There is something I need to do and I will be back soon.
Please worry not.
Kandi.

"I'm sure Kandina is fine," said the maid, trying to calm her. "She could be anywhere."

"Precisely," Averil retorted. "She could be anywhere! No indication of where she was going," Averil waved the note helplessly. "If she left last evening, she could be half way to

Drasmil by now!" Then she stopped with a horrified frown. "Or lying in a gutter somewhere..."

"You could try to contact her," the maid suggested.

Averil shook her head. "No, Kandi has never communicated before, it would only scare her. Get me the captain of the guard. He can send soldiers out looking, and they will not give up until they find her."

* * *

Prince Calib of Drasmil rode out on patrol with his troops. As he rode his mind wandered. His father's strange behaviour had passed beyond the established bounds of his long term madness. The King seemed uncharacteristically happy with himself, as if he were a child who had just done something immensely satisfying yet terribly naughty.

Calib knew it had something to do with his brother Atwin, it always did. But he could not fathom what his father might have done. Surely it was not just happiness that Atwin was out of the picture, chasing after his kidnapped princess.

The Prince had an idea that his father was hiding a dark act and a small part of him dreaded the thought that maybe the King had something to do with Princess Nettayna's kidnapping. Calib desperately hoped he was wrong.

Calib was shaken from his reverie by a commotion ahead. The Prince had ridden ahead of his men as scout, and now sat his horse watching, his soldiers far behind. A small band of thugs had waylaid a lone traveller and the scene looked about to turn ugly.

Moving closer, the Prince saw five men surrounding a small figure in the livery of Shirall. He wondered what a page was doing this far from home. The lad was scowling at his attackers, brandishing what looked like a carving knife.

Quietly, the Prince dismounted, drawing his sword as the men closed in on the boy. With a sneer, the thug leader sent two of his minions into the fray as the lad waved the knife about. There was the briefest struggle, before the boy was overwhelmed by the two men, his knife sent skidding across the cobbles as his wrists were captured. The thugs dragged the lad to their master, who laughed.

"Give me your purse, boy," snarled the thug leader.

The plucky boy shook his head. At a nod from their leader one of the thugs twisted the boy's arm painfully behind his back and he cried out in pain.

"You're a page, yes? You must have a purse of moneys for whatever business you're on. Now hand it over."

The boy whimpered. Calib had seen enough. Stepping silently up to the leader, he pressed his sword into the man's back.

"Unhand the boy and call off your thugs."

The thug leader spun, heedless of the sword, a sneer on his grizzled face.

"How dare you point a knife at me?"

The Prince raised an eyebrow. "You are a cocky one," he said mildly. "I repeat. Unhand the boy and call off your thugs."

He pushed the sword point hard against the big man's stomach and the thug drew in his breath sharply.

"Or what?" said the man, sneering.

The Prince shrugged. "Or I will give my sword its head!"

The thug leader threw his head back and laughed as his men closed in on the Prince, but Calib only smiled.

"If you are looking for a fight, I should warn you. You have chosen the wrong opponent."

With that the Prince stepped back and took stock, sword at the ready. All five men closed in, surrounding him. Calib turned slowly, sizing up each man. Two held swords and looked like they knew how to use them. The others carried knives but only the leader looked confident.

As they fell to the attack the Prince was already in action, quickly disabling the two hesitant men and turning his attention to the leader and his two swordsmen. The thug leader held back, letting his henchmen do the work.

Calib knew the tactic, sending the boys in to tire him first. This leader was a typical bully, hiding behind his men who he ruled by fear. The swordsmen were moderately well trained, but Calib had spent years sparring with his College trained brother, and these men were no match for the Prince at his best.

The sword fight was over quickly. The first man lost his blade as Calib slashed his wrist and sent his sword skittering across the road and into the bushes. The second fought hard, and eventually the Prince was forced to stick him in the side. The man fell to his knees, one hand pressed to his side and the other raised in front in submission.

The leader snarled, but made no attack. Instead he turned his back on the Prince and stalked off, his four injured men slumping after him. Rising to his full height, the Prince sheathed his sword and squared his shoulders. Then he turned to face the frightened page.

"Well, lad, what are you doing this far from Shirall?"

The boy looked up from where he huddled in fear. His eyes widened.

"Calib?" the boy whispered. "That was incredible!"

But that wasn't a lad's voice. Nor face for that matter despite the dirt, streaked with tears. Calib's eyes narrowed.

"Who are you?" he said.

The page lifted a hand to push back the hood of the orange and yellow liveried surcoat. Long red hair fell to her waist. The Prince gasped and his heart jumped in his chest.

"Kandina?"

* * *

SEVEN

King Gerard sat idly in his great carved throne, crown lopsided as usual. He had long since stopped worrying about appearances. He knew that however well he presented himself the people who came to petition would sneer and whisper. The snake had done a good job turning his people against him.

Lounging back against the cushions, one leg over the elaborately carved arm, he yawned as the latest idiot begged for mediation in some petty land rights dispute. The King had no idea how many of these undeserving cases would pass through the hall today.

He wished he could trust his advisers to take audience for him, but they were all in thrall of his traitorous son. A shout, muffled through the big double doors, caught the King's attention.

"Your Highness, you cannot enter, the King is in audience!"

The supplicant stuttered and stumbled over his words, glancing at the closed doors.

"I have waited long enough, Calib," said a female voice. "If I had not needed to make myself presentable I would have come straight here. Why would I wait for some peasant to finish talking?"

The King sat up straight in his throne. Finally some excitement, he thought as the doors burst open.

A pretty young woman stormed in, dressed in a fine silk

gown with light red hair piled high on her regal head. The King raised an eyebrow. Now what was the little princess doing in Drasmil?

The Princess Kandina stalked toward the King, Calib following close behind.

"I am sorry, Father, she would not be stopped."

The King raised a hand. "No matter, Calib, let her speak," he smiled at the Princess. "To what do I owe this unexpected pleasure?"

Kandina scowled. "No pleasure, Your Majesty."

"Oh," the King said, taken aback. "Then why are you here?"

The Princess glared at him through narrowed eyes. "To give you a piece of my mind."

The King chuckled. "Clear the room, Calib," he said.

"Yes, Father."

The Prince quickly rounded up the advisers and courtiers who stood about and shuffled them out the door, then returned to the King's side.

"You too, Calib."

"Oh," he said, looking nonplussed. "Yes, Father."

When the big double doors closed on the Prince, King Gerard focused on the girl in front of him and smiled. This was going to be fun.

"Now, little princess," he said. "How have I offended you?"

Kandina glared. "You had my cousin kidnapped," she accused.

The King widened his eyes innocently. "Who, me? Now why would I do that?"

"I know it was you, and I regret ever putting the idea in your head!"

"You have an over inflated opinion of yourself, little princess. What makes you think it was anything you said?"

The Princess scowled again. "I am not blind, I know you heard everything I said at Netta and Atwin's joining feast. I saw the look in your eye, but in my own pain I realised not what I had said. You should not have sought me out further, and you should not have taken me seriously."

The King threw his head back and laughed. "You are clever, little princess."

"Why did you do it?"

He shrugged. "You wanted her gone, I wanted her gone. Why not? You cannot tell me this is not exactly what you wanted."

"No it is not!" she cried. "You had no right!"

"I had every right," he snarled. "I will do everything in my power to stop that snake from stealing my throne."

"What are you talking about? What snake?"

"Without the Princess to give him Shirall he will never gain influence over the council and he will never get hold of Shirall's armies. My throne is safe."

"Do you mean Atwin? He is your son and heir. Why would he want to do any of that?"

"Because he wants my throne, and he will stop at nothing to get it."

The little princess shook her head. "He would never do that. Quite the opposite. He worships you."

"You silly little girl, this is politics. You have no idea what he is capable of."

"No," she snapped. "You have no idea what he does for you behind your back!"

"I can well imagine," he sneered. This girl was too much. How dare she speak to him this way!

"No you cannot imagine, obviously," she continued. "Atwin has had the council on his side for years. It is because of him that you are still king!"

"How dare you!" the King yelled.

"No, how dare you!" she yelled back. "Atwin does everything he can to keep you on your throne. He defers to you in all his dealings with the other kings. He works tirelessly to do what a king should do, and constantly gives you credit for it. He gives you dignity and respect, and all he gets in return is hate. You are an evil, twisted man who should have abdicated long ago!"

The King gasped, feeling his illness take hold, his breath stopping in his throat and the dizziness blackening his vision. Then he felt a sharp pain in his cheek as the little princess slapped him across the side of the face. His fit stopped as his eyes snapped open in surprise.

"You will not run away from this," she snarled into his face. "You will sit there and you will listen to what I have to say. And you will hear and understand!"

He stared at her. Nobody had ever dared to slap him like that. Nobody had ever stopped an attack like that before. How had she known that they were fake as often as they were real.

He had certainly underestimated this little princess. Kandina stood before him, breathing heavily, tears streaking her face. Now what? He may be mad but he still hated seeing a girl cry.

"I just wish you would stop and really look at your son and see him for what he really is. You hate him against all reason and without any evidence. All he does belies everything you say. Against all your hate, all your accusations, your son has stood by you. He has kept your name alive. He never once spoke out against you, he never allowed anyone else to speak ill of you. I cannot believe you do not see it."

King Gerard gritted his teeth. "If what you say is true, why would he put his own picture above my throne?"

Kandina stopped, then lifted her eyes to the painting on the stone wall above the King's head. As he watched, she gazed at the painting, her tears falling unheeded, and the King grunted in satisfaction, certain that now she saw all the evidence she needed.

She shook her head. "Is this all your proof? Do you really believe this portrait is your son's?"

The King snarled. "Of course it is."

She shook her head again. "He looks so like you, Your Majesty, but this portrait is not Atwin. The eyes are the wrong colour."

Gerard frowned. "What are you talking about?"

"Just look at it," she said. "Atwin's eyes are light golden brown. This portrait has blue eyes."

The King spun in his chair and stared at the picture. He had never really stopped to look at the painting that caused him so much pain every time he saw it.

"How long has this portrait been here?" she asked.

"I... know not," he murmured. "Why do you ask?"

"Because, Sir, this is not Atwin. It is you. It is your coronation portrait."

"It cannot be..." he murmured.

"Did you forget, Sir?" she whispered.

He shook his head. He remembered sitting for that portrait, just days after he was crowned king, years before his marriage. He remembered sitting in the garden for hours, the servants fanning him in the sun and bringing cool drinks. How could he have thought it was Atwin?

"Your Majesty," she said then. "Look at me."

The King turned in his throne to face her again.

"I am nobody," she said. "I have nothing to gain from this. I am not even old enough to attend the council. But I am not a child and I am not blind. Because nobody notices me I see things and I listen. I think you have been under a delusion for a very long time. I think it is now time to let it go."

The King stared, heart stricken and mind in turmoil as she continued in that soft voice.

"I hear what people say about you. They talk about your madness and how it has changed you, and yes they bemoan the fact that Atwin should be king. But they do it out of respect for who you once were. Every time such a comment is made, it is tempered with remembrance of what you used to be."

King Gerard sat in stunned silence. He could hardly believe what this slip of a girl was saying. But he listened and he heard. He could not believe he could have been so mistaken.

"Sir, do you know what they say about your son?"

He shook his head, bemused.

"They say how much he is like you. They compare him to the King you once were. They say he is just as brilliant as once you were. They respect him for his resemblance to you in all he does. These are not the rumblings of a council that wants you gone. It is the respect of a council that regrets your fall."

The King sobbed, the anguish of his long years of paranoia manifesting in physical pain as his mistakes overwhelmed him.

"Please, do not continue this persecution of the one person who has stood solidly for you at every turn, against every accusation you threw at him. He never stopped loving you, and he deserves your respect and your thanks. Please, Your Majesty. Drop this madness and be king and father once more."

Her words rendered him speechless. She turned and left him there, his own guilt flooding his heart and his head exploding with shattered illusions.

Calib watched appreciatively as the Princess breezed

into his study a good hour after his summons. She stood before his desk, with hands on hips and a look of disdain. She was stunning.

"What do you want?" she said rudely.

Calib rose from his chair and walked slowly around his desk, pretending to consider his words. He motioned to an armchair in the corner and bade her sit.

"What are you planning to do now, Princess?" he asked quietly.

She seemed confused. "I said what I came to say," she shrugged. "I suppose I should go home. Maybe I will stay here for a while. Nobody will care."

Calib frowned. "Does your mother know where you are?"

She shrugged again. "I am not a child, Calib. I can do as I please."

"I see," he mused. "I think we should contact her," said the Prince.

Kandi raised her eyes sharply. "Why?"

"Do you not think she deserves to know? I am sure she is worried."

"She cares not what I do."

"I cannot believe that, Princess."

She shrugged again, bottom lip trembling slightly. Calib studied her, trying to see through her bluster. All that confidence was a ruse, he realised. She was afraid.

"Are you worried that she will be angry?"

The Princess shrugged. "I deserve it."

"I am sure she will be glad to know you are alright."

Kandi sniffed. "It is not that," she whispered.

"Then what frightens you?"

The Princess shrugged again, but her eyes darted about and her lip trembled even more. Calib studied that fascinating lip, licked his own unconsciously.

"Is it the journey that scares you?" he said.

She looked up then, meeting his eyes, unshed tears glistening. He nodded in sympathy. She was afraid of meeting more ruffians on the road.

"You need not worry, Kandina. I will get you home safely."

She sobbed her thanks.

"Now, shall we contact your mother?"

"I know not how," she wailed. "Mother never taught me."

"Well then, it is high time you learned."

He knelt before her and held out his hands. With some hesitation, the Princess took them and smiled, eyes radiant through the tears. Ignoring the spark of her touch and the fluttering in his chest, Calib closed his eyes on the sight of her and began the spell.

For three days they rode in silence. At night they made camp, ate and slept without a word. Calib steadfastly held himself aloof, unwilling to admit the effect her presence had on him.

He was certain she did not return his interest, though at times he caught her looking at him and wondered. He maintained a respectful distance, his sense of propriety and chivalry overpowering his fascination.

Late in the afternoon on the third day, as Calib rode ahead to avoid looking at her, he caught a flutter of movement in the bushes beside the road. Pretending not to notice, he continued on, listening intently. Hearing a scrape and a gasp behind, he spun his horse to find a group of bandits had come between himself and the Princess.

Kandi was shaking her head as they approached, and her horse sidled skittishly as the men advanced. One of the men yelled and Kandi's horse reared, throwing her off his back and bolting into the trees. One man closed in on her while the others turned to meet Calib's charge.

Sword drawn and horse flying, the Prince galloped straight at them, swinging and cutting down the first, pulling back hard and turning the horse on its hind legs and chasing down another.

The bandits turned and fled. Seeing Kandi huddled in the dirt, Calib sprang from his horse to help her up. Sobbing, the Princess clung to him, head buried in his chest, and in spite of himself his arms went about her. He told himself he was just giving comfort.

"Why did they do that?" she cried, pulling away. "What did they want?"

He shrugged. "They probably just wanted your purse. I do not think they would have tried anything else with me here."

She shuddered. "Calib, I am afraid!"

He reached out to lift her chin with one finger. "I promised you I would get you home safely," he murmured. "And I will."

She was so beautiful, so vulnerable. He wanted to protect her from the world, wrap her in his arms and keep her safe. The Princess stared at him, tears staining her cheeks, lower lip trembling.

On impulse, he leant forward and kissed her. He felt her stiffen and instantly regretted it, but she softened and responded. Then she pulled back and slapped him hard across the face.

"How dare you!" she exclaimed.

"I am so sorry, Your Highness," he gasped. "I should not have done that!"

"No, you should not," she retorted.

"I think it is high time we got you home safely," he said. And with virtue intact, he thought ruefully.

"But I lost Swiftly!" she sobbed, the image of a strong willed, confident young woman crumbling away again to show that lost, frightened girl.

"He will not have gone far."

He helped her up onto his own horse and swung up behind her, reaching around her with some hesitation to take the reins, ignoring the trembling in his hands that he could not quite hide.

"Shall we go find him?"

He clicked to his horse and they set off, following the trail Swiftly had made as he crashed through the shrub. It was not long before they came across the gelding quietly cropping the grass in a clearing.

Calib strode into the audience chamber at Shirall, Kandi hurrying along in his wake. At sight of the Princess, Averil rose quickly from her chair and hurried to meet them.

"Kandi!" she cried, smothering her daughter in her arms. "I was so worried." Then she pulled away with a scowl. "What were you thinking?"

"I... I am sorry, Mother."

"What possessed you to ride off to Drasmil like that? On your own! You could have been killed."

"I know," Kandi sobbed. "I really am sorry!"

"Why did you do it?"

Kandi looked about, stony faces staring back at her. She hung her head.

"I... needed to talk to the King."

"Gerard? What could you possibly have to say to him?"

"I... I wanted to make him bring her back."

"Who?" said Averil, then her eyes widened in comprehension. "Netta?"

"It was my fault!" Kandi blurted.

Averil narrowed her eyes. "How was it your fault?"

"I put the idea in his head, at Netta's joining feast. And then the next day, he came to speak to me about it. I am so sorry, Mother! I never intended for her to be taken by the kalkar."

"Wait," said Calib then. "Are you saying my father was behind the kidnapping? And... it was your idea?"

Kandi sobbed and nodded. Calib's face clouded over as he stared at her. She took a step toward him but he backed away, shaking his head. Then he turned on his heel and stalked from the room.

EIGHT

The search party sailed due east. The days wore on, and as the leagues passed by with no sight of land the sailors grew restive. Atwin spent his days standing at the rail, staring forward at the interminable expanse of water separating him from his love.

Evelar joined him infrequently, spending the time turning things over in his mind. He reluctantly avoided making contact with Miyam, since the mental tests required a mind linkage with the examiner, and any interference would be noticed immediately.

Instead, he thought about Kandina's strange effect on Naali, and the events surrounding Netta's kidnapping. Something was there, but he could not make the connection.

As the third week came to a close, the mood amongst the sailors became ugly. The Captain came to Evelar with a suggestion that they turn back.

"Have we used up half the supplies?" asked the revealer.

"Pretty much."

"How much?"

The Captain hesitated. "Well, there might be a few more days afore we reach half, but we canna risk havin' nothin' over fer an emergency, now can we?"

"I'm afraid we must," said Evelar firmly. "You agreed."

"But in a few days I'll be havin' a mutiny on me hands. We must turn back now."

"I'm sorry, Captain. In a few days we should hit land, if

my instinct serves me right."

"Beggin' yer pardon, but I happens to hold little faith in 'instinct', effn ye don't mind. We'll be turnin' back now."

The Captain turned to leave, but Evelar took hold of his arm in a vice-like grip. He drew a dagger from his belt and pushed the point suggestively against the Captain's ample stomach.

"We'll be turning back when I say so and not a moment before," he said in a deadly quiet voice. "Is that clear?"

The Captain looked him in the eye for a long moment. "Perfectly," he said between clenched teeth.

The mutiny began with an attack on Evelar. The first mate and two others jumped him from behind, only to find that here was a fighter well used to combat. The two sailors had an unexpected swim and the first mate found himself on his back with a sword pointed at his throat.

"Are we going to forget this nonsense?" the revealer said pointedly.

The first mate fumed, but gave a curt nod.

"Glad to hear it." Evelar left him there.

Less than an hour later, the crew gathered in an ominous group at the stern. The Captain pleaded with Evelar to let him turn back, but the revealer was resolute. The Captain addressed his men, but they scowled angrily. One stepped forward and calmly struck the Captain across the jaw. He fell to the deck, unconscious.

With a roar the crew surged forward at the watching passengers. Atwin and Ordel pushed Delsi behind them and met the attack, while Evelar leapt upwards, climbing quickly into the rigging. As the battle was joined, the revealer worked feverishly, loosening ropes.

The two princes fought well, keeping the angry crewmen at bay. These were burly men, more used to brawling than planned battle, and two trained warriors had no real trouble dealing with them. But, they would soon have to give way to the sheer force of numbers.

Atwin glanced upwards to see what Evelar was doing, and the revealer gave him a signal, simultaneously implanting a thought in his mind to pull back. Atwin pulled Ordel back with him, disengaging from the fight.

The sailors hesitated a moment, surprised by the sudden withdrawal. At a noise from above, they looked up as one, and several gasped. It was too late to run, as they were smothered in a group by the huge mass of the fallen mainsail.

The ship sat idle in the water. As the crewmen struggled to burrow their way out of the confining folds of canvas, the two princes gathered rope and tied the men into a bundle within the sail. Evelar continued to climb upwards, towards the crows nest, and the man who had remained above, watching eagerly.

The crewman noticed the revealer and panicked. He tried to climb down before he was caught, but Evelar was too fast. He caught the man by the scruff and held him out over the side of the crows nest, letting him dangle in the air. The poor man kicked frantically, crying out in desperation. He happened to be facing the bow of the ship, and Evelar yelled at him to be quiet and look.

Finally, the man fell silent, his fear shutting him up more quickly than the voice of the revealer could. He stared down at the deck far below and whimpered.

"Be quiet and look up," Evelar ordered in a voice to be obeyed.

The man did as he was told. He swallowed in shock and blubbered out something.

"What was that, friend?"

He blubbered again.

"I can't hear you."

"L-l-l-land h-ho," he whispered.

"Can't you be a little more enthusiastic? How are your mutinous friends supposed to hear you, hmm? Come now, use those salt-ridden lungs of yours and I might just pull you up."

"Laaand Ho-oooooo!!" the sailor yelled.

"Now that's more like it."

The revealer pulled the frightened man up and straightened his shirt for him. Then he patted him on the back.

"Good man."

Evelar swung over the side and climbed briskly down to the deck.

By evening, they had cast anchor in a small cove, and the passengers struck out for shore in the row-boat. The Captain accompanied them, and set the men who had rowed to finding driftwood for a fire. A second boat brought more sailors ashore, and the Captain sent them off to hunt for game. Tonight they would feast on the fruits of this new land.

They found sparseness all around, but somehow managed to gather enough fresh food for a reasonable feed. The passengers sat apart from the sailors and discussed their next move.

"Does Naali recognise Netta's trail?" asked Delsi anxiously.

Atwin nodded. "It is faint, but she did come this way. And kalkar have definitely been here recently."

"We'll know for certain if we wait until morning," said Evelar. "It will be easier to find physical evidence in the daylight. But I agree with Atwin. This spot feels right somehow."

"In that case," said Ordel quietly, "we should get some rest."

"I'll take first watch," said Evelar. He stood up and strode to the edge of the camp, looking out into the gnarled trees bordering the beach. He reached out over the miles of ocean, and found his other self within Miyam's subconscious mind, waking her from a deep sleep.

'Evelar?' she said quickly. 'Where are you?'

'The new world!' he said jokingly. 'And it stinks of kalkar. I think perhaps we've found their homeland.'

'Netta?' she asked.

'We're still on the trail. It shouldn't be long now.'

'I hope you're right, for her sake. I hate to think what they're doing to her.'

'Are the mind tests finished?"

'Yes, I begin stealth tomorrow. I'll be glad when this is over.'

'I'll be glad when I can speak to you without interrupting your testing, my love.'

Two days from the sea, Atwin awoke with a gasp from a deep sleep. He looked about himself nervously and Evelar, who had been standing watch, knelt beside him. Atwin looked at him.

"The visions have returned," he whispered.

Ordel spoke quietly from the bed roll he shared with Delsi. "Returned?"

"Yes, sir," said Atwin. "Leena went into some form of protective state and stopped sending images. All I could get was a direction for a long time. But now the visions are back."

"Why the change? Do you know?"

"They seem to have stopped moving. Leena must feel more secure now."

"Where is she?" asked Delsi tensely.

"I am unsure. I think she is underground, in a cave somewhere. The kalkar have locked her in. It is dark down there," he shivered. "Cold and damp."

"We must find her," said Delsi. "What is the direction?"

"East, still."

"Then let us go," she stated, rising from the blankets.

Atwin exchanged a look with Evelar, who shrugged. They struck camp and rode out into the dark night.

* * *

On a cold and blustery night, after weeks of trudging through thick grassland which burned in their wake, Netta and her captors reached the foothills of a huge mountain range. They began to climb, higher and higher, the Princess growing weaker by the day.

Her illness had not abated, even after finding fresh water to replenish her bags and rehydrate her body. Each day, while the two remaining kalkar stood dormant in the sunlight, Netta hunted, filling her pack with small animals that she cut and dried in the stifling heat, spreading them out in the sun each day.

She knew Atwin was coming after her, but this interminable journey had taught her to find food at every opportunity. She had no idea if she was doing it right, but she knew that dried meat might save her life. But no amount of food could calm her churning stomach.

Every bite of every meagre meal went down reluctantly and came back up more often than not. Even water sat uneasily in her rebellious gut. She had a bad taste in her mouth day and night, and the plain water in the two sacks she carried tasted foul even when they were freshly filled.

Worse was the new symptom, the dizziness that came on suddenly and sent her retching to the ground, sometimes to the point of blacking out. The Princess knew she must have picked up something nasty, from something she had scavenged to eat somewhere along the trail.

But she was so weakened now she had given up hope of ever feeling better. Netta had long since stopped counting the days. There was no point. This journey would never end and Atwin would never find her.

Soon she would grow so weak that the kalkar who dragged her when she could not walk would leave her to lie where she fell. Now, as they climbed higher into the mountains she knew that day was close.

But then something changed. Her two captors were becoming more animated with every step. The ground they passed through was now barren and blackened, and the small animals had disappeared.

Bare dirt and rock passed under her feet and not a sound could be heard. But the burnt smell that hovered over everything sent her sensitised stomach reeling.Then finally, at the end of another long painful night, a dark cavern yawned ahead. The Princess sobbed as fear gripped her heart.

With no energy left to fight, she allowed the kalkar to drag her into the dark. Down a long stone passage, they led her toward a distant glow, the smell of kalkar thick in the stifling air.

The glow at the end of the tunnel burst upon her as they entered a large cavern. Kalkar were everywhere, some passing through and some tending the objects that rested in niches along the walls. In the centre stood a huge pillar of rock, filled with more niches, and each and every hole in the rock contained a glowing light and a large roundish object.

But her captors gave her no time to make sense of the scene, dragging her through toward another tunnel as the denizens of the cavern raised their glowing red eyes to watch as they passed.

Moving on into the new tunnel the darkness seemed even deeper than before. Eventually, when she thought her legs might finally give way, she was tossed dismissively into a small cave, the pack leader entering after. With a low growl of anger the kalkar raised a clawed foot and slammed it into her stomach with the full heat of his flesh uncooled.

"That is for my pack mates who were lost because of you," he rasped in his horrid guttural voice.

The Princess fell to her knees, the blow sending pain through her as the pack leader stormed out of the cavern, and a barred gate was closed across the entrance. Body racked with convulsions, she lost the pitiful contents of her stomach. She knelt there in the dark, weeping in despair.

NINE

Dawn broke with a chill. As the party continued on into the crisp winter morning, the sun rose, a glorious golden blaze in the east.

Atwin sighed. "How can a sunrise be so beautiful in a place like this?"

"We may be in a foreign land, surrounded by the devastation of kalkar, but nature still lives," Delsi murmured. "She is beautiful ever, and here she is more so because her spirit has not been broken. She speaks in me still."

Evelar nodded solemnly. "Kalkar may not appreciate her, but that is only because they do not need her to survive. They need only the sun and shelter from the rain. She welcomes our presence."

Atwin stared out over the waving grassland, appreciative of the display. Evelar rode ahead, examining the ground before him. As the Prince watched, he dismounted and bent to the ground. He ran a hand through the dry grass, noting burnt patches speckled with the green of new growth. He frowned. He gently broke off a handful of old grass and held it to his face, absorbing its smell. He stood and beckoned to Atwin and the others. As they joined him he pointed out the blackened stubble.

"Kalkar have passed this way recently, perhaps a week ago." He looked out over the flat plain. "If only there was a hill from which to spy out the land. I'm willing to bet this trail would stand out like an arrow, pointing the way."

"Can you follow it anyway?" asked Ordel quietly.

Evelar nodded. "Easily, but a better view might confirm that they went east and might warn us of a change in direction." He remounted. "Still, we should continue."

They struck out over the golden grassland.

When the sun reached its zenith, the travellers stopped for a meal and rest. Still worried for Netta, Delsi suggested Atwin try to contact Leena again. He concentrated, holding Naali in his right hand. His lips moved silently, as if he were talking. His forehead creased in a frown. Then his eyes snapped open, staring at nothing. He shook his head in fear. Then he doubled over with a cry of pain, as if he had suffered a blow to the stomach. He groaned. Delsi reached out toward him but he flinched away from her touch.

"What happened?" she asked in concern.

Atwin shook his head, refusing to speak. He pulled his knees up to his chest and wrapped his arms about his legs, rocking back and forth. He stared downward, unresponsive.

Delsi shivered, her blind eyes showing her concern and Ordel slipped an arm about her. Evelar frowned and knelt beside the Prince. With only a brief glance at Ordel, he placed a hand on Atwin's forehead. He had not wanted to reveal his mental power, College policy forbade it. But he had no choice.

He reached into the Prince's mind carefully, felt the trauma and probed at it gently. It was a mess in there. The Prince had somehow become linked to the Princess, through the amulets. Evelar would have to separate them before Atwin could return to his own body. He explored the images bouncing around in the conscious mind.

The stone walls seemed to close in all around. It was cold, and the damp seeped into the bones. It was dark.

Kalkar did not need light to see, so they had no conception of the human need for light. The darkness felt worse than the walls.

There was hunger. The Princess had barely eaten enough to survive; Kalkar did not need to eat. Leena had been keeping her alive by slowing down her metabolism and suspending the growth of the child within.

Child? Leena had needed to protect it, not only from starvation, but from the blows that the kalkar were so fond of inflicting. No wonder she had shut down.

Evelar tried to separate the Prince from those experiences, but something blocked him. He examined closer. Leena had grabbed onto Naali in a grip like iron, and was now using his energy to supplement her own. There was no way to separate them without destroying both minds.

Reluctantly, the revealer slipped out of the Prince's mind and removed his hand. He looked at the Queen and her husband and shook his head.

"What did you find?" asked Ordel.

Evelar looked strangely at the Prince Consort, surprised that he seemed to know what he had been doing.

"There is nothing I can do," he said, telling them what he had found.

Delsi clutched at her husband's hand. "A child? In those conditions? We have to find her."

Her voice broke and Ordel held her gently to him.

"We must continue," said the Prince Consort unhappily.

Atwin was led unresisting to his horse and he mounted mechanically. He trailed behind, staring blindly ahead, the stallion bearing his unresponsive rider with head held high.

For many days they rode, with Atwin in another world. Finally, a ridge of mountains on the horizon signalled an end to the seemingly endless grassland.

*

They rode through another dull, cold day as the mountains grew to fill the sky. It was the highest range Evelar had ever seen, rising thousands of feet to the snow-covered peaks. He signalled a halt and they dismounted to discuss their next move.

"Now we know why the trail has been so straight," said Ordel. "Those mountains must be riddled with caves. The perfect place for kalkar to hide from the rain of winter."

"It could be a problem," said Evelar.

"Oh?"

"Once we hit rocky country, the trail will disappear, and Atwin is unable to tell us where to go next. We cannot hope to find the cave where Netta is held without communicating with Leena."

"Perhaps we should try to reach Netta ourselves, using the ancient spell of communication," Ordel suggested.

"Yes," said Delsi eagerly. "That could work."

"But we can't be sure she can tell us how to get to her," Evelar cautioned.

"There's only one way to find out," Delsi replied.

Evelar watched the Queen and her husband for a moment. Then he sighed and gave a sharp nod. They sat in a circle and joined hands, including Atwin in spite of his dubious state.

Delsi began incanting the ancient spell. The mind they finally encountered was barely recognisable as the Princess. She had completely closed in on herself. At first they could not even make her acknowledge them.

Finally, when she realised what she was hearing, she grabbed eagerly at the contact, but she was incoherent. She mumbled the word 'help' over and over and would not answer any of their questions. Then, all of a sudden, she gave a sharp cry of fear, and then screamed in agony. Her mind was ripped away and those in the circle came back to themselves, heads throbbing.

"What happened?" said Delsi shakily.

"I think they heard us," Ordel whispered.

"They hurt her!" Delsi said, stricken.

"I know, love. We were not to know."

"Now what do we do?" she said in despair.

"Keep going," said Evelar. "We can at least get as far as the mountains."

They rode on in silence, the trail still straight and true as Evelar took the lead, his mind far away.

'Have you found Netta yet?' Miyam was saying.

'Unfortunately, no,' he hesitated. *'We have a problem.'*

'Oh?' Miyam said worriedly.

'Atwin is out of commission. We can't use Naali to find the direction.'

'What's happened?'

'Naali is with Leena in spirit, and has taken Atwin with him. He is totally unresponsive. I've tried to separate them, but I can't without sending them both mad,' he sighed. *'I need you here, Mym.'*

'You know that's impossible.'

'One can always hope,' he said.

'I miss you too, dear...' she broke off and called to someone.

'Who's there?' he said.

'You must be out of it if you can't feel your own sister!'

'Hello, Opal,' he projected through Miyam.

'Who said that?' he heard echoing back.

Miyam laughed, and Evelar chuckled in spite of himself.

'Have I caught you at a bad time?' he asked then.

'Not really. Have you forgotten how to count the days, dear?'

'You're in a rare mood, my love. And no, I haven't

forgotten. Congratulations. Should I leave you to it?'

'Why don't you hang around? Since I can't have you here in the flesh, this is the next best thing.'

'What a nice idea,' he replied.

'Stop yapping, you two,' Opal broke in via Miyam. *'We have a ceremony to attend. And you forgot to congratulate me, Sand. Your baby sister has finally caught up to you.'*

'Now, Opal, you were never a baby. Congratulations, Lady Artisan!'

'Thank you. Now can we get moving?'

'Oh, Mym,' said Evelar.

'Yes, dear?'

'Are you wearing your mote knife?'

'Yes, of course. Why?'

'Oh, nothing. I have an idea, that's all.'

* * *

Miyam stood nervously in line outside the huge double doors to the great hall at the College. She had joined the collection of other new journeyers, while Opal made her way to join the two other new artisans, both many years older than her.

They still wore their old colours, since the new would be presented to them during the ceremony. The ascendants stood in their separate groups in the large waiting hall, while those ranks below them slowly emptied from the room to take part in the ceremony. It seemed to be taking forever.

After a long hour, the new novices had finally all been inducted and the new apprentices had filed out of the waiting hall to take their places in line.

Finally, the new journeyers were called from the waiting hall and lined up. Every few moments, the line took a step forward as another was admitted into the presence of the entire collected membership of the College. The ascendant journeyers around her all seemed more excited than nervous, but for Miyam it was not so easy to feel good about the ceremony.

She felt like a stranger amid a close knit family. None of her old friends were with her, and she had made very few new ones. Worse, she had been placed at the end of the line. The Maestro had warned her that she would be introduced as a special case, and she did not like the idea.

Evelar stayed in her mind, ready with reassurance when her nerves got the better of her.

'Relax, my love,' he said. *'There are enough people out there who will remember you to ensure that you're welcomed.'*

'I hope you're right,' she replied.

Then it was her turn at last. Miyam took a deep breath and strode into the Great Hall, her brown bordered apprentice cloak flowing out behind her. She tried not to glance around, keeping her eyes front. Nevertheless the Maestro, sitting stiffly in his gilded "throne", caught her eye and gave a wink.

As Miyam climbed the stairs to the dais the old counsellor at the podium, in his grey bordered cloak, read out her name. She carefully removed the brown sash from her head, palming the tiny mote knife in its sheath, and approached the Apprentice waiting to take her old cloak and nameless badge from her.

"Now, this young lady," the old counsellor began, "has come to us..."

"Yes, Wind, thank you," said the Maestro suddenly, standing up.

The crowd murmured in surprise. The Maestro never spoke at the ascension ceremony. Wind looked at him in utter shock.

"You may be seated, old friend."

The old man tottered to his seat, grumbling under his breath.

"Now," the Maestro continued. "I wish to speak to you today about this young woman. Unusual, I know, but that's my prerogative, I hope. Miyam has proven herself under, shall we say, unique circumstances.

"I think most of you will remember the affair a few years ago concerning the one called Mist. As a result of those events, Miyam was removed from the College under protest.

"Fate has brought her back to us, and I have seen fit to set a precedent in this case. She was ever a fine student and will make an excellent member of the College. I could not expect any less of the daughter of Mist.

"She has proven her abilities by ranking top of this year's complement of aspiring apprentices, despite her long absence. I would like you to join me now in welcoming her to active duty."

He began to clap. The counsellors looked at each other, then joined the Maestro in applauding Miyam. Then the rest of the hall burst into applause, as in a great wave they stood and cheered.

The double doors burst open and the waiting ascendant masters, adepts and artisans clustered in the doorway. Opal pushed her way to the front and cheered the loudest of them all.

As the noise continued, the Maestro took the new green bordered journeyer's cloak from a waiting apprentice and draped it over Miyam's shoulders. He took the name badge that had belonged to her mother from another apprentice, and fastened the cloak securely. He wrapped the new green sash around her hooded head and tied it, while she slipped the mote knife in underneath. Then he wrapped her in a bear hug.

'Well done, my love,' said a voice in Miyam's head. The Maestro pulled away and looked at her strangely.

"What was that?" he said

"Oh, nothing," she replied timidly.

He examined her face uncertainly, then gave a shrug. He turned her to face the assembly and raised a hand for silence. The crowd hushed.

"My friends," he said proudly. "I give you... Mist."

He handed her a shiny new College-made sword, light and perfectly balanced, as the applause came anew.

* * *

As night fell they climbed higher into the foothills, eventually taking shelter for the night in a gully by a stream, where a few stunted trees fought over the water.

"Will you be taking first watch?" Ordel said to the revealer.

Evelar did not answer.

"Evelar?"

"Hmmm?" He shook himself and looked absently at the Prince Consort. "Excuse me, Your Highness?"

"I asked if you were taking first watch."

"Oh," he said vaguely. He was listening to the voice in his head. "Ah... I'll be back," he said, striding off into the trees.

"Where are you going?"

Evelar did not answer.

Ordel looked after him uncertainly. Then he shrugged and set about building a fire. It was cold, and a hot meal would do them good.

* * *

The great hall had become the site of a wonderful banquet. The meal was simple but generous; roasted meats and bread, steamed vegetables and roasted tubers. Mist sat silent between Jepsa and Sylvan, now using the College names Foss and Blue, as they made small talk over her plate. They tried to draw her in with their giggling banter, but Mist said nothing.

As soon as the meal was ended they left her for their male companions, who had both managed to be in residence for the ceremony, leaving Mist alone with the loving presence in her head.

The dancing was energetic. Mist sat with her young brother Domyn and her mental visitor, turning down many an offer. She watched the assembled members pairing off, cloaks flowing with their movements, colours blending on this one occasion where rank mixed with rank.

Couples of unmatched rank left their peers to mingle openly across all colours, and Mist wished Sand could have been there. She appreciated Opal's occasional visits between dances with Dock, her husband, and pretended to listen to Domyn's excited chatter, but neither could quell her loneliness.

Finally, as time wore on, she rose and walked slowly onto the floor. Domyn fell silent as his sister left him there without a word. She stood in the middle of the floor, bathed in solitude, and looked slowly about her. Her body followed as she surveyed the room, leading her into the swirling first movement of the dance of separation.

In the stunted forest of the great mountains half a world away Evelar, too, danced the De'iungi.

The crowd watched Mist reverently. Her unconscious grace was captivating, but her isolation was heart-wrenching. The dance continued, its whirling movements proclaiming her despair.

Almost, the audience could see an invisible partner, shadowing her movements. Finally, she slowed. The dance ended and she stood, head bowed, alone.

Evelar stood alone in the forest, with eyes closed, his head also bowed in sadness.

Slowly, Mist raised her eyes to look at the Maestro, watching her from his place on the dais. He stood and came down the stairs, walking toward her. He held his arms wide, and she rushed into his embrace, burying her face in his fatherly chest. Then, quite suddenly, she disappeared.

The Maestro looked about in shock. From the crowd, a young boy yelled out.

"Mym!"

TEN

The boy ran at the Maestro screaming, with fists pummelling the old man in the stomach.

"What have you done with my sister?" he screamed.

A nearby master came to the Maestro's aid, catching Domyn's arms from behind. The boy struggled, angry tears flying. The Maestro held a hand up to the Master.

"It's alright, Pond."

The Maestro bent before Domyn and placed his hands gently on the boy's shoulders.

"I promise you, Dom, I have done nothing to your sister," he said kindly.

The boy stopped struggling. "Then where is she?" he scowled.

The Maestro hesitated. "I can't say for sure..."

The boy began to struggle again, but the Maestro hushed him with a finger tap to the chest.

"But I can tell you what I think has happened."

Domyn considered, then reluctantly nodded.

"There is an old power. Some revealers are able to use it, but it is very rare. So rare that it has not been seen in living memory. I think we have just seen it."

The boy cocked his head. "What power?"

"It's called translocation, the ability to transport objects from one place to another. Although, I've never heard of it being used to transport a person."

"But who would do that?"

The Maestro smiled. "In my opinion, there is only one man who just might be able to do this."

Domyn's eyes opened wide. "Sand?"

The Maestro chuckled. "Most likely, Dom. Who else would want to?"

The boy nodded, face breaking into a grin. The Maestro straightened, ruffling the boy's hair with one hand. Then he looked about the room, noting the confused faces and hearing the rumbling whispers. He needed to calm this now.

"My friends," he said with hands raised for quiet. "Mist is unharmed. She has gone to join her teacher on assignment. I know her method of departure was a little unorthodox, but then Sand was never one to follow protocol or established tradition. Please, continue with your festivities."

The murmuring continued as the assembled members milled about, discussing the incident. But the music kicked up again, and couples began to once more fill the floor as the Maestro made his way back to his table. He shook his head, mumbling to himself with a rueful smile.

"That boy never ceases to surprise me."

* * *

The woman felt strong arms close more tightly about her, and felt comforted. There was a breeze on her back, and she shivered a little. She turned her head to the side and opened her eyes. It was dark. The moon shone down through the branches overhead.

"Maestro, why are there trees in the great hall?" she murmured.

"There weren't the last time I looked, my love," said Evelar.

Miyam pulled away slightly and looked up into the man's face. She could not believe her eyes.

"How did you..." Translocation, she thought.

He shrugged. "Does it matter?"

Her mind raced. The sixth sign! Could it be possible that Evelar was the Awakener? Very carefully, Miyam buried that thought. If it were true, Evelar had to find out for himself.

"My Sand," she whispered proudly.

"My Mist," he replied with a twinkle in his eye.

She smiled and reached up to touch his face. "I love you, my husband," she whispered.

He grinned. "Good!" He kissed her deeply.

After all the difficult weeks of study and testing, separated for far too long, they melted into each other body, mind and soul, forgetting the hostile world around them.

After sharing a meal with his wife, Ordel went in search of the revealer. He had been gone a long time. Ordel was concerned by the man's strange behaviour earlier and felt obliged to see if he was alright.

The Prince consort picked his way through the tangled growth along the stream, looking for signs of the revealer. He came out into a small clearing and stopped short.

He saw two figures standing in the darkness, wrapped in each other's arms. A flash of red in the moonlight told him that Evelar was one of the figures, but who was the woman and how had she come to be there, a vast ocean away from human civilisation?

He peered closer, carefully to avoid being noticed, but he had a feeling they would not notice him even if he were to light a bonfire at their feet. Who was she? Perhaps it was a kalkar trap to lure the revealer away and dispose of him.

But no, kalkar did not work that way. Then he realised that she, too, was wearing a revealer's cloak, but he could not see its border in the darkness. Their amorous activity was becoming more... enthusiastic and he turned away, thinking he should not be watching.

He walked slowly back toward the glimmer of the fire, turning things over in his mind. Evelar could look after himself and he would not do anything to endanger himself. But where had she come from?

Ordel knew the College taught some strange things. He had learned some of the tricks as a child when he lived there with his father, though he had lost the knack since. Perhaps this was something new they had developed.

"Ordel, what is it?" said Delsi, sensing his mood as he entered the circle of warmth by the fire.

"I have just seen something incredibly strange," he murmured.

"Oh? Did you find Evelar?"

"You could say that. But he was not alone. I did not disturb them."

"What are you talking about?"

"He was with a woman, another revealer. They were... being friendly."

Delsi raised an eyebrow.

"Exactly what I thought!" said Ordel, bemused.

"How did she get here?"

"I have no idea."

It was after dawn when Evelar returned to camp. He appeared alone at the edge of the trees, and Delsi turned toward the sound questioningly. Ordel watched impassively, but Evelar did not enter the camp. Instead he turned sideways slightly, looking behind and a woman appeared, in a green bordered revealer's cloak. She passed Evelar and stood in front of him and he put his hands protectively on her shoulders. Together they looked at the Queen and her husband.

"Miyam?" said Delsi uncertainly.

"Good morning, Your Majesty," Miyam replied. "How did

you know it was me?"

Delsi shrugged. "I... sensed it. I know not how, but I just seem to know things."

"You have never mentioned that before," said Ordel.

"It is getting stronger," she replied. "I sense a lot now, almost as much as I used to see. What are you doing here, Miyam?"

"I thought I might pop in."

"Pop in?" said Ordel dubiously. "That is rather an understatement."

Evelar shrugged. "It's accurate."

They moved forward then and joined Delsi and Ordel at the fire.

"But how?" said Delsi.

"Ah... it's a little trick we worked out," Miyam replied. "It's a bit complicated."

"Are you really here?"

"Of course."

"Since when have you been a member of the College?" said Ordel suspiciously, remembering a long-ago discussion with the Kings about trust and familiarity.

"Since I was about ten years old, though I was away for a few years."

Ordel shook his head. "I thought I knew you."

"You can never really know anyone, Your Highness. We all have our little secrets."

Ordel nodded. His own secret was known only to his wife and his father. Even his daughter did not know that her grandfather was a revealer.

"And how long has this other little secret been going on?" said Delsi archly, indicating their joined hands.

The two revealers looked at each other and smiled.

"That's a secret," said Miyam with a twinkle in her eye. "Right now, I want to see what I can do about Atwin."

"Of course." Ordel indicated to where Atwin sat, staring straight ahead at nothing.

Miyam went to him and placed a hand on his forehead. Evelar knelt behind her and listened mentally.

"I think I know what to do," Miyam told him.

She offered her hand and he took it without question. With Miyam as the focus and Evelar giving her the energy, the two revealers probed into the Prince's ravaged mind. Miyam stroked at the edges of the trauma until he let her in.

Then she followed the link back to its source. Leena. The Queen's amulet resented the contact, but slowly Miyam was able to loosen her grip. Finally, she broke through to the Princess.

Netta's fear had in part caused the problem, and Leena's own despair had magnified it. Miyam managed to implant the seed of hope, so Netta would know that help was on the way. Leena relaxed, and finally allowed Naali to pull Atwin out of the link.

Miyam sent the Prince to sleep and withdrew from his mind. She sagged against Evelar and relaxed her grip on his hand.

"Well done, my love," he murmured.

"That was not easy," she said softly.

"Will he be alright now?" asked Delsi worriedly.

"Hopefully," said Miyam. "We'll have to wait until he wakes before we can know for sure."

Taking the opportunity to rest, the travellers settled about the fire, with Ordel sitting on watch. Some four hours later, Atwin began to stir. When he finally opened his eyes, he looked about frantically. Miyam calmed him and he looked at her with surprise.

"It's a long story," she said to him quietly. "Are you able to travel?"

Atwin nodded. He did not seem to want to speak, but he was definitely back among the living.

At noon they stopped. Something had to be done. They had no idea how far the kalkar had taken Netta before going underground. They did not want to miss the entrance to the cave system. But how would they find it? They could not risk losing Atwin again.

"Why don't you see what you can find out from Netta," Evelar said to Miyam.

She shrugged. She closed her eyes and reached out with her mind to the Princess. She saw the cave where she was being kept. It was cold and damp and very dark, but the Princess was in no mental state to tell how she had come to be there. Miyam examined her position in relation to where she was herself standing. The Princess seemed to be higher and a little to the left. She came back to herself and told the others.

"But that could mean anything," said Delsi in frustration.

Ordel nodded. "The entrance could still be anywhere above or below her position and to either side. We could be searching about up here for months."

"Do we have any choice?" said Evelar.

They all turned to Atwin. "Do you think you could find out anything?" said Delsi.

Atwin looked dubious.

"I don't think we should risk that again," said Miyam quietly.

"I could try..." said Atwin, almost inaudibly.

"No," said Delsi. "Miyam is right."

"We cannot sit here doing nothing," said Ordel harshly. "We have to find her."

"I know, dear."

* * *

ELEVEN

Mavick the fisherman sent his young son into the rigging of his small boat to furl the sails. It was time to pull in the nets. To the east the sky grew light with the coming dawn and a warm breeze took the chill off the night air.

The nets had been set overnight off the beach of a small island, one of many in the southern archipelago known as the Sunrise Islands. The gulls were diving, and Mavick hoped for a good catch. To the east he could see another flock winging in and he hurried to set the winches, and called the boy down to take a handle on the crank.

A strange smell carried on the breeze, like smoke but with more tang. He wondered where the fire was and what was burning to bring such a smell this far out to sea.

"Papa!" the boy called from aloft. "What's that?"

Mavick looked to where the boy pointed. The birds were much bigger now, but whatever they were they were not birds. He could see black shapes against the eastern sky, flushed orange now with the coming sunrise. Huge wings, long thin arms and legs with clawed talons on all four limbs, and glowing red eyes. The air was much warmer now, but Mavick shivered.

"Chasper, get down now!" he cried, fear adding an edge to his voice.

They headed straight at the boat, coming out of the dawn like a swarm from the nether world. The boy hurried to climb down, but not before the leading edge was on them.

A wave of heat came ahead of the horrific flock as they flew low above the boat. One struck the top of the mast in passing, breaking it off and setting the furled topsail alight. The force of the impact caused Chasper to lose his grip on the rope.

For a moment the boy hung there, legs flailing, before he managed to right himself and scramble down the rigging. The dreadful flock passed over, heading for the small island behind the boat as the sun threatened to peek over the horizon. The vanguard settled to land and a strange keening sounded.

Chasper covered his ears, and Mavick looked on helpless as the creatures gathered on the island. The swarm came on, seemingly endless as the sun threatened to rise. The keening grew louder and more insistent.

Finally the last of the flock was passing over head, the bulk of them already landing on the island when, with a shaft of bright light, the sun broke over the sea. The keening stopped and the remaining creatures fell into the water with a resounding hiss of steam that echoed over the waves in the sudden silence.

The water roiled and bubbled where the last of the flock had fallen, boiling with the heat of them and cooking the fisherman's unlanded catch where it waited in the nets. The bodies of the creatures dissolved in a toxic foam, spoiling what live fish remained.

Mavick the fisherman stared at his lost catch, several hundred fish now floating on the polluted waves, ruined and unsalvageable. The salt vats in the hold would remain empty, but he still had a long day ahead clearing the nets.

They would have to stay out another night and find a new spot to lay the nets again. Then, with his stocks replenished, Mavick would head home to Zelona and find some officer of the King, to report this unearthly army.

* * *

The King of Zelona stood on the battlements of his small castle on the south east fringe of the Barren Wastes and stared out to sea. The news the fisherman brought of a large force of kalkar on wing had come as a disturbing interruption to his otherwise quiet town. Since then everything had changed.

His people had begun preparations as soon as they heard the report, but nobody had any idea how to prepare for a kalkar attack. All the usual defences had been prepared. All ships had been sent up the coast to find a safe place to ride out the coming enemy storm. There were now a series of deep water filled ditches between the town and the harbour.

Artillery had been gathered behind the walls, thousands of arrows and three large ballistae, stocked well with fist sized balls. But something ate at Lenent's heart. He knew he had missed something. He had no idea what, but he knew the battle would be hard and the city would fall.

He stood now, staring out over the harbour as the sun set in flame behind him, picking up the red highlights in his hair. He could just see in the distance the nearest of the Sunrise Islands, peeking its crown over the far horizon. His scouts told him the enemy gathered there, and in a long scattered front on every island behind it.

This would be a battle for survival, but it would only ever be a first defence. The King was determined to keep his people safe, and if that meant an early retreat he would not hesitate. He hated himself for being so pessimistic before the battle even began, but he knew from what little he had learned at the Conference of Kings the year before that this enemy was implacable and unstoppable.

As night fell the King watched the darkness, his heart filled with foreboding. He stood there for hours, waiting for the first sign of the enemy. He could smell it on the air. They were coming. The night air was cold but a warm breeze came off the sea, a breeze that should have been cold but was not.

He saw the dark shapes, gliding in on huge wings, a moment before the sentry gave the call. Giving the order to his captain standing by his side, the King marshalled his troops.

Skerf stood next to Captain Poppel, the commander of this hastily formed civilian army, and watched the first wave make landfall just outside the outermost ditch. He smelled their heat on the air and shivered.

"Stand ready, Skerf," said the Captain.

The enemy studied the ditches for a moment, hesitating at the sight of the water, then in a coordinated push they jumped as one, crossing the first ditch easily. There was not a word spoken, not a grunt to indicate the sophistication of the manoeuvre.

The archers took aim and fired into the enemy ranks as they approached the second ditch. Arrows rained down, striking the kalkar with killing force, but most bounced harmlessly off their leathery hide. Those that did penetrate burned on contact, causing no great injury. Not a single kalkar fell.

"Damnation!" Captain Poppel cursed.

The second ditch posed no more obstacle than the first. Again the arrows rained down and again there were no fatalities. Now the gathered human defenders murmured in rising fear.

This enemy could not be killed. The kalkar progressed to the last ditch, one last small gap separating them from the humans and the city behind.

"Stand firm!" yelled the Captain.

A man hissed at Skerf from behind, whispering in his

ear in their native tongue.

"Shall I give the order, Sir?"

Skerf hushed the man, glancing nervously at Captain Poppel.

"Not yet, Harti. Send Estra and Korv to me and spread the word," he said, fingering the ornate ivory horn that hung about his neck. "We move on my signal."

"Yes, Sir."

The man hurried away. Across the small ditch, the kalkar had paused, another jump blocked by the palisade of sharpened stakes on the human side. A strange noise was echoing across the city, a hum multiplied from every kalkar throat. The people glanced about in terror.

"Stand your ground!" yelled the Captain.

As the hum grew steadily in pitch and took on a strange ululating warble, the front rank of the enemy leapt across, impaling themselves on the palisade. The keening cry of the enemy horde reached a horrific crescendo as their fellows died.

But as they gave their lives to the human defences, the heat of their dying bodies set the stakes alight, burning them to the ground.

Two men sidled up beside Skerf, unnoticed in the commotion.

"Are we really going to do this, Sir?" said one.

"You know the answer to that, Korv," said Skerf quietly. "Our families will suffer if we don't."

"Yes, Sir."

"Shall we go then?"

As the enemy as one jumped across the last ditch, the three men turned their backs and walked calmly toward the castle.

"At the ready!" they heard the Captain yell.

As human and kalkar joined battle, the three men

walked on, closing their ears to the sounds of mortal combat behind them.

Up on the battlements the King watched, cursing as far too many humans fell in the dirt to be trampled and burnt by the enemy horde. He did not hear the scuffle behind, so engrossed was he in the horror before him.

He was made aware of the commotion only by a shout from Captain Mortel beside him as he drew his sword. The King spun, pulling his own sword and standing at the ready as he surveyed the scene.

Two of his guards lay dead, a third holding off three strangers who sneered in their contempt. The fourth guard and the King hurried to join the fray. But these men were fearless and the fight was vicious. Lenent's guards managed to kill one, but the second killed a third guard and the leader came straight for the King.

Lenent eyed the man warily, hearing his last guard grunting with effort as he struggled to finish off the other attacker.

"Who are you?" he asked the man.

"Skerf, of the tribe Alacot."

"Why are you doing this?"

"Because I have no choice."

The man fell savagely to the attack but the King defended easily. All was quiet, the other two had seemingly finished each other off. The King was on his own as this determined assassin moved in.

Lenent fought desperately. This man was quick and agile, showing no fear and no fatigue, easily parrying the King's sword and almost breaking through his guard. For the first time, the King began to worry that he might not survive.

Showing remarkable skill, the tribesman forced the King

backward until he found himself pressed up against the parapet. Seeing a flicker of movement the King attempted to draw the man's attention further.

"Are you sure you want to do this?" he said. "Is treason worth whatever you are fighting for?"

The man snarled. "Yes!"

He raised his sword for the killing blow. But at the last moment he drew in a sharp breath as another sword pulled hard against his throat. The final guard had risen from his faint and captured the assassin from behind. The King raised a hand.

"Wait, Mortel. I want to find out more."

At that the assassin sneered. He threw away his sword and drew out a small, curved knife. He held the knife up in what might have been a gesture of surrender and with the other hand he took hold of the horn at his chest. Raising it to his mouth he blew three short sharp notes, twice.

Then, before the guard or the King could stop him, he aimed the knife at his own chest, driving the curved blade in under the sternum and piercing his own heart.

Down on the battlefield the call of the horn was repeated, echoing eerily over the city. In every regiment on every corner of the field, in every street of the city, one in ten turned on his fellows and human killed human.

The tribesmen who had appeared somehow from within the city itself had turned on the innocent people of Zelona at the sound of the failed assassin's horn. Lenent had been forced to evacuate. The kalkar had overrun his city sweeping over all in their path, with no regard for the people who lived there.

His people had fled into the night, and many had not made it out alive. The kalkar had pursued relentlessly and many more had perished before the sun rose on that first day.

The first wave had been followed by a second and a third, each night bringing more from the direction of the Sunrise Islands to join with their fellows as they hounded the people fleeing west.

Now, Lenent looked out over a broken people, settling into a scattered camp beside the long road across the Wild Plain. His had been a peaceful town, with no standing army. He had hated leaving his home in the hands of the kalkar, but he had been powerless to prevent its fall.

North was the desert, so they headed west. Leaving the horde dormant and turning their backs on their lost home, they had crossed the mountains. They travelled along the great trade route toward Nella Fillenga and the land of the Fillens. Lenent was determined to see his people safe.

"Captain Mortel," called the King.

"Yes, Sir!"

"I am putting you and your cohort in charge of the non-combatants. I want you to round up all the civilians and take them west. When we get to Nella, you will take all who want to join you, and continue on to the west coast, hide out in the lands between the mountains and the sea until this war is over."

"But, Sir," he hesitated. "What if we lose? What then?"

"Just get the people settled and safe. Stay there as long as necessary. I have no idea when you will be able to return. I am trusting you with my people, Mortel. Do not let me down."

* * *

TWELVE

Four Zjobock Dhort stood on the bluff outside the great hatching cavern, body shut down in daytime dormancy, mind roiling in turmoil. Her consciousness could not rest and her mind flew over the many days to where the packs were meeting.

The great mind of all had joined them as one and those left behind were there in the mind too. Leena the terrible was close now and her mate, the mighty murderer was following. Now was the time, now that those two were removed from the human world, the new incursion had begun.

The packs would continue the journey west, following the chain of islands that linked the two lands through the cold waters of the southern sea. Many packs had already gone, only to face death at the hands of the humans.

But the Leader allowed no pain at the loss, gave no chance to mourn the passing of thousands. It just ordered more packs to advance, sending forth wave after wave to attack the humans again and again.

Somewhere far to the south in a place close to the dreaded great water, a huge force stood in the sunlight waiting for the night. The grasses were blackened, a charcoal stain covering a vast plain. A haze of smoke rose in curling drifts, smudging the air and hovering like a miasma over the land. Silence reigned.

Somewhere buried in that host was the one for whom Four searched. The one she would have mated if this war with the humans had not taken all the packs away. She had no quarrel with the humans. None of them did. If the Leader had not come to take the great mind under Its control she was sure this would not be happening.

After the first great mission to prevent Naali the mighty murderer from coming once more into the light had failed, the packs had faced horrible slaughter at the rejoining of the murderer with his mate, Leena the terrible.

The packs had come home defeated and decimated. They had tried to forget, to rebuild. But then there was the Leader, the one who drove them to this new war. The one who now forced her to take the wrong male as mate.

Too many had died. And now, with these forced matings, the ceremony of adulthood had become dangerous. Too many females were dying as they were made adult by the male's knife at the mating ceremony.

Four had no intention of dying. She intended to be alive and unmated when her true mate returned from the war. If he returned.

But she knew there was only one way for that to come about. She had to get away, leave her pack, take her life into her own hands and somehow hide from the Leader, who knew all and connected them all in the greatest melding of pack minds that had ever been. She had no hope of succeeding, but she was determined to try.

* * *

As the travellers began to climb higher into the mountains they came across a lone kalkar sizzling quietly in the late morning sunlight. Evelar dismounted and examined the dormant creature cautiously.

"Why is it out here by itself?" said Ordel. "Should it not be with its pack?"

Evelar shook his head. "I don't know. Most unusual," he mused.

Miyam dismounted and joined him, opening her mind to read the creature's dreams. She looked at Evelar in surprise. "It's female!" she said.

"I did not think they had such a thing as a female," said Ordel in bewilderment.

"Apparently they do," Evelar murmured.

"Well, whatever she's doing out here, we don't have time to muse about it," said Miyam matter-of-factly. "Let's keep on."

The travellers set up camp in a protected gully and, while the Queen and Atwin rested, Ordel wandered restlessly. Evelar and Miyam began an exhaustive exploration of the surrounding countryside in an attempt to pick up clues, but when they returned to camp they had little to report.

Since landing at the beach, they had not sighted any kalkar, but for the lone female of that morning. Neither could fathom why. As the shadows grew long, the little group sat dejectedly by the fire.

Atwin had improved over the day and spoke more readily. His frustration was infectious and at nightfall they were no closer to an answer. They sat long into the night, speaking little, confounded by the futility of it all.

Finally, Delsi drifted off to sleep, followed by Atwin soon after. Ordel spoke quietly with the two revealers until the early hours of the morning, but a solution did not present itself. Then, an hour or so before dawn, Atwin awoke with a cry of pain. The others gathered around him in concern.

"Kalkar," he whispered.

The party readied for attack, but it did not come. Evelar glanced to the east, noting the lightening sky. On the early morning breeze wafted a faint smell of acrid warmth. Kalkar were about. Finally, a movement to the west caught Miyam's eye and she pointed. A lone figure approached hesitantly.

As it came closer, the two revealers looked at each other. It was the female. She raised a hand appealingly.

"I greet you," she said in a soft voice.

"You speak the common tongue?" Ordel strode toward her, his sword pointed warningly in her direction. "Come no closer," he said harshly.

"Please," she said. "I mean you no harm."

"What do you want?"

She hesitated. "I want to help you..."

Ordel and Atwin exchanged a bewildered look.

"Why?" said Delsi.

"Please," said the kalkar woman. She glanced nervously to the east. "I have very little time."

"Why should we trust you?" said Atwin with venom in his tone.

"Because I can lead you to her."

"How did you..."

"The sun rises," she said raising her arms, pulling the hood of skin over her head and wrapping the wing membrane about her thin body. "Please wait for me to wake... Let me explain..." The sun peeked over the horizon and the kalkar woman stood frozen before them, the ground sizzling at her feet.

"She is definitely alone," said Evelar.

He and Miyam had spent the morning searching the countryside for signs of other kalkar.

"We have nothing to fear as yet."

"But where did she come from?" said Atwin. "Her pack must be close by."

"Maybe she has no pack," said Delsi.

"I find that hard to believe," said Ordel.

"We know nothing about the females," Miyam reminded them. "Perhaps they don't run with the packs."

"What makes you say that?" asked Ordel.

"Did you notice her voice?"

"The one that spoke in Atwin's vision had a harsh, guttural voice," Evelar said, picking up Miyam's thought.

"Perhaps only the males fight, which means the males alone run with the packs," Miyam concluded.

"We cannot be sure of that," Ordel replied.

"No, but I think we should hear what she has to say."

"We're not in any danger," Evelar stated.

"Besides, what choice do we have?" Miyam continued.

"It's our only clue," Evelar concluded.

As night fell, the five travellers positioned themselves in a circle around the kalkar woman with weapons drawn and waited for her to wake. The sun sank slowly below the horizon and, with a little crack, the female came to life, the grey colour of dormancy washed from her flesh by the mottled green of activity. Shrugging the skin membrane off her head and letting the wings fall so that they draped much like a cape, she noted their hostility and sighed.

"Please," she said in her soft voice. "You will not need those weapons. I am no danger to you."

"We apologise if we seem distrustful," said Atwin. "But can you blame us?"

"Of course not," she said. "That is why I will answer any question you care to ask."

"Why do you want to help us?" said Delsi.

"Because I do not like what the Leader has done."

"The Leader?"

"The one who controls us."

"Who is he?" said Atwin.

"We do not know. It is not male, nor female. It is the Leader."

"Has this Leader always controlled you?"

"No," she replied. "It came. Now It controls."

"We have noticed," said Evelar then, "that kalkar have been acting strangely. Banding together when previously you have not, and joining with certain humans against us. Is this the work of the Leader?"

"Yes. It makes the packs join. It forces us to do things which are not our way."

"Where is your pack?" asked Miyam quietly.

"I... left."

"You ran away?"

The female nodded.

"Why?"

"I... did not like the male the Leader chose for me. And..." she hesitated and raised a thin green hand to her throat. "I did not want my throat cut."

Delsi gasped. "Who wanted to cut your throat?"

"Please, do not misunderstand. It is our way. When a child becomes an adult, the throat is cut, to change the way the voice sounds. Then all will know that a new adult is among us."

"Who does this?"

"The male does it to himself. The female has it done by her male on the mating night."

Miyam shuddered and exchanged a look with Evelar. He took her hand and squeezed it reassuringly. Delsi raised a disbelieving hand to her own throat.

"If this is a normal custom," said Ordel, "why did you not want it?"

"Sometimes, a new adult dies from the wound, but since the Leader came it has happened more often. We do not know why. I was afraid," she admitted.

"What is your name?" asked Ordel then.

"Name?"

"What do others call you?"

"Call?"

"How are you identified?"

"Oh. I am Four Zjobock Dhort."

"Your first name is a number?" said Ordel incredulously.

"It is a rough translation. I am the fourth hatched in the moon Zjobock of the sun Dhort," she explained. "That is my designation."

"Is that not a rather cumbersome system?"

"It is our way," she shrugged.

"I am..." Ordel began.

"Ordel," she said. She faced each of them in turn. "Delsi. Atwin. Miyam. Evelar. I have been... listening."

"How can you help us?" said Ordel then.

"I know where your friend has been taken. I can lead you there."

"What do you hope to gain from us?"

"I... wish to come with you, to your land," she said, looking about warily. "I want to help you destroy..." her eyes flicked about nervously. "It will hear me."

"So kalkar can communicate mentally," said Ordel quietly.

"Before the Leader came, we could only hear those of our own pack. Now we hear all, because of It."

"It knows you are a traitor, then," said Atwin.

"Please," she replied. "Do not misjudge me. I want... Things have changed so much. It has changed us. I like It not. Help me."

"You can lead us to Netta?" said Atwin eagerly.

"I can."

"Then lead on."

The female kalkar led them higher into the mountains, and the cold of winter deepened. As they travelled, they discussed strategy. Finally, Four halted them with a raised hand.

"You can plan forever, but it will not help you," she said bluntly. "The Leader knows what I am doing. I cannot hide from Its awareness. It will be ready for you."

"There must be a way," said Atwin stubbornly.

Four shrugged. "It may not spring the trap."

"What do you mean?" said Delsi.

"You are not the Leader's main target, neither is your child. It is entirely possible that It will let you go."

"Are you sure?"

Four shrugged again. "I sense that it may be so. The diversion has served It well."

"Diversion?" said Ordel. "I like not the sound of that."

Four looked at him, her red eyes burning. "Your child was taken to bring you here, to get your amulets out of the way. Your land is in far more danger than you."

"What?" said Delsi. She clutched at her husband's arm. "Ordel, we must hurry."

"I know, love."

"Come," said Four. "We are almost there."

Delsi, Atwin and the rest of the party gathered at the base of the embankment. The almost stagnant river flowed stickily behind them, its brown depths hiding any number of nameless objects. Four shrank away from the polluted water, lying flat against the rise of the embankment in her fear.

"When you enter," Four explained, "you must look like you belong. I will give you a designation to use and teach you a few basic words of our tongue, but you must not speak unless it is absolutely necessary. Your voice will give you away. Hopefully, you will be mistaken for a child and left alone, but you must not rely on that. The Leader will have alerted the packs to your presence. One will escape detection where several will not. Who is chosen?"

"I will go," said Atwin without hesitation.

"Your amulet will not hide you from a determined scan. Most would not bother to scan you, but if the packs are ready for you they just might. You will enter through an escape tunnel. It opens into a small storage chamber next to a large cavern. There will be a lot of activity, so you must be careful."

"What manner of place is it?"

"That is not your concern. Now, once you are through the large cavern, a passageway will lead straight to where your friend is kept. Once there, you must disguise her and bring her out as quickly as you can. If asked, your designation is Seven Tokrus Fliech. Repeat."

"Seven Tokrus Fliech," Atwin repeated obediently.

Four proceeded to educate the Prince in the basic elements of the language, hoping that if by chance he was addressed by a kalkar he might be able to pick up the sense of what was said to him, just maybe saving himself from capture.

"The Leader knows we are here," said Four nervously. "It has heard me. You must move quickly."

"Should we not wait until day?"

"It will make no difference inside, there is always a lot of activity. Speed is more important now."

"First we must warn Netta. Things might get a little tense in there," said the Queen.

Delsi drew the others to her and began the communication spell. The minds of the party melded and reached out to the missing girl. In answer, the group detected a faint presence. A confusing array of feelings flowed through the group, fear the strongest. The Princess was alive, but nothing more could be established. Within seconds the fragile contact was severed with a wrenching burst of almost unbearable pain.

The Queen broke down, barely controlling her panic.

"Please, Atwin, you have to get her out of that horrible place!"

"Believe me, Your Majesty," he said, his own concern for the girl clear in his voice. "If it is my last living act, I will bring her to safety."

From the top of the embankment, the small mouth of a tunnel was just visible in the side of the mountain. Two kalkar stood on guard. The Prince led the way through the dark night, circling to one side of the guards with Ordel while Evelar and Miyam circled to the other. As Delsi and Four watched from behind the embankment, they closed in and jumped the guards, silencing them quickly with water from the dead stream.

Atwin dragged the rapidly cooling remains of one of the guards down the hill away from the entrance. Its head was mostly dissolved by the water but the rest of the body was intact. Taking out his knife he began cutting at the wing membrane, drawing a startled gasp from the kalkar woman.

"What are you doing?"

"You said I have to look the part."

He continued his work, carefully separating the wing membrane from the body. The creature's blood steamed as it oozed from the cuts, tarnishing the blade and causing blisters where it touched his hands, but finally he had the flesh free. It was heavy and slick, slightly oily. Waterproof, he remembered suddenly.

Atwin donned the gruesome disguise, hiding his human features under the voluminous folds, and bowing his head to cast the membrane hood's shadow over his face. It reached almost to the ground, not quite hiding his booted feet. He shrugged. Maybe they would not notice.

"Are you sure you want to go alone?" said Evelar.

"I must, it is her only chance. She must be brought out quickly and quietly."

They all watched anxiously as Atwin disappeared into the dark hole of the tunnel, then Ordel and the two revealers rejoined the others in the shelter of the embankment and settled in to wait.

THIRTEEN

Atwin moved along the tunnel at a crouch, for the roof was low. His whole awareness was geared to the mission at hand. After a gruelling journey, through a passage which rose and fell with alarming frequency, he emerged almost too suddenly into an underground cavern.

Following the perimeter, he found an opening which led into a huge echoing vault. A soft glow radiated from holes in a crystalline structure in the centre of the cavern, and several kalkar moved about in the semi-darkness, tending to the contents of hundreds of small niches in the stone walls.

The Prince set out across the cavern, trusting in the dubious protection of the kalkar wing skin.

"Unke," a voice croaked peremptorily.

Atwin hesitated.

"Ha skhelte," the creature beckoned.

The Prince moved slowly toward the rasping voice, keeping his head lowered.

"Unke satik khomdab skheltarg?"

Atwin nodded, hoping that was the right response.

"Unket igt nomklenatcha?"

Atwin recognised the word for designation. "Seven Tokrus Fliech," he said very softly.

"Unke kitne?" You are a child?

Atwin nodded.

The kalkar thrust something at him. "Skhektekka ghot

egra human."

Egra human? Egra meant female. Something about Netta, then. The Prince nodded again and moved off.

"Tokrus," the kalkar said.

Atwin paused.

"Hok rratach," the kalkar pointed.

The Prince nodded again and made his way from the cavern.

Moving cautiously, Atwin edged his way along the passage, listening and watching for any sign of the girl. Soon he encountered a group of guards and crept closer to listen.

"Achemp kallak merg skeef," said one harshly.

"Klokka skeefrigte lyccham," another stated.

A third cackled and they moved off.

Atwin followed at a distance. The young man seethed with anger as sounds of sadistic punishment and human terror floated to his ears from a remote cell.

Outside, Evelar had been listening mentally to Atwin's progress. On hearing those sounds of torture, he exchanged a worried look with Miyam.

"Perhaps we should go in after him," said Miyam quietly.

"You cannot," said Four adamantly.

"He just might do something silly if he catches them in there with her. He might need help," said Evelar reasonably.

"It is too dangerous."

"Didn't you say that the leader already knows we're here?" said Miyam then.

"Did I?"

"It seems to be leaving Atwin alone," said Evelar.

"It might leave us alone too," Miyam continued.

"You cannot know that," said Four. "The Leader is only

waiting for the right time. If you go in there, It will spring the trap and catch you all. Then It can continue the incursion into your land without having you turn up behind the packs to cause trouble."

"And what will happen to Atwin if he's caught in there with Netta and we're not there to help him escape?" said Miyam.

"It will know you are in there. What possible good could you do?"

"It may know we're in there," said Evelar, "but we're not kalkar."

"It can't read us," said Miyam. "Therefore It can't locate us once we're in there."

Four sighed. "Fine, go ahead. When It has you killed, I will send your friends back to your land without you."

"You do that," said Evelar. "Now give us names and I'll take the wing membrane off that other guard."

"That is only one of you. What about the other?"

"Let me worry about that. I can imitate the voice and confound their eyes if I have to."

Evelar and Miyam moved cautiously through the long tunnel, finally breaking into the small chamber. Moving to the opening they peered cautiously into the great cavern. In the glow of the central crystalline structure, they could see the attendants moving about.

They watched one as it reached into a niche and brought out a large spherical object. The kalkar turned the object over in its hands, examining it carefully. Then the attendant returned the object to its niche and moved on to the next.

The two revealers moved out boldly and made their way across the cavern. They had nearly crossed when a kalkar hurried in their direction. As it raised a hand to signal them, another intercepted it, distracting it long enough for them to exit and continue down the next passage.

"That was too close," Miyam whispered.

"We must hurry," Evelar replied.

Hearing footsteps approaching from a side passage, they ducked out of sight in the shadows, hoping they would not be seen. Two guards passed close by, too busy to notice the huddling figures. The two revealers caught part of their conversation and Evelar closed his eyes to reach into their thoughts, lips moving silently as he stored the language in his mind.

Evelar and Miyam followed the two guards down the corridor. As they drew closer, they prepared to subdue them. Miyam lifted a water bag from under the membranous cloak and drew her knife, ready to slit the bag, but a footfall from behind stopped her. As Evelar turned to face the follower, weaving a spell of disguise to make himself appear as kalkar, Miyam replaced the water bag under the cloak.

"Hattak khomdabi kallak sattubi oflimkit," said a rasping voice. "Unket igt nomklenatcha?"

"Six Zagros Trrask," Evelar replied in an equally raspy voice, quietly assimilating more of the language. "Hok Three Flogg Summack," he indicated Miyam. "Skheltarg vis egra human."

The Prince followed the sounds until he reached a heavy iron door, which stood open. He heard the Princess screaming and it took all his power to stay outside until the noises ceased.

He was outnumbered in here and a fight would only bring others running. Finally, the guards emerged, cackling gleefully at their fun.

"Hok satik rrubrik," one of them rasped as he pulled the door closed with a thud. "Etch egrat klokkarat spegtra."

They continued onward and, almost before he was sure

they were gone, the Prince threw himself against the door in an agony of despair.

The girl's whimpering could be heard from a dark corner as the Prince burst into the cell. At his abrupt entry, there was a cry of panic. Atwin closed the door behind him and stood, shocked into immobility.

The horrid cell was less than six foot in diameter, completely dark, without even a straw mattress on the cold stone floor. A whimper of terror drew his attention to the farthest corner, and in the dimness he could barely make out the girl's cowering form. He took a step toward her and with a cry, she shrank further into the corner, hiding her already bruised face from any possible blows.

With a curse, Atwin threw the cloak of skin away from him. He took another step and spoke soothingly to the huddling figure.

"Be not afraid, Netta," he murmured. "It is me, Atwin. Look at me." He knelt near her, letting her see his face. "Do you not remember me?"

The girl gingerly uncovered one eye and stared covertly. The Prince sat perfectly still, his eyes begging her to remember. Her face changed expression constantly, her once habitual mask no longer able to hide her emotion. The Prince watched her in what little light there was and saw a girl almost unrecognisable.

She had been horribly abused and was covered in welts and bruises. Her clothes were rags and her hair hung matted about her shoulders and face. She made no attempt to brush it from her eyes. She had been so long a prisoner that her defences had been rotted away. Slowly, her face changed.

Abject fear gave way to a tentative hope, disbelief and finally awed recognition. The girl relaxed, almost imperceptibly at first, and leaned tentatively toward him, one arm stretching out across the floor in a heartbreaking gesture of appeal.

She could barely speak and she mouthed his name, an incredulous hope glimmering through the fear.Slowly, the Prince moved closer, careful not to startle her. He knelt in front of her, studying the ever-changing face and gently reached out to brush the straggling hair from her eyes.

She stared in wonder at his very welcome face and a small sob escaped her. She mouthed his name a second time and he took her tenderly into his arms.

Once her trembling calmed, the Prince gingerly coaxed her out of the corner and turned to the door. Though it caused her fear, he donned the gruesome cloak of skin. Then he lifted her off her feet and carried her through the doorway. He halted, face to face with a guard, and mercifully Netta fainted.

Atwin backed into the cell, carrying Netta's limp form with him. The kalkar advanced menacingly, its red eyes blazing.

"Latche skhekteknin egra human?" the kalkar croaked.

Atwin looked downward, hiding his face. He did not understand the words, but he heard the threat. "Egra hurt," he said haltingly.

"Unke kitne?" the kalkar said. "Unket igt nomklenatcha?"

"Ah... Seven Tokrus Fliech."

The kalkar nodded in satisfaction. "The Leader warned me of you," it said in the common tongue. "Your plan has failed, human. Put the female down."

Atwin gently laid Netta down and turned to face the kalkar, standing tall and letting his face show defiantly.

"Sit," said the kalkar harshly.

Atwin stood firm.

"I said sit, human. You are in no position to resist." Atwin turned his back on the kalkar to check on Netta.

"That will be all," said a rasping voice. Another kalkar had appeared in the doorway.

The first kalkar turned in surprise. "Unke nenomkle," it said in its own language. "Unket igt nomklenatcha?"

"That is not your concern," the other replied in common. "The Leader has made new arrangements for the humans. I am to take over."

The first kalkar hesitated.

"You may go. The Leader will see to you later."

"How dare you threaten me? I know who you are!"

Atwin watched incredulously as the newcomer calmly thrust a hand into the other's chest and the guard fell down dead, his fire cooled.

The second kalkar entered the cell, making way for the female who had been hidden behind him. While he bent to work on the fallen guard, she moved immediately to where the Princess lay. Atwin stood in her path.

"What do you intend?" he said suspiciously.

The female touched his hand reassuringly. The touch did not burn, and Atwin looked at the hand in surprise. She was human. She knelt beside Netta and touched her forehead. The Princess woke. She flinched away from the woman, who hushed her by taking the Princess' hand in both of hers.

"Be calm, princess. You are safe."

"Miyam?" said Atwin then.

The woman hushed him.

"Come," rasped the kalkar in the doorway. "We must hurry."

Atwin looked from Miyam to the kalkar and back. "How...?"

"There's no time," Miyam said.

She gave the Princess her cloak of skin and ordered her to put it on. Reluctantly, Netta allowed Atwin to drape it over her shoulders.

"What about you?" asked the Prince.

The new kalkar passed the woman the skin membrane he had just carved off the body of the fallen guard.

"The Leader has chosen to let you go," said the kalkar. "But you must hurry, before It changes Its mind."

They made their way quickly from the cell and headed back in a tight group to the large chamber, the kalkar in the lead and Netta huddling in their midst.

They drew a few glances, but were not questioned. The kalkar walked with authority and others left him to conduct his business. They continued on, through the small, winding tunnel and finally emerged into the dark night.

Delsi and Ordel ran to the Princess in relief and took her from Atwin's supporting arm, half carrying her between them. The Princess sobbed uncontrollably and Delsi sat her down, ignoring her own trembling. Ordel noticed the kalkar and stood in his path, preventing him from entering the camp.

"I mean no harm," said the kalkar.

The waiting female made her way eagerly to where the other kalkar stood. Miyam followed, reassuring Ordel and sending him to join his wife and daughter. Four stared at the kalkar in open interest.

"I know you not," she said in the language of the kalkar. "What is your designation?"

"That is not your concern," the kalkar replied. "Four Zjobock Dhort, the Leader commends you for your involvement in this matter. It recommends you return to your pack, before It sees fit to subject you to discipline. You would be wise to comply."

Four nodded hastily. "On one condition."

"You are not in a position to..."

"Have you a female?" she said suggestively.

Miyam stiffened at the tone, though she did not catch all of the words. Four reached out quickly with one hand to touch his face, but Miyam stepped in front of her warningly.

"Don't even try," she said. "This one is not for you."

Turning her back on Four, Miyam reached out to take the bony green face between her own two hands and forced the red eyes to lock on hers. Four's eyes widened when the woman's hands did not burn.

The figure began to shimmer, and the features to shift and change. Returned to human form, Evelar sank to his knees, his flesh ashen. Four gasped. Miyam knelt beside him and he leant against her, his breath wheezing out in his fatigue.

"How did you do that?" said Four.

"That's not your concern," Miyam replied. She found the pouch at the revealer's belt and took out a small yellow pill.

"Have you any Zestina?"

Evelar shook his head. *'The pill will be enough,'* he said mentally.

"Barely," she replied. She called to Atwin, asking for a cup of water. When he brought it, Miyam dissolved the pill and fed the mixture to Evelar. Then she forced him to lie down. "You will have to sleep off the rest," she said.

"No," he said, sitting up again. "We have to move, before they come after us."

"I thought you said the Leader let us go."

"Still, It will not let us simply walk away."

"Hush, dear."

"Your mate is right," said Four then. "We really must go. We must use the rest of the night to get as far away as possible."

Miyam shook her head. "He has not the strength."

"You know we have no choice," said Evelar.

Miyam sighed. "I don't like this."

"I know, my love. I'll be alright for a few hours."

"Are you sure?"

"I promise I'll sleep later. Don't worry, my love. Help me up."

FOURTEEN

They rode through the rest of the night at a fast trot. Netta rode with Atwin, cradled in front as she huddled against him. Her long captivity had made her nervous and she jumped at everything.

Miyam rode Lumen behind Evelar, her arms wrapped about his waist as she fed him energy in a constant stream. Finally, as dawn lightened the sky, Miyam called a halt. The revealer had slumped forward in the saddle, his weariness too great to fight any longer.

Miyam dismounted and caught him as he half fell from the saddle. Atwin laid out a blanket and Miyam guided the revealer to it, laying him down tenderly. With a weak smile for her, Evelar drifted into a deep sleep.

Miyam settled down beside him. She had been giving him most of her strength, and now that he was asleep she could give in to her own weariness.

Four sizzled quietly nearby, absorbing the morning sunlight. While Atwin lit a fire, Delsi sat her daughter down and began combing out her matted hair. Ordel quietly boiled some water so that the Princess could wash, and then he began to prepare a meal.

When the Queen had finished she pulled Netta's hair back into a long plait and wrapped a blanket around her. Ordel brought a bowl to Miyam and she thanked him gratefully. It was a tasty broth and she ate with relish.

Sitting behind the Princess, Atwin pulled her into his

embrace while her mother attempted to feed her some broth. Netta shook her head but Delsi insisted and she managed to choke down a few spoonfuls. Delsi suggested to Netta that she should try to sleep, but the Princess shook her head again.

She huddled in Atwin's arms, unwilling to lose contact. But before long she slept in spite of herself. She felt safe for the first time in weeks and had relaxed noticeably since her rescue. Atwin laid her down gently and Delsi called Miyam to the circle.

"We need to communicate with my sister," she said quietly. "I did not want to subject Netta to the experience as yet."

The four joined hands and Delsi began the spell.

DELSI? said Averil. *WHERE ARE YOU? HAVE YOU FOUND NETTA?*

WE HAVE HER WITH US, Delsi replied.

I AM GLAD. BUT THERE IS SOMETHING YOU SHOULD KNOW. NETTA'S KIDNAPPING WAS ONLY A DIVERSION.

YES, said Delsi. *WE KNOW.*

HOW?

WE HAVE HAD... HELP. WHAT HAS HAPPENED THERE?

Averil sighed. *KALKAR HAVE INVADED AND ZELONA HAS FALLEN. LEN HAS TAKEN HIS SURVIVORS TO NELLA FILLENGA, WHERE HE AND DERREK ARE PREPARING FOR A SIEGE OF SORTS. KALKAR HAVE A STRANGE WAY OF WAGING A WAR. BUT I WILL EXPLAIN ALL THAT WHEN YOU RETURN. WHEN CAN I EXPECT YOU?*

PERHAPS A MONTH, IF WE ARE LUCKY. MAYBE A LITTLE MORE, said Delsi.

PLEASE HURRY. WHO KNOWS WHAT WILL HAPPEN BETWEEN NOW AND THEN.

WE WILL BE THERE AS SOON AS WE CAN. IS THERE ANYTHING ELSE I SHOULD KNOW?

WELL, she said hesitantly. *SOMETHING STRANGE IS GOING ON WITH KANDINA. SHE RAN AWAY NOT LONG AFTER YOU LEFT AND CALIB BROUGHT HER BACK. SHE HAD GONE TO SEE GERARD, OF ALL PEOPLE. SHE TALKED WITH HIM ONCE BEFORE, AFTER NAALI WAS BROUGHT HOME, AT THE JOINING FEAST. SHE BLAMES HERSELF FOR THE KIDNAPPING.*

WORRY NOT, SISTER. ALL WILL BE WELL.

I HOPE SO. MAKE HASTE, DELSI. WE NEED YOU HERE.

With sword in hand the woman danced, working the patterns with unconscious grace and beauty. The Artisan watched with undisguised fascination. She performed every move with perfection, holding the sword in her left hand, her face a study in concentration.

When the Prince sat next to him the revealer barely noticed, transfixed by her. The woman made her way through the pattern, meeting each stroke perfectly. But then she faltered, the sword resisting the next move and ending at an awkward angle. She cursed, letting the point drop and hanging her head, breathing heavily. Then she gathered herself, assumed the first pose and began again.

"What happened?" murmured Atwin. "What is she doing?"

"She's retraining," said Evelar. "She's learning to fight left handed."

"Why?"

"You remember her injury last year? The arm never regained full strength."

Miyam stopped again, head shaking in frustration. She took a deep breath and started again.

"Why is she struggling so?" asked the Prince.

"Fighting left handed is tricky. It's not as simple as just swapping hands. Every stroke has to be reversed."

"I never thought of it like that."

They watched as she worked her way through the pattern again, faltered again, started again.

"Why are you not helping her? You should work the pattern with her."

The revealer hushed him. "I've never seen her practice before."

The Prince chuckled. "Ah so you are watching with your... heart," he said with a wink. "Not your head."

Evelar smiled but did not reply, eyes fixed on his wife as she practiced.

"Are you seriously telling me that after a year of marriage this is the first time you have seen her practice?"

He shrugged. "We were still keeping secrets most of that time. This is really the first chance I've had to see it since I learned of her past in the College."

The Prince shook his head. "You revealers and your secrets. You know things would be a lot simpler if you just talked about things."

"Maybe," Evelar smiled. "But not half as much fun."

Miyam struggled again. Her frustration was starting to effect her concentration.

"You should be helping her," said Atwin.

"Why? I like watching."

"You are the artisan! You are supposed to be teaching her."

"So?"

"So teach her!"

Evelar sighed, but he was grinning. "As you command, Your Highness!"

He rose fluidly, hand reaching for his own sword. As the Prince watched, the revealer strode out to meet his flustered wife. She jumped as he placed a hand on her arm and stopped her movements, looking at him. Taking up position opposite her, Evelar stood at the ready and met her eyes.

"Mirror me," he said.

The rest of the party were waking now, joining Atwin to watch the display. Netta sat next to the Prince and slipped in under his arm, while her parents stood behind, Ordel whispering a commentary to his blind wife.

The two revealers flowed with the moves, executing the pattern in a flawless mirrored dance. With Evelar to guide her, Miyam moved effortlessly past the point that was giving her trouble and finished the first pattern perfectly.

"Good," he said. "Now the next pattern."

They continued, working each pattern together, and as Miyam gained confidence the movements became faster, more fluid. She was smiling now, eyes locked on her husband's, working easily through the exercises as her mind finally picked up the trick of reversing the patterns she already knew so well.

"Well done, my love," he grinned as the final pattern took form, her lithe body flowing easily through the moves, sword an extension of her arm.

They completed the final move in perfect unison and stood in the end pose, swords pointing straight up close against their bodies. They stood still for a brief moment, then Evelar brought his sword away from his body, planting his feet at the ready and pointing the blade directly at his wife. An invitation to spar.

With a delighted grin, Miyam copied Evelar's move and they progressed to simulated combat. The previous work on the patterns now flowed seamlessly into active use, the moves guiding their hands, the parry and thrust of swordplay tempered by practiced technique.

Beneath the cut and dodge the observers heard grunts

of effort, the force of the movements peppered by the timed vocalisations that added power to the swing and brought mind and body together. This was no easy bout.

It was not an even fight. Miyam, less experienced and still raw with the left hand, could not be expected to match the Artisan in his prime. He held back none of his strength, yet she matched him for a while. Still the first cut went to Evelar.

"What is he doing?" said Delsi to her husband. "He has drawn blood!"

"Hush, love," said Ordel. "It is their way. It would not be a real test if there were not the risk of injury. Miyam knows that."

They watched, Evelar cool and calm, Miyam holding her ground with teeth clenched and face set with determination. With a cry of triumph, Miyam slipped through his guard and scored the second cut. Evelar just grinned and she laughed delightedly.

"Don't get cocky, my love," he murmured.

They threw themselves into the fight for the third cut, which would end the bout. Miyam danced, light on her feet, quick and agile. Evelar stalked, his movements weaving through and around hers, accepting them calmly and answering with power and precision.

Amid the grunts and growls, laughter bubbled, the adrenalin of a wildly enjoyable bout getting the better of them both. The clash of sword on sword rang out again and again, meeting and rebounding, locking and releasing until quite suddenly all sound, all movement, stopped.

They stood, swords crossed between them, pushing against each other but drawing closer in their effort. His wide grin belied the stalemate, and her shrewd look from under lowered brows showed that she knew he was playing with her.

The observers murmured, thinking the fight over, but Atwin hushed them.

The Artisan took his right hand away from the hilt of his sword, holding it firmly in his left. The freed hand slipped sensuously about her waist and pulled her close, pressing them both hard against the swords between them.

Over the top of the crossed swords, he leant forward and planted his mouth firmly on hers. In perfect unison, they slowly drew their swords outwards and free of their bodies. At the exact same moment both swords dropped to clatter on the ground. Evelar's arms tightened about her and her arms slipped about his neck as the kiss deepened.

Ordel began to chuckle. Atwin lifted a hand to quiet his father-in-law.

"It is not over, Sir," he whispered. "Watch."

Miyam's right hand was doing something strange behind the Artisan's head. She gave an almost imperceptible jerk of the wrist and something glinted in the sunlight as it danced above them, laughing at the passionate embrace. The watchers held their breath as the tiny silver knife dipped and cut, slicing through the red sash that was wrapped about Evelar's brow holding his hood in place.

The scarf fell between them, catching on their noses and he pulled away, one hand clutching at the red cloth as it fell. He stared at it for a moment, then his eyes widened as he felt the tiny blade at his neck. His gaze was captured by the glimmer of triumph in his wife's brilliant green eyes.

His hand went to his neck as she held his eyes and allowed the knife to slowly and gently brush the skin of his neck, drawing a thin line of blood, a mere scratch.

She had won the third cut. Atwin laughed aloud and Ordel chuckled. Netta smiled and her mother just shook her head. With a smile of pure unadulterated pride, Evelar caught the tiny knife between his fingers and brought it back to her, sliding it once more with a click into the ornate sheath hidden in her green sash.

"Well done, my love," he murmured as he took her in his arms again. Then he pulled away with a hurt look. "You cut my sash!"

She laughed, snatching it from him. "I guess I'll have to mend it now!" she said with a grin.

The party approached the beach where the crew had been ordered to wait for their return. They had discussed the problem of Four. She could not be taken aboard without endangering the ship, not to mention the reaction of the crew if they were to see a kalkar in their midst. So far, no solution had presented itself. Ordel rode ahead to speak to the Captain, while the others waited out of sight.

"So, ye decided to return from the stinkin' depths of this almighty rat-hole ye brought me ship to," they heard his non-too-gracious welcome. "We was about to leave wi'out ye."

"I thought we had your word you would wait," Ordel said pointedly.

"Aye, that ye did. But me men ain't cut out fer waitin', effn ye catch me meanin'. They was ready to turn on me again."

"Well you can tell them we are going home now," Ordel said.

"Ho, Froyd," the Captain called to his first mate. "Ye can tell the boys we're on our way."

"Aye aye, Cap'n." The mate ran off to spread the news.

"Now, Captain, we have just one slight problem," said Ordel quietly.

"Oh? And what might that be, effn ye don't mind me askin'?"

"Ah... I think it is easier if I show you."

The Captain shrugged and followed Ordel to where the others waited. As he rounded the bushes he stopped in his tracks.

"Are ye crazy," he cried. "What ye think yer doin' bringin' that thing 'ere. I winna be carryin' that on me ship, effn ye don't mind."

"Keep your voice down, Captain," said Atwin. "Do you want the men to hear?"

"Ain't they goin' to know soon enough anyways?"

"Not if we can help it," Atwin replied.

"It'll burn a hole in me ship!"

"That is why we need to find a way to carry her safely," said Ordel reasonably. "Have you any suggestions?"

"Aye. Douse it with water and leave it behind."

"Not an option, I'm afraid," said Evelar then. "She's too valuable. Perhaps you have a metal crate down in the hold that she could stand in?"

"Nay. Metal wouldna stand up to the heat. It'd melt through. There ain't no way we can bring it along."

"Ah..." said Four timidly. "I can fly..."

"Out of the question," said Delsi. "You would never make it."

"It is how they brought your child here. It is not that far," Four argued.

Netta flinched, rubbing at her arms in remembered pain. The burns from being thus carried had faded but the memory had not.

"No," said Delsi.

Four shrugged. "Then there is only one option. Bring the metal box."

"But it winna work," the Captain insisted. "I told ye, it'll melt."

"Trust me," she replied.

"Not bloody likely," he said with a shudder.

"Just do it," Four said in exasperation.

"Alright, but I still dinna think it'll work."

The Captain strode off, mumbling to himself.

"Now," said Four. "You must half fill the box with sand. Just before the sun rises and I go dormant, my body temperature will cool considerably for a few moments. I will wrap my wings about myself and lie on the sand. Then fill the box to the top, so that I am totally covered."

"You will die!" said Delsi, shocked.

"No. Nothing can harm me when I am dormant. I will only cool. Put the lid on and take it aboard. The crew will never know what is in there."

"Bury you alive?" said Miyam. "We can't do that."

"I will be dormant. I will not notice."

"Will you not wake when you are covered and you no longer feel the sunlight?" said Ordel then.

"No. There will not have been enough time for sufficient energy to be stored. I will not wake. Within the sand sunlight will not reach me. I will stay cool and I will remain dormant. When you reach your land, stand me in the sun and I will warm again, waking when night falls as normal."

"I like this not," said Delsi.

"It is the only way," Four said. "I will not be harmed."

"Are you sure?"

Four shrugged. "I will be a little drained for a few nights, but that will pass. I assure you, this is what must be done."

* * *

FIFTEEN

Prince Calib strode down the corridor on his way to his father's chambers. He still could not believe the change in Gerard since the Princess Kandina's unexpected visit. Though he had heard upraised voices, Calib had never discovered what passed between them. But since that day, the King had mellowed.

He had withdrawn into himself, his neurotic behaviour a thing of the past. Taking advantage of that mood, Calib had slowly worked on his father in Atwin's favour. The King had accepted Calib's arguments without the irate reaction that such comments would previously have engendered.

The way was now clear for Atwin to return to Drasmil in honour rather than disgrace. It made Calib glad, for his brother's sake. Atwin could at last take control of the country, with the army behind him. Calib had worked hard to keep the legions under Atwin's control, by feeding the King's fear that if they were taken from him he would lead them in revolt.

But Atwin would never turn on Gerard, he had proven that time and again. Perhaps now it would not be necessary. The Prince gave a knock on the door to Gerard's chambers and, when he heard no answer, entered quietly. The King was not in the outer chamber, but on the desk was a sealed letter.

Curious, Calib approached the desk. Gerard never left paperwork in the open like that. He was too worried about

Atwin's "spies". Calib picked up the letter. It was addressed to Atwin.

"Father?" Calib called.

There was no answer. He replaced the letter and made his way to the inner chamber. Opening the door slowly, Calib entered. The room was empty but, thrown negligently on the four-poster bed, lay the empty scabbard of Gerard's sword. Calib shivered, a cold chill touching his spine.

That sword had not been drawn in over ten years. Worried now, Calib searched the King's apartments. There was no sign of Gerard, but the ward room was in a shambles, as if the King had been searching frantically for something. Calib looked about in consternation. Then he froze, a terrible picture forming in his mind.

He should have realised that Gerard's strange behaviour was a prelude to something. He looked about. He returned to the main bedroom and looked about in there. Then he saw it. The double doors to the King's private balcony stood ajar.

Why had he not noticed that before? The King had not opened those doors since the night of the Queen's death. She had been murdered on that balcony and the King had been terrified that an assassin might come for him also. Cautiously, Calib edged toward the doors.

A cold wind whistled through the small gap between door and jam, seeming to express for him the fear in his heart. The Prince took a deep breath and stepped out onto the balcony. His breath caught in his throat and he raised a hand to his mouth.

Gerard was there. He lay sprawled on the stone, face down, arms flung out to the sides. His sword, so long unused, protruded from the middle of his back. The King had killed himself, falling on his sword like a disgraced soldier.

* * *

In the twin town of Nella Fillenga, the survivors of Zelona had enlisted into the mercenary army of the Fillens, and King Lenent had joined Derrek in the palace. The ditches that had failed so disastrously at Zelona were dug wider and deeper at Nella Fillenga.

The water from the great River Nort was diverted to fill the ditches, forming a long narrow lake half circling the city, the southern edge of the town protected by the high cliffs and deep fiords of the coast.

For miles about the twin city the river delta fanned out over the plain, forming a sprawling marshland with many small rivers breaking off and heading for the cliffs of the coast to cascade into the cluster of deep narrow inlets that formed the fingers of headland that gave the town its name.

The two kings sat long into the night with a hastily gathered court and council to plan for the coming siege. The lesson of Zelona was foremost in all their minds. The port town on the edge of the desert had failed to utilise the one weapon that could have defeated the inhuman enemy. Water.

"We have a natural defensive perimeter here already," said King Derrek. "With the river now surrounding the city and the marsh all about, the kalkar will have a tough time reaching us."

"Perhaps," said Lenent. "Unless they fly, which they will."

"Your Majesties, we need new weaponry, not just defensive ditches and streams."

"What would you suggest, General Moster?" said Derrek.

"New missiles, made to fire from the existing ballistae, filled with water."

"It is a commendable idea," said Lenent. "But do we have time for something that sophisticated?"

"Perhaps we can put something together quickly from what is at hand," suggested Derrek. "Gather up any wineskins, canvas bags, anything that can be waxed to hold water, fill them and fire them. They do not need to hold together long, just so they reach the enemy and burst on impact."

"Yes, Your Majesty," said the general. "I'll set the men to arrange it."

"What about the archers?" said Lenent, remembering with a pang of regret the failure of the arrows at Zelona. "Can we rig something similar for them?"

"Leave it with me, Your Majesty," said General Moster. "I'll see what the men can think up."

As night fell the kings waited, watching for the approach of the enemy, giving orders to their generals and preparing their troops for battle. At last, around midnight, the word came that kalkar had been sighted, making their way across the plain toward the great delta of the River Nort.

At the farthest edge of the marshland the kalkar horde stopped and waited. The force continued to build and still they waited. There seemed no end to the approaching enemy. The gathering force finally stopped an hour before dawn, spreading out over the plain. Still they did not advance further. Instead they stood and waited for the sun.

At dawn the kalkar army went dormant and Lenent sent his men out into the marsh, armed with as much water as they could carry. They marched all morning, six leagues through marsh and bog, to where the enemy stood.

The first kalkar stood in a menacing line, spreading out for over a mile in both directions along the edge of the marsh. The ranks behind filled the plain to the horizon and beyond.

Captain Poppel stood at the head of his troops, ignoring

the murmuring behind him. He summoned the leaders of the cohorts. As the men watched, the Captain shrugged a water bag off his shoulder and walked forward. He studied the creature for a moment, taking this chance to see the stuff of nightmares up close.

The creature stood covered by a strange cloak made of living skin, its head and body completely hidden, only its clawed feet visible. The Captain reached out to touch it, but stopped when he felt the heat radiating from it.

Instead he uncorked the water bag and slowly poured it over the creature's head. The water sizzled and bubbled, steam rising in a cloud, but the kalkar stood unharmed as the water ran off the slick protective membrane and fell harmlessly to the ground.

Pulling out his sword, the Captain slid it in under the membrane covering the head, slicing through the thin skin and watching it fall about the creature's bony shoulders to show the alien head underneath. Captain Poppel grimaced. The eyes were closed, the thing's breathing almost imperceptible. It had no hair and the scaled skin over the head was dark olive green mottled with light grey. Patches of skin about the tiny holes that served as ears and spreading down, around the neck, glowed yellow.

Reaching out with the water bag again, the Captain poured it over the now unprotected head. The flesh began to blister and bubble and the Captain jumped back in surprise. The creature's flesh melted away, the water running down under the rest of the membranous cloak and melting the body too. All that remained was a steaming, stinking puddle of goo.

"Take your cohorts and spread out," said Captain Poppel to his men. "Take down as many as you can."

The men worked all day, slowly making their way further into the plain, killing rank upon rank of the enemy. Then, as the sun dipped low in the west, Captain Poppel called a halt and pulled his men back into the swamplands.

"Let's see what these things do now," he murmured to his first officer.

The last ray of sun winked out. With a reverberating crack that stuttered and echoed through row upon row to the horizon, the kalkar horde came to life. A piercing wail, beginning low and soft but building rapidly to a high pitched ululating crescendo, blasted across the plain as the enemy mourned their fellows.

Protective skin fell back, showing slender limbs and mottled flesh, spattered with fluorescent markings. Clawed hands reached forward and the first line of kalkar rushed headlong into the marsh. The next line followed and the next, until several thousand kalkar struck out through the swampland.

The humans stood firm, watching the approach. The leading rank was the first to fall. The taloned feet sank into the boggy soil, deeper with each step. Screams of pain could be heard as legs melted on contact with the wet mud. More and more began to falter, legs giving way and bodies falling into the mire to melt away in gut wrenching screams.

The keening cry of grief came again, sending shivers up the spines of the watching humans. Captain Poppel grimaced at the sulphurous smell rising in steam from the melted ranks of the enemy. The army had not raised a sword, the kalkar destroyed before they even came in range.

The greater part of the horde stood, red glowing eyes staring menacingly, at the edge of the swampland. Slowly, the kalkar horde opened wings, the skin membrane pumping full of what passed for blood and spreading wide.

Captain Poppel felt a rush of warm air on his face as thousands of great wings pushed the horde off the ground.

They came straight at the humans, one never ending wave of hot menacing flesh. They passed overhead, and without a backward glance the enemy flew toward the city, their massed bodies blocking out the stars.

"Well, now," said the Captain. "That was fun."

On the plain outside the wall, Lenent marshalled the troops. Night had fallen and the enemy was coming. A cry from the east tower alerted the army to the coming horde. Lenent sent the Captains out to ready the catapults and ballistae, to set the archers on the walls and to gather the cohorts in the streets of the city. The King watched as a dark smudge covered the sky, billowing and growing as the kalkar horde approached.

"Hold firm and watch for the archers!" he cried, his voice echoing as he called encouragement to the troops.

Certain that he had done his best to prepare the defence of the city, King Lenent of Zelona headed up to the battlements. Climbing the stairs inside the wall, the King emerged on the walk, staring out over the plain. For a moment the incoming invasion threw his mind back to his own fair city and the sudden devastating attack that had sent his people to flight.

"Archers, ready to fire!" he called.

The enemy came closer, but he held the archers back, hoping to get as many in range of the new water tipped arrows as possible. Each arrow head had been covered with a small sack of water. It was hoped that on impact the arrow head would pierce the sack and water would leak into the wound. It might not kill but it might cause some damage. Barrels of water were collected on the wall for a second defence.

"Ready!" cried the King. "Fire!"

Arrows flew overhead, arcing upward into the kalkar as

they closed in. Arrows bit into kalkar hide, water splashed over exposed flesh, kalkar screamed. A few fell, and Lenent smiled in satisfaction. It was not a rout but it was something.

"Ready catapults!" he yelled. "Fire!"

Large skins of water the size of melons flew upward into the now looming kalkar force. They hit with a series of sickening thuds, bursting open to saturate their targets. This time the screams were deafening.

The creatures were hit front on and the water melted into their flesh, quickly penetrating to the vital organs and sending the remains crashing to the ground before the wall. Others were hit on a wing, melting away the membranous flesh and sending them falling, screaming but still alive.

A few were hit on a limb but continued on to land amongst the humans on the wall, or in the streets below.

"Stand fast," Lenent called. "Ready the next round."

Combat raged around him as he watched the next wave approach, the men working in pairs to slash with sword and splash with water from the barrels.

Again he gave the word. "Fire!"

From somewhere inside the palace behind, Lenent heard a trumpet call. Three short sharp notes, twice. He stopped and turned with eyes wide, his blood cold and his heard thudding in his chest.

"Your Majesty?" said a voice at his side. "What is it?"

"Derrek!" he murmured. "With me, Captain."

Without a backward glance, the King ran, breath ragged in his panic and fear filling his soul. He prayed that he would make it in time, but deep inside he knew he was already too late.

Lenent entered the room, his captain behind him and stopped short. His eyes were drawn to three bodies in the middle of the floor, the Queen and her two children, all dead. He saw King Derrek a small distance away, beside the body of the assassin. His sword still protruded from the traitor's chest.

"Captain, the city is lost," said Lenent quietly.

"Are you sure, Sir?"

"That call was a traitor's signal. Tribesmen will have already turned on our troops, from within our own ranks. Call the retreat."

"Yes, Sir!" said the Captain as he hurried off.

King Derrek lay still, a pool of blood growing around him to mingle with the blood of the assassin. Lenent knelt by the King, seeing the knife buried to its hilt at an angle that pushed the blade up under his ribs, hearing the rattling sound of his shallow breath.

"Oh, Derrek," he said, shaking his head. "I told you to get them away."

The dying king's eyes focused on him, pain and regret shining as the light faded. Lenent sighed.

"Sleep well, my friend," he murmured as the final breath rattled out and the eyes fluttered as the life in them died.

King Lenent sat on the floor beside the dead King Derrek, looking around at the complete destruction of a royal bloodline. Reaching forward he gently closed the King's eyes. He shuddered as he pictured the uncertain future now ahead for the Kingdom of Nella Fillenga.

Lenent shivered. His own beloved Zelona had narrowly escaped the same fate. He suddenly realised how precarious his own kingdom was. He had no family to be saved, or to take over when he died.

The King of Zelona sighed, his own regret at a life wasted now becoming startlingly clear. He had never taken a wife, never tried to secure his kingdom for the future. The one woman he had ever cared for had married another, and even when her husband was killed he had held back, waiting for a right moment that had never come. Perhaps the right time was now.

A light step and a sob brought him back to reality, and he hastily wiped his eyes, rising to his feet and turning to face the newcomer. A young woman, shuffling her feet and wringing her hands in anguish.

"I... I am sorry, Sir," she whispered.

"No, child," he murmured. "Who are you?"

"I am Mirta. I have only been here a week..."

Lenent sighed. "Come then, child, we should get you to safety."

"What safety?" she sobbed.

"One of my captains is leading the civilians west, you can go with them."

"But I want to help."

"Some have stayed to do what they can to help the army as we march north. You are young and there are very few women staying, but if you feel you are able I can take you to the captain in charge of the civilian cohort."

"Thank you, Sir."

The King of Zelona crouched in the darkness, watching from the bushes as row upon row of sizzling forms marched past. The King of the Fillens had accepted his counsel, but it had not been enough. On the death of King Derrek, Lenent had ordered the city evacuated.

Now, Nella Fillenga stood abandoned, left to the possession of the kalkar horde. Derrek's army, the rival only of that of Drasmil, had failed to repel the invasion of the evil ones.

Now, Lenent crouched in the darkness, having sent the army on to Yerterma ahead of the invading horde. He had lost his horse the first day, stolen from his camp while he slept. There were refugees everywhere and they were all desperate.

He hoped to somehow evade the kalkar and head north. Not wanting to involve anyone else in such a perilous task, Lenent had slipped away alone. He had taken it into his own hands to get word to the other kings.

King Lenent had been totally unaware of the tribal presence in his city, and had almost been killed. King Derrek, too, had been ignorant of it. It had cost him his life. The other kings had to be told that their lives were in danger, and their families too. He had to get to Shirall, where perhaps he might yet save his lost love.

SIXTEEN

Averil was waiting on the dock when the ship came in on the evening tide. She embraced her sister and Ordel, and watched with a smile as Atwin led the Princess to her. Netta returned the smile and Averil opened her arms in invitation.

The Princess accepted the embrace. She had begun to heal during the voyage, and was almost her old self. Atwin embraced Averil and planted a kiss on her cheek.

"Miyam?" said Averil, noticing the girl with the revealer. "Where did you come from? And when...?" she indicated the green-bordered revealer's cloak.

"Ah... It's a long story."

Miyam looked to where the horses had been brought ashore and noticed the box being unloaded.

"Should we let her out yet?"

"No," the Queen said. "I think we should get her safely into the palace grounds. The town is not the place for her."

"Who?" Averil asked.

"I will explain later," said the Queen.

"If Your Majesty agrees," said Evelar, "Miyam and I will look around town before coming up to the palace."

"Yes, that might help," said Delsi. "And perhaps I should pay a visit to Algernon."

"I can handle that," said Ordel. "You should see Netta settled."

"Alright, dear." She ordered two of the sailors to follow

with the metal box carrying Four, and took hold of her horse's bridle. "Let us get indoors."

An hour later, the two revealers made their way to the inn to meet Ordel before returning to the palace. He was waiting at a corner table, nursing an ale which he had no real intention of drinking. Algernon wandered over and offered to bring one for Evelar.

"No, that won't be necessary," he replied with a grimace of distaste.

"Shall we go?" said Ordel, eager to leave his warm ale.

"Not just yet, Your Highness," said Evelar.

"We need to mingle a bit first," Miyam finished.

"Of course you do," the Prince Consort replied.

At that moment, the door opened and a pair of revealers breezed in. Miyam and Evelar turned to watch from their corner. One was an artisan, and her companion wore the purple border of an adept.

"Will you excuse us, Your Highness," said Evelar.

Ordel shrugged.

Miyam and Evelar made their way to where the newcomers had settled into the shadows beside the hearth. As the Artisan looked up, Miyam smiled with pleasure and Evelar chuckled delightedly.

"Well met, Seiliar."

"Hello, brother. You know Jondras."

"Greetings, Dock."

"Hello, Sand."

"I see you found Miyam for us," said Seiliar with a grin. "She had us all rather worried when she disappeared so suddenly."

Evelar shrugged. "How did the Maestro take it?"

"Oh, he knew where she was as surely as I did. You could at least have warned us."

Evelar grinned. "I'm sorry I startled you."

"Oh, it was fun! Shook up a few of the counsellors rather drastically. That made the shock worthwhile. Some of those old totterers need a jolt every now and then."

"My dear sister," Evelar laughed. "You've grown so cynical in your old age. Has that splash of red gone to your head?"

"Never, brother dear. It's just that I've finally broken free of your shadow. I'm no longer blinded by the light of your success!"

"Do I hear a touch of bitterness?"

She waggled a finger at him. "Don't even think of it. If not for you I would never have come so far. I'm terribly proud of you, you know."

"The feeling's mutual. Where are you headed?"

"Mytar. Apparently there's been a lot of activity in the mountains and King Erris is worried. You know the invasion is not going well for us."

"I had heard something like that, yes. But we've been a bit out of touch."

"So I gathered."

"What can you tell us?" asked Miyam.

"Oh, you'll find out soon enough. This I can say; the Fillens are on their way north. Nella Fillenga has fallen and Derrek was killed, along with his entire court. The people and what's left of the army are filtering into Yerterma and Mytar."

"We've heard rumours that the tribesmen are on the move," said Evelar then.

Seiliar nodded. "But they're headed south, to join up with the kalkar. It does not smell good."

"That's an understatement," said Jondras quietly.

Riding together on his stallion, Lumen, with Prince

Ordel following behind, Miyam and Evelar finally returned to the palace. They headed first to the stables in the ruined courtyard where they handed the horses to a stable boy. Miyam scanned the stalls, hearing a nicker and looking for a familiar muzzle.

"Come, my love," said Evelar as he turned to leave.

"Wait," Miyam said, shaking her head. "I need to see Cheena first."

She moved closer, looking into each stall until she found the one she wanted. Atwin's wild stallion, already rubbed and fed, looked up and snorted at her as she passed. Lumen was being cared for in the stall opposite, and Ordel's horse was next door.

Then she saw her, standing in the darkness of the corner stall farthest from the door. The beautiful mare stood looking over the stall door, whiffling and flicking her ears. Miyam rushed to her.

"Oh my beautiful girl!" she cried, hugging the mare about the neck. "I'm so sorry I had to leave you here."

"I'd forgotten she was still here, my love," said Evelar, close behind.

Miyam looked up at him. "I have her back now," she smiled, tears in her eyes. She buried her face in the horse's mane. "I'm sorry I was gone so long."

The next morning, there was a conference in the Queen's private drawing room, off the main audience chamber. Four had been stood in the sun inside the walls of the ruined above-ground palace.

"The remnants of Derrek's army are being led by a corporal by the name of Blad," Averil explained. "The civilians from Nella Fillenga and the surrounding area are gathering under the control of a farmer known as Freakles. This man has some remote connection with the royal family, and the army is pressuring him to assume the throne. They say he is the closest living kinsman of the late king."

"What happened to Lenent?" asked Delsi.

"I wish I knew," Averil sighed, clutching her hands together to prevent their shaking. "Our reports say he was with Derrek when he was killed and that he ordered the evacuation. But now he seems to have disappeared, and it worries me so. I am hoping he will turn up in Mytar or Yerterma with one of the smaller groups who have yet to join the main march."

"I am sure he will turn up soon, sister," said Delsi.

"Let us hope," said Ordel. "Algernon says the people are getting nervous. They need to be organised into some sort of home guard. Is the army ready to march?"

Averil nodded. "They await your command. I have also had word from Drasmil. Calib has the legions marshalled and ready for your arrival, Atwin."

"Good," Atwin replied. "I will leave as soon as we are finished here."

"Ah... belay that, if you would," said Averil.

"Why?"

"Calib will explain when you see him. Things will not be as you expect. Perhaps you should warn him first of your imminent arrival."

Atwin narrowed his eyes in suspicion. "What is afoot?"

"It is not my place to say," said Averil. "Just do not go unprepared."

Atwin looked about nervously. "What is going on?"

Averil said nothing. Then she coughed. "Ordel, Tarnel awaits you at Tellemot. He thinks it best that you join forces and march to Yerterma."

Ordel shook his head. "That will leave the coast open to further attack. There could be kalkar advancing across the Barren Wastes. Tellemot is too important to abandon now."

"In which case he will need you even more."

"I will take the legions down to Mytar," said Atwin. "Yerterma will be hit first, so Erris needs to keep the passes over the Dragons and the heights under strict control. From what we know of the alliance between kalkar and tribesmen, we need to clear the mountains, or we will lose both Yerterma and Mytar in one stroke."

Ordel nodded. "We could be fighting a war on two fronts. Tellemot is as much a target as Yerterma and Mytar, but we cannot hope to defend both against the horde."

"Perhaps I can help," said Evelar.

"How?" Ordel replied.

"I have a few connections."

"The nomads?" said Atwin. "Do you think you could get them to help?"

"If the kalkar are advancing across the desert, the nomads will want to defend their territory. We have already seen that the kalkar are quite willing to enter the Wastes in force. The nomads could slow their march."

Ordel nodded. "That would help. If you could have the nomads fall back to Tellemot, then we could take a larger force to Yerterma."

"But will they follow you?" said Atwin.

"I have access to Old One and they follow him. They will come."

"Perhaps we should ask Four where they march," said Miyam then.

Delsi nodded. "She could tell us where the main strike will come."

"It would be nice to have advance warning," said Ordel ruefully.

"So that is why you brought that thing here," said Averil with a shiver.

"Judge her not, sister dear," said Delsi. "She may be

different on the outside but she has a keen mind and a good heart and she deserves respect. She has risked everything to help us and she has already proven herself useful. She may yet turn this war around for us."

"Then let us adjourn 'till this evening. We can plan further when we know what to expect."

At nightfall they gathered in the old palace and watched as Four came to life. She looked about uncertainly.

"What is this place?"

"The old palace at Shirall," said Delsi. "How do you feel?"

"Weary. I must have been asleep for a long time."

"Just over three weeks."

"We need your help," said Averil.

Four looked sharply at the woman.

"This is my sister, Averil," said Delsi. "She will not harm you."

"How may I help?"

"We need to know where the packs march," said Ordel. "We suspect they may be moving in two separate forces."

Four concentrated briefly, her green brow furrowed slightly. Then she sighed. "They move on both fronts," she said and sank wearily to the ground.

"Are you alright?" said Miyam quickly.

Four nodded. "I need to rest. My fire is not fully charged as yet. I need another day of sun."

"Can we help in any way?"

"No. You may leave me here, if all is safe. I suspect you too need rest."

"I would like stay with you, if you do not mind company," said Averil then. They all looked at her in surprise. She smiled. "I have never had the chance to learn about your people. I would like to talk with you, if you do not object."

"If you wish," Four shrugged.

*

In the Queen's drawing room in Shirall, a group had gathered for a final discussion before going their separate ways. Four had been led carefully down into the audience chamber and stood now off to one side, carefully avoiding the expensive tapestries and rugs, the stone floor impervious to her sizzling flesh.

Atwin would leave soon for Drasmil and Ordel would take Shirall's small army south by sea to Tellemot. Evelar and Miyam would accompany the Prince Consort as far as Tellemot, where they would continue on into the Barren Wastes in search of the nomads.

"I want to come with you," Netta cried. "Why must I stay?"

"Netta, we talked about this," said Delsi. "You are too weak and we must protect the child."

"You know your mother is right," said Atwin. "You need to be monitored."

"But I feel fine and I could help," she argued. "You know how much stronger we are together. The amulets could defeat this threat if we stay together!"

"Netta, you cannot use your power while the child is so small," said Delsi. "You are four months and not showing. It worries me. Leena was protecting you while you were captive, and slowing the child's growth, but now you need to stay safe and recover, to bring this child back to full health."

The Princess sat between her husband and her father, one hand clutching Atwin's and the other resting on Ordel's arm. She did not want either to leave.

"Please be careful," she said in a small voice.

Atwin smiled reassuringly.

"Ordel, did you find out anything more from Algernon?" asked Averil.

"The people are getting nervous," the Prince Consort replied. "Perhaps they should be organised into some sort of home guard. It would keep them occupied."

"Are you sure that's necessary?" said Delsi.

"Your Majesty," said Evelar then. "There may be a more pressing need for some sort of security organisation within the city."

"Oh?"

"Tribesmen are about," said Miyam.

"Over the past few weeks they've been filtering into the city," said Evelar.

"They're planting their... spies in the most worrying of positions," Miyam continued.

"Worrying?" said Averil.

"They're worming themselves into positions close to the most powerful men in the city," Evelar explained.

"Several have taken up places on the docks, one even in the office of the Customs Manager," said Miyam.

"Some even made it into Algernon's network," said Evelar.

"He's using them to gain more information," Miyam stated.

"They may even have a few plants within the palace itself," Evelar concluded.

"Oh dear," said Delsi.

"We must weed them out," said Averil.

"That may not be possible," Evelar replied.

"If you let them know that you're on to them," said Miyam, "they may get nervous."

Evelar nodded. "You'll force their hand and then we'll have a much greater threat to deal with."

"Such as?" said Delsi.

"Such as a full scale battle within the city itself," said Miyam.

"Without a standing force to combat the tribesmen, Shirall could fall into their hands," Evelar finished.

"What shall we do?" said Delsi.

"Be prepared," said Miyam.

"And watch yourself," Evelar warned.

SEVENTEEN

Atwin walked slowly through the garden in the underground palace at Shirall. The servant followed a pace behind, eager to please. Since he and the others had returned the Prince had been unable to shake the feeling that something was terribly wrong.

As always, he felt uneasy about appearing at his father's palace unannounced, but this was something more. Averil had been acting strangely toward him ever since he and the others had arrived, and he felt sure it had nothing to do with the kalkar invasion.

She had mentioned that they had discovered his father's role in the kidnapping from Kandina. The Princess had confessed her own part in it all when she returned from her unexpected visit to Drasmil. He had no idea that Kandi's feelings were so very strong.

He had decided to send a private message to his brother before he made the trip himself. The Prince heard a light, determined footfall on the path and dismissed the servant with a short, precise letter for Calib.

"Belay that order," said a mild voice. "It will not be necessary."

Atwin turned sharply. He faced his brother with a look of surprise at his seemingly miraculous appearance.

"Worry not, brother," said Calib. "I have not suddenly developed supernatural powers!" He took the letter from the servant and dismissed him. "A messenger was on his way to me as soon as your ship was sighted. I needed to catch you here."

"You must have pushed your horse to the limit."

"I had a fresh mount waiting half way. There is news you must know before you appear in Drasmil."

"What has happened?" That curious sense of foreboding came rushing back.

Calib hesitated appearing to cast about for words. "Our father is dead," he said finally. "Your Majesty."

Atwin stared at him, uncomprehending at first. Then conflicting emotions warred for dominance and Atwin made no attempt to hide his changing expressions. He did not know what to feel. Was it disrespectful to be relieved, to be silently glad?

"Wait, there is more," Calib said, forestalling comment. "Please do not say anything until you have read this." He handed his brother a sealed letter.

"What is it?"

"You shall see."

Calib turned and walked away. He thought he knew what the letter contained, and he respected his brother too much to be present to witness his reaction. He left the garden and went in search of Netta. The Princess was already looking for Atwin.

"Did you tell him?"

"Yes. He is going to need you soon."

"Where is he?"

"In the garden. I will make sure you are not disturbed."

Atwin sat on a bench under the spreading leaves of a simpa tree. He began to read slowly, fighting the swelling emotions which threatened to overwhelm him.

My Son. When you read this, my soul will have joined

my ancestors. Before I go there are a few things I wish for you to know, but any words I may write cannot do justice to the depth of my feelings.

Throughout the last several days I have spoken many times with your brother Calib, and he has at last made me see the error of my ways. My treatment of you has been unforgivable. I know now how wrong I have been.

You cannot know how deeply I regret the agony I have caused you over the years. Excuses are not enough, for there are none. I know that what has passed cannot be changed, but I can endeavour to somehow ease your pain.

The seed of doubt was planted long ago and the more it grew, the more lost and confused I became. Now my life is forfeit. I hope I have not totally destroyed yours, for then I could never hope to regain your affection.

My heart grieves for the years we have lost. Now I will never be able to prove to you how much I care. You are my eldest son and I would see none but you in my place.

Atwin paused and closed his eyes, drawing a shuddering breath. Then, reluctant but compelled, he continued reading.

I owe you many things, not least of which is my gratitude. For so many years you have kept my name alive in the hearts of the people, when it should have been your name they called. I have not deserved your loyalty.

Now it is with great gladness that I give to you that which should have been yours long ago. Atwin, my beloved son, you are king.

My heart swells with pride and respect for you. I long

to tell you in person the depth of my love for you, but now it is too late.

Goodbye, my son. May your life be long and full. Rule well and wisely, Atwin. Forgive me if you can.

Your repentant father, Gerard.

Atwin crumpled the letter in his lap, head bowed. Netta had arrived in time to watch him read the last of the letter and was worried by his rapidly disintegrating figure.

She moved slowly toward him and knelt quietly by his knee. Gently, she took the letter from his unresisting fingers. She stood, turned away and began to read. She did not see him look up and follow her with tortured eyes.

When she had finished her tears flowed freely and she turned to Atwin in sympathy. He was standing now, drawn by the comfort of her presence, and their eyes met.

"Why do you cry?"

"I cry for you," she said and wrapped her arms about him.

For a moment, he clung to that contact, but then he sighed heavily and pulled away, stubbornly regaining control. She clutched at his hand, wanting so desperately to help him, to ease his pain.

He walked away from her, unable to face such pity. She could only watch helplessly as he moved spasmodically, agitation manifest, his eyes wild. He found himself on the bridge, looking into the water of the little underground stream, hands clutching the rail.

Netta moved up behind him and placed a hand on his arm. He jumped at the contact. Then he took a deep breath.

"I... hated him... for so long."

"I think not."

He jerked around to face her. "What do you mean?"

"I think deep down you worshipped him. You did

everything in your power to earn his respect. All you ever really wanted was for him to notice you and to be proud of you."

He lowered his eyes in dejection. "I tried... so hard," he whispered with difficulty. There was an audible wail in his tone.

"I know."

"I could never do anything right."

"The fault was not yours."

"I keep thinking... I should be glad that he is gone, but..."

Netta wordlessly put her arms about him, pulling his head down onto her shoulder.

"Let it go," she whispered. Then, very softly, she began to sing. It was a meaningless song, a mixture of ballads and lullabies and hymns, but its cathartic energy did its work. With an anguished sob, Atwin slipped from her grasp and sank to the ground, clutching at her skirts in his agony.

Netta lowered herself to his level and sat down, heedless of the mud, cradling his head in her lap. Her voice rose in song, muffling the sounds of his grief until his racking sobs eased.

As his upheaval calmed, her voice lowered, until she was again singing very softly, stroking his hair, as he lay drained but calm. Finally, he rolled over onto his back, his head cushioned in her lap, and her song ended. He took her hands in his, kissed the palms, and held them to his chest.

"ATWIN!"

Netta looked up and in a flash Atwin was on his feet.

"Kandi, you can't go in there!" A second voice cried out, warning them of the cyclone headed their way.

Quickly, Atwin offered a hand and helped Netta up. They looked ruefully at the mud all over their clothing, and

Atwin shrugged. He led the Princess to the rail and both looked into the water, for all the world like nothing was amiss. Both had felt a warning jolt from the amulets at Kandina's approach.

As the younger princess stormed into the quiet of the garden, Atwin turned so that she would see only his back. The girl stopped and took in the scene with a glance. She saw the mud and she saw the hands resting together on the rail.

She saw the closeness of the two bodies and she felt the tingle of electricity which surrounded them, joining them together like no mere physical connection could ever do. Kandina stared, her jealousy overwhelming. When she spoke, her voice was dangerously quiet.

"Well, I see I interrupt."

"Not at all," said Netta.

"Of course, you would say that. But I am not blind. Atwin, what is going on here?"

"I really do not think that is any of your business, Kandina," he said without turning around. The use of her full name and the refusal to face her, made the girl seethe.

"Well. I am so sorry, Your Majesty," she said sarcastically.

"What are you doing here, Kandina?" he asked, cutting across her tirade.

"I wanted to see if you were alright. I thought you might need comfort."

"That is really not necessary. I have all the comfort I need." Atwin looked at Netta and smiled. Kandi could not see his face, but she caught Netta's reaction to the look and fumed at the tenderness she saw there.

"Well excuse me for caring, Your Majesty. In future, I will not bother, since you choose to forget our friendship. You turned from me the moment you fell into the clutches of this... pseudo-royal interloper..."

At that, Netta took a step toward her in surprised indignation, but Atwin detained her with a hand at her waist. The embrace calmed Netta, but it infuriated the younger princess. She opened her mouth for another cutting remark.

"That is quite enough, Kandina!" Averil had entered unnoticed, summoned by Calib when Kandi had stormed past him into the garden. The girl spluttered and turned to face her mother, an indignant retort on her lips.

"Do NOT even think about it, young lady."

"But..."

"Enough. I want you to apologise to Atwin and to your cousin, his wife!"

"Never!"

"Then you are confined to quarters until further notice. Calib will see that you go there and a guard will see that you stay."

"You cannot do that!"

"Oh yes I can."

Calib took a step forward and took the Princess by the arm. The girl pulled away and ran toward Atwin and Netta, but before she could reach them he turned to face her. She stopped and took a step back, staring at his ravaged, tear-stained face. His grief had given way to a carefully controlled anger and he clenched his fists at his sides.

"Go away, Kandina," he said in a voice that was tightly controlled and very cold. "Get out of my sight."

She stared at him, her bottom lip trembling. For a moment, he returned the stare, then he turned away in disgust. Kandina watched as Netta came back to him and laid a hand on his arm. Atwin's anger dissipated like mist and his carriage dissolved to reveal a crushed and broken man.

Almost convulsively, he pulled Netta close and clutched

her to him, hiding his face from view. Netta quietly stroked his hair and hummed softly. Kandina watched for a few moments more then turned on her heel and stormed out of the garden.

With a brief look at Averil, Calib followed. The Princess Regent watched her niece as she comforted Atwin. She wanted to reach out to this man who was like a son to her. With a sigh, Averil turned and began to walk away.

"Highness..." said Atwin softly.

As she turned back he looked up to face her.

"Thank you," he said quietly.

Averil smiled. "Be comforted, Atwin. The storm has passed and the sun is breaking through. You have much to do. Heal yourself and then begin to heal your country. Know that in this I am your friend and ally."

She left them alone together.

The little princess sat in front of her mirror in the privacy of her rooms, quietly seething. She had tried to leave earlier, to find the promised guard standing stiffly at her door.

She had spent some time pacing the floor, muttering choice curses under her breath. Her anger had kept her moving and every so often she would find something breakable to make a satisfying crash on the wall.

Finally, around midnight, her anger had burned itself out, leaving her emotionally drained. She sat now, staring at her tattered reflection in the polished brass of the mirror. Atwin had been hers, until Netta appeared. She had been sure that he would take her to wife.

She had allowed herself to conveniently forget that he was destined to marry the next queen. She had been gone and seemed likely never to return. But then Netta had appeared from nowhere, at the Queen's side, claiming to be the long lost princess.

Kandi groaned. She had welcomed Netta because she was lonely for a friend, but she had not dreamed how quickly the returned princess would take Atwin from her.

She cursed the destiny that gave her prince to another. It was clear now that Atwin did not love her, Kandi, even half as much as he did Netta. The way he had spoken to her had cut into Kandina's heart like the keenest blade.

Why had she thought he could ever be hers? Worse, how could she ever have thought that getting rid of Netta would bring him back to her? She should have known that such an act would alienate him forever.

What a fool she had been. Now Atwin hated her and everyone knew what she had done. Her mother would never trust her now, and she would be forever the fool. Kandina bowed her head and finally, gently and ever so silently, she began to cry.

EIGHTEEN

Four returned upstairs to the ruined palace to absorb energy through the day. Atwin and his brother had left for Drasmil some time earlier, and Netta had retired to her rooms. Ordel had made his last goodbyes and was preparing to leave. He and Delsi sat with Averil in the drawing room, with the two revealers on hand. They had ceased worrying about the possibility of success and now merely awaited the outcome.

There was very little conversation when the messenger entered. All as one looked up. The messenger bowed to the Queen and turned to Evelar. Without a word he held out a note. Evelar took the paper with a nod and the messenger bowed again to Delsi and backed out of the room. With a look at Miyam, Evelar broke the seal and began to read.

His face was a mask. He read placidly, and nothing in his stance showed his reaction to the news. But almost imperceptibly, his hands began to tremble. When he finished, the note fell from his grasp and fluttered to the floor.

He raised one shaking hand to his head and pushed the hood back, the sash that held it in place falling to the floor behind him. The revealer strode to the hearth and stared into the flames for a long moment.

Miyam bent to pick up the paper and the red sash. She read the note and handed it wordlessly to Averil. Evelar pulled his long hair out from beneath his cloak and drew his knife. Then he grasped the hair in one hand and raised the knife to it, sawing roughly.

The long hair came away in one hand and he flung it into the fire. As the Princess Regent read the note aloud to the others, Miyam moved to stand silently behind Evelar.

Sand, I regret to inform you that the one known as Opal, who was your sister and my wife, has fallen at the hands of a traitor. A spy called Kratis took her from behind.

I have sent her back to the College with my assistant and am in pursuit of the spy. If you wish to join me, he is travelling south west towards Mytar.

We will have vengeance. Dock.

Evelar unclasped his Art name badge and removed his red bordered cloak. He rolled it up into a bundle and raised it in his hands, ready to hurl it into the fire after the hair.

Miyam placed a hand gently on Evelar's arm and took the cloak from his grasp. He dropped his hands to his sides and bowed his head.

When Evelar finally raised his gaze to meet Miyam's, she could see the tears standing in his eyes. Without a word, he turned and strode brusquely from the room. There was silence as they all stared at the back of the door.

Miyam gazed at the empty space where Evelar had been and gave in to her own grief. Seiliar had become a good friend and now she was gone. She stood by the fire, holding the Artisan's cloak to her. Suddenly she pulled it away from her and stared at it, her mind racing.

The seventh sign was rebellion. Acting outside the law. Could this be it? Miyam looked across to where the Queen sat stunned with her husband and her sister.

"Will you excuse me, Your Majesty," she said with

dignity.

Delsi nodded, and Miyam headed toward the door.

"Wait," said Averil then.

Miyam turned to face her.

"Why did he remove his cloak? I have never seen him without it."

"He's gone to exact his revenge on the spy. He does so without sanction from the College of the Art. By discarding the cloak, he's declared himself outside College law. In effect, he's resigned. He is no longer a revealer." Miyam turned and followed Evelar from the room.

"Now what do we do?" said Ordel in exasperation. "Without the nomads Evelar promised to bring, we cannot hold Tellemot against the kalkar horde."

"We are lost," said Delsi.

"Let us not jump to conclusions," said Averil. "I do not think Evelar will desert us. He has proven himself trustworthy time and again."

"But he has never been bent on revenge before," Ordel argued. "His grief controls him now, not his reason. We can no longer count on his aid."

"We cannot back out now," Averil said. "Our plans are laid. Atwin goes to marshal his troops and yours await you already aboard ships in the harbour. It is too late to stop it. This war will happen, regardless of whether or not we have the help we need."

"I know," he replied. "But I like it not."

"Nor I," said Delsi, her worry plain in her voice. "Let us not tell Netta about this. It would damage her so."

Ordel nodded. "I agree. I shall take the army to Tellemot and await relief from the nomads. If they do not come, I will take a smaller force to Yerterma. We will have to make do with what we have."

*

Miyam rode in a frenzy. It was impossible to catch Evelar. After storming from the throne room, he had gone straight to the stables and ridden away at breakneck speed. Miyam could barely manage to keep him in sight. He rode through the night, refusing to halt for rest, pushing his horse to the limit.

Finally, two days out of Shirall, Lumen collapsed under him. Miyam soon rode up, her mare lathered and wheezing, close to collapse herself. Evelar was frantically tugging at the reins, trying to force Lumen to rise. The valiant steed tried to comply, but could not get his feet under himself long enough to stand. Miyam forced the reins from his desperate grasp and he sank to the ground at Lumen's head.

"Are you trying to kill him?" said Miyam harshly. "That won't bring her back."

Evelar looked up at her, his face stricken. Then he looked down at Lumen and lifted the stallion's big head into his lap. He stroked the strong neck tenderly.

"I think it's time you settled down a bit," said Miyam. She knelt beside him and touched his leg gently. He jumped. "You need sleep," she said softly.

He looked at her then. "As do you," he murmured.

She smiled. "So we rest now?"

He nodded.

The next morning they rode on, much more slowly. The horses were weak, barely able to manage a walk, and Evelar was impatient.

"He's getting away," he moaned for the umpteenth time.

"At least your horse still carries you," said Miyam. "Things would be a lot slower if Lumen was dead."

He frowned. "I realise that, Mym."

"Then stop complaining. It's not my fault you almost killed him."

He said nothing, but his frown deepened. Miyam sighed and pulled to a halt. Evelar stopped and looked back at her.

"Why have you stopped?"

"I will not ride with you until you snap out of it. I'm not your enemy. I loved her too." She turned her horse and began to ride back the way they had come.

"Mym, wait," he said.

She halted but did not turn around.

"Please don't go."

"Why should I stay?" she said without turning.

He rode back to join her and looked deep into her eyes. "Because I can't do this without you. And because I love you."

Her lower lip began to tremble. "You've never said that before..." she whispered.

"How remiss of me." He bent over, closing the gap between the horses and kissed her tenderly. "Well I do," he murmured. "I love you. And when this is over, you will be my wife officially."

She laughed. "You know that doesn't matter," she said. "But I accept."

He grinned. "Now let's go kill the spy who killed Seiliar."

Evelar and Miyam stood over the body of Jondras, known as Dock. Sadness engulfed her as Miyam remembered his wry smile and dry humour. The husband of Seiliar had been a good man, and his revenge had led to this. Fate was not always fair.

Evelar stood as in a trance, his eyes focused on nothing. Jondras had been the one link he had to his sister's murderer.

"He must have caught the spy and been killed," Evelar said, cursing under his breath.

Jondras had always been impetuous and, with grief

spurring him on, he would never have thought to wait for help.

Evelar cursed again. "It's my fault. If only we'd reached him sooner, but the horses were so exhausted," he moaned in his grief. "If I hadn't pushed Lumen to the edge of death, this might not have happened."

Miyam knelt beside the body of Jondras and gently reached out to close his eyes. As she did a glint of silver caught her eye and she pulled back his shirt at the neck.

"Evelar," she said. "What's this? It looks like an amulet like Netta's or Atwin's."

Evelar knelt beside her. "That belonged to Seiliar. It was our mother's. Jondras must have taken it from her body before he sent her back to the College."

Evelar unclasped the necklace and took it from the body of Jondras, reverently placing it about his own neck. Miyam saw a quick flash of blue light as the amulet touched his skin, gone as suddenly as it came.

Evelar bowed his head as he gave in to grief, and when he lifted his gaze there was an unfamiliar gleam of gold fire behind his eyes.

Evelar shook his head, a small sound of despair escaping him. He searched the ground for clues, but there were none. Miyam listened as he searched with his mind, but even the psychic echo had been erased.

The spy was good at covering his tracks. Evelar cursed yet again. He raised his face to the sky and let out a scream of rage. Then he spun on his heel and leapt onto his stallion's wide back, spurring him to a gallop.

Miyam called after him but her voice, ripped away by the wind, brought no response. It was her turn to curse. Laying a blanket carefully over the body, she climbed into the saddle and followed.

*

When she finally caught him up, Miyam slid down from her horse and stared. Evelar was standing, arms outstretched above him, staring up into the sun. A strange light surrounded him and his voice came whispering to her as he conversed with the heavens.

She moved toward him, but stopped when she heard a voice reply. The voice was soft and musical, but it had a depth to it that no mortal could acquire. Evelar said something else and a different voice answered. This time it was higher, more lilting, but still with that softly resonant quality.

A light began to shimmer in the air before him and one by one, forms began to emerge from the light. What had been a white glow broke up into all the colours of the spectrum as each figure assumed its own individual hue. Miyam gazed, dumbfounded, as the forgotten spirits appeared in all their glory.

The whole world was singing and the earth itself seemed to resonate with their coming. Miyam knelt on the dry ground, watching. Her lips moved in silent song, as her deepest soul responded to the divine presences. Evelar spoke long with Zayus, leader of the council. The ultimate power in the universe spoke as friends with a mortal man, and the other spirits stood and listened as the world around them sang in jubilation.

Here before her was a stranger. Here was a man of such power and purity, it awed her. Evelar was speaking with the divine council and tears of wonder slid unheeded down her face. She knew with a frightening certainty that what she had suspected was true.

This was the eighth sign. Evelar was the Awakener. All that remained was his own realisation, which would be the ninth and final sign. Miyam watched and her soul soared with the heavenly choir.

This was the heart of the universe and the event toward which all history had been striving, and she was privileged enough to witness it. As she watched, one of the beings of light separated itself from its companions and came toward her.

Miyam watched silently as the shimmering figure halted before her and smiled gently. Miyam lowered her eyes reverently, but the spirit reached out and lifted her chin. Where he touched her she felt a warm glow, which spread throughout her body to engulf her in a feeling of pure love. She gazed at him in wonder.

"Fear not, oh faithful one," he said in a voice of liquid gold. "Turn not thy face from mine."

He shimmered in a golden light. It was the light of the sun and she knew who it must be.

"Are you Pollon?" she whispered.

"Called am I thus by thy people," he replied. "Before thou didst forget."

She hung her head in shame.

"Be thou not aggrieved," he said. "Long ago did it happen and the fault is not thine. Satisfied am I that thou, of all thy people, canst remember."

"Is Evelar..."

"He is whatever thou wilt. His destiny doth lie on a dangerous path. He wieldeth power that no mortal shall ever wield, but for him. Thou art the centre of his strength. Be thou a light for him to follow."

"But he's the Awakener. He doesn't need me," she blurted, her deepest fear leaping to her lips before she could prevent it.

"Degrade not thyself in the light of his greatness," Pollon replied. "Thou art the reason for his power. Without thee he is no more than thy equal."

"But how can that be?"

"Has it not ever been the way of thine order to join two together for greater power? It is thus even for the Awakener. Thou shalt see the truth of this."

"But I have no such power..."

"Knowest thou not thy destiny? The Awakener is partnered not by one without power. It is thine to wield. Thou shalt find the strength within. Come."

He held out a glowing hand to her and she took it without thinking. Then the spirit pulled her to him and wrapped her in his divine embrace.

"I am Pollon, reader of the star trail. Know that I speak truth. As mine energy thou feel, so shall the Awakener feeleth thine. Thou art his strength and his life. Without thee he is lost. He feeleth this even now as surely as thou feelest me. Go, my beloved and accept thy destiny."

* * *

NINETEEN

After many days of walking, hiding from the advancing kalkar army which seemed to never end, King Lenent of Zelona finally found himself left behind and free of the enemy. Setting a small fire he sat and prepared to send a communication. Without his horse he could never make it even to Mytar in time, let alone Shirall. He had to get a message through.

Closing his eyes, the King began to mumble the ancient words. The world spun and his mind began to fall into the blackness. Then he found the presence he was looking for and made himself heard.

LEN? she whispered in his head. *IS THAT YOU?*

YES, AVVY.

WHERE ARE YOU?

I AM...

He could not complete his thought. A powerful force swept over his mind, a great reverberating negative, forbidding the communication and severing the link, throwing him to the ground. Clutching his head he groaned, looking about nervously.

"Alright," he said to the air. "I get the message. No communication. Sorry!"

* * *

In Shirall, the Princess Regent clutched at her head, eyes squeezed shut. The shock wave had ripped through her mind leaving a throbbing pain in the back of her skull.

"What happened?" she whispered in fear. "Len?"

* * *

King Lenent rode almost due north across the Wild Plain. He had found the horse wandering in the grasslands, saddle and bridle still clinging to him. The King had no idea what had happened to the rider, but the horse was a blessing. Now he could entertain some small hope of succeeding in his self-imposed quest.

Lenent rode day and night. He knew that he would soon be on the heels of the kalkar horde and he also knew that somehow he had to get past them if he had any hope of getting the message delivered in time. He just wished he knew how he was going to do it.

He stared ahead at the blackened grassland, immune now to the sight of such devastation. He was headed for Yerterma, where he could warn King Umbro of the danger from tribesmen within the city.

Then he would cross the Heights to Mytar and King Erris, after which he would ride on to Shirall and Drasmil. He knew that tribesmen were lurking in the Dragons and he knew he should stay clear of those mountains.

There was a safe pass just below Yerterma, he just had to get there. Hopefully, it was still under Umbro's control. But as he came closer to the enemy he saw the extent of the kalkar force and knew he would need the shelter of caves if he were ever to survive in the midst of the horde.

As the sun stood high on a cloudless day, Lenent finally caught up to the enemy. They stood sizzling, the bright sun filtered and blurred, rendered mute by a thick haze of smoke. He rode east along the rearmost fringe of the horde, looking for a way past, but the mountains loomed before him with no end in sight.

Reaching the first gentle hills as afternoon deepened, the King of Zelona began to search for a safe camp. Once the enemy came to life at nightfall there would be no hiding.

He had to be out of sight before then. He finally settled for a rocky outcrop in the lee of a hill, facing away from the massed kalkar just a few miles away.

Passing an anxious but uneventful night, Lenent set off at first light to once more catch the horde. He rode at breakneck speed, trying to close the distance, but it was late afternoon before he finally caught them once again. This was never going to work.

Now that he was amongst the enemy he could never ride fast enough nor far enough to pass them by, not if he had to hide at night. He had to find a way.

Riding further into the foothills, Lenent hoped to get far enough away from the kalkar march to allow travel at night. But the higher he climbed into the mountains, the more chance he had of running into tribesmen. Maybe they would not see a lone rider as a threat, but he could not take such a risk.

As night fell, the King found a cave. He set about concealing the entrance and spent a fitful night, ears listening for the slightest noise and sleep disturbed by the sound of trickling water somewhere deep in the cave. Rising again at first light he prepared to set off again. Only then did he notice the depth of the cave and the shimmer of light reflected off water on the back wall.

Intrigued, he moved closer. The cave seemed to go on forever. The reflected light came from a point way back in the darkness where he could see a small pinpoint of sunlight hitting a tiny rivulet of water.

Feeling his way cautiously to that point, Lenent found the cave opened out, and further ahead he could see a glimmer of daylight. Returning for his horse, the King moved toward the light, hoping it was another exit.

*

Emerging into the sunlight, the King found himself in a secluded valley, strewn with boulders and closed in on both sides by high canyon walls. The land was lush and green, no kalkar had been there. There was movement in the undergrowth and birdsong in the air. Leading his horse, Lenent moved forward into the bright sunshine.

Lenent walked day and night, stopping neither to eat nor sleep, leading his horse through the rocky valley. Only riding when the boulders thinned, Lenent travelled along the length of an ancient river, now a mere trickle. After three days the valley opened out into a large plateau covered in grassland and wild flowers.

Finally able to ride safely, Lenent mounted and kicked in with his heels, racing headlong across the plain. As the sun rose, Lenent sat a lathered and exhausted horse, staring out over the Wild Plain.

He had reached a high rocky outcrop from which vantage point he could see to the horizon in three directions. The kalkar were nowhere to be seen, the long grass of the plain pristine and unburnt. Either they had taken wing and all was lost, or he had by some miracle managed to pass them by.

* * *

The combined navy of Sar Sor and Sar Let had been called together under the command of the Prince Consort of Shirall, boosting the force under his control to significantly more than twenty thousand men. He posted three brigades, a little under two thousand men, as a home guard.

From a fleet of one hundred triremes and twenty quinqueremes, Ordel posted about a third as a coastal guard. The cavalry, two thousand strong, he sent by land to Tellemot, while the rest of the army, some five thousand soldiers, was divided amongst the main fleet, consisting of sixty five triremes and fifteen quinqueremes.

Each trireme was heavily loaded with fifty soldiers and each quinquereme carried roughly a hundred. In addition, the fleet was rowed by fifteen thousand oarsmen and crewed by one thousand five hundred men.

This formidable force made its way steadily toward Tellemot. There, Ordel was greeted by King Tarnel, who had gathered together a small army of roughly five thousand soldiers. Together they began to prepare for the defence of Tellemot.

The navy had made the journey without incident and they now waited for the cavalry to arrive. Tarnel's five thousand had joined with Ordel's force and all were now camped outside the small city.

"You say the nomads are coming?" said Tarnel.

"That is my hope."

"You don't sound too sure, Your Highness," said the man who stood to the King's left.

"It is true, Mandra, that I cannot say for certain whether the nomads will come. I am hoping that the revealer will be able to convince them. Unfortunately, he has suffered a bereavement, and I fear he has forgotten his mission in his thirst for vengeance."

"I knew it was a mistake to trust a revealer," Tarnel murmured.

"Forgive me, Your Majesty," said Ordel, "but I have seen Evelar in action, and I have every reason to believe that he will complete his mission."

"But you cannot be sure."

"No, but Miyam is with him. If he does not remember, she will."

"The girl? You know I do not trust her."

"Your mistrust is unfounded, Your Majesty."

"What makes you think she can bring him and the nomads here?"

"Oh, she has quite a hold over him, you know," Ordel said.

"I still think we need to plan without them," said Mandra.

"A wise precaution," said Ordel.

"How do you suggest we proceed?" said King Tarnel.

"I must head for Yerterma as soon as I may," said Ordel. "I will leave the naval contingent here to bolster your troops. I will take with me the main body of the army and the cavalry."

Mandra nodded in satisfaction. "That should help."

"If the nomads do not come, you may have to abandon the city to the kalkar," Ordel continued. "If you cannot hold against the horde, fall back to Shirall and join the home guard there."

Tarnel frowned. "I like this not."

"Nobody likes war, Your Majesty," Ordel said harshly. "Now, if the nomads do come, hold out as long as you can. It may be that the aid they can offer will not be enough to withstand the horde. If, even with their help, the city cannot stand, send them to me and take yourself and your troops to Shirall."

Tarnel shrugged. "It is as good a plan as any."

"It is better than no plan, Your Majesty."

King Tarnel gathered his army outside Tellemot. He had brought Ordel's men off the ships to join his own, leaving only the boat crews on the water. One small ship had been dispatched to Shirall bearing his wife and family to safety.

He had no idea how long he had before battle would be joined and he had no idea how many to expect. But he knew that water was his greatest weapon, and he wanted to be ready.

He set the men to digging a trench, stretching from the south east corner of Port Tellemot to the coast of Tellem Cove in the north. It was a mammoth task which kept the army occupied and fit while they waited for the invasion force.

When it was done, Tarnel ordered it filled with water, forming a moat ten yards wide and three yards deep. The town was now totally surrounded by water. Then, he ordered the moat covered with reeds and branches to make it look like the surrounding landscape.

Tarnel stood on the battlements watching the approach of the dark horde. The army stood ready, water barrels set in catapults. Under a waning moon, the kalkar rushed toward the town. In the dark, the human army had been ordered to stay well behind the moat, to avoid stumbling into the water and giving it away. So they watched. The night grew late and the horde drew closer.

The King held his breath. The kalkar raced toward the town. When the first ranks hit the moat, they actually made it across, but they were soon cut down by the water shot over the walls into their faces. The reed covering over the moat began to burn from their passing.

The ranks behind followed, thinking the fire to be the normal reaction of grasses in their path. They almost reached the other side before the covering grew too weak and they were dropped in the water.

The momentum of the dark march kept them moving for some moments more before they realised the danger and slowed to a halt. A good portion of the force had been lost and the deadly water was near boiling from the heat of the ones who had fallen, the rising steam obscuring the view from the parapet.

The still huge kalkar army stood in milling ranks,

keening their grief and staring at the walls so close and yet so unattainable. They stood watching and waiting for dawn.

Far to the south, another wave was arriving on the coast near Zelona. The death of so many had alerted the Leader to the defeat, and It was determined to win. It had no doubt that the kalkar existed in sufficient numbers to wear the humans down; it was only a matter of time.

The Leader laughed, and every member of the dark horde stopped momentarily, listening to the sound. Then It sent forth the new troops, pushing tirelessly northward on huge wings.

Throughout the day, Tarnel sent his men out into the sizzling ranks of kalkar with water barrels, which they poured over the standing force. Steam rose in billowing clouds from the battlefield, and at the end of the day a great number stood blackened and smoking.

Tarnel made his way down from the walls for a few hours' rest. After a hot meal, he collapsed gratefully onto his bed and was soon asleep. He was awoken by a soft sound. He lay still and opened his eyes.

There it was again. A scrape of leather on stone, faint and well muffled. If he had not been so lightly asleep, anxious about the war unfolding about him, he would never have heard it. Someone was in the room.

He forced his breathing to slow, as it would in sleep. The assassin crept up from behind, thinking his prey unaware of his presence. There was a very faint sound of scraping metal as the assassin drew his knife.

Tarnel strained to hear. The assassin was barely breathing, controlling the sound. But as he raised his arm, he drew in his breath, ready for the killing blow. That was the signal Tarnel was waiting for.

As the knife came down, the King rolled from under it,

and it buried itself to the hilt in the mattress. Tarnel raced for his sword, sheathed and standing against the wall by the door. It was gone.

He looked about in panic. His eyes lit on the pitcher of water on his night-stand. Grabbing hold of it in both hands, Tarnel threw the water at the assassin's scowling face. Then, while the man was gasping, the King broke the pitcher over the man's head and ran for the door.

Tarnel yanked the door open, calling for his guards. The two soldiers lay on the floor outside his rooms, in a spreading pool of blood. The King grabbed a sword from one of the bodies and turned back to the room.

The assassin had staggered after him and stood in the doorway, blinking his eyes to clear them of water and the blood that trickled from a gash in his forehead. Enraged, he charged recklessly at the King, who held the sword level and waited.

Half blinded, the assassin must not have seen the blade before him. Or perhaps he was too intent on driving his knife into the King's unarmoured body.

The force of the charge lent strength to Tarnel's arm, and the sword slid almost gracefully between the assassin's ribs. The King caught the man's wrist, holding the knife away from himself.

The man thrashed for a moment, and finally collapsed at Tarnel's feet. The King stared at the man for a long time. Then he jogged off down the corridor in search of men to clean up the mess.

When night fell over Tellemot, the doused kalkar did not wake, and their companions stood staring about them. The horde squatted where they stood, and Tarnel hoped they had been defeated. But eventually they rose again and each spread wings and lifted off the ground.

"Ready the catapults," the King yelled.

As the horde crossed the moat, water was fired from the walls. Many fell, and the force that made the near side was a fraction of that which had started, but victory for the humans was far from certain. As the diminished kalkar strode forward, a lookout cried out a warning.

"Look to the south!" he shouted.

Tarnel stared, and his courage left him. Making its way across the sky from the south came a force larger even than that it would replace. Without hesitation, the King ordered the evacuation signal to be given. Tellemot was lost.

Tarnel's army sailed north toward Shirall. He had sent messengers by land to warn the towns on the way, and taken to the water. He had lost many in the brief battle through the streets of Tellemot.

The replacement horde had landed right inside the town, causing panic amongst the people, already frightened by the sudden order to evacuate. Where they landed, streets melted and thatch caught alight. Soon the retreat had become a rout.

Now, his diminished force was easily accommodated aboard the small fleet, and he hoped to reach Shirall within a day or two. He planned to send the Queen and her daughter north, out of harm's way, and join in the defence of the city. But his optimism was gone. He had seen the kalkar force doubled overnight, and he knew that ultimate victory would go to the horde.

* * *

TWENTY

The night was dark, the clouds overhead hiding the stars. Evelar and Miyam crept through the growth by the road. The campfire glinted in the trees ahead. The spy was being careless again, and Evelar was still unable to fathom why.

His best guess was that on defeating Jondras the spy had thought he was safe from attack, and had covered himself only long enough to get away from the scene. After the death of Jondras, the spy had been meticulous in covering his tracks. But now, it seemed almost as though he wanted to be found.

Jondras had been buried with all possible ceremony, and he would be exhumed and taken to Eeasto for proper burial at the College once peace was restored. Zayus had given Evelar the spy's location, and he and Miyam had struck out in that direction.

The spy left no trail, but Evelar trusted the spirit's words, and soon the spy grew careless. Small signs began to appear that pointed out his path. Evelar was pleased, and as the signs became more obvious he chuckled delightedly to himself.

"Don't get complacent, dear," Miyam warned. "He may be careless, but he managed to kill Seiliar and Jondras. I don't want to see him kill you as well."

"Don't worry, my love," he smiled, eyes gleaming. "With your help, I can do anything."

Miyam and Evelar split up and circled around the man, just outside the light of the fire. Evelar crept up behind him, sword drawn.

"Well met, Sir Artisan," said the spy.

Evelar lowered his sword cautiously.

"You didn't think I was unaware of you?" the spy continued. "Come now, Sand, I'm no fool. I know who it was I killed. I was hired specifically for the task."

"To what end?" said Evelar.

"Why to catch your attention, of course. The Leader is most annoyed with you."

"The Leader?"

"Don't play the innocent with me, Sand. The Leader was most impressed when you infiltrated the lair of the stinking ones. It finds you quite interesting. It wonders who you are that you can take such risks without fear and succeed."

"I am no one of consequence."

"Perhaps. Still you are different."

"No different than any human is to another."

The spy shrugged. "As you wish."

Evelar raised his sword to the spy's throat. "Enough talk, Kratis."

"By the way, Sand," the spy said, ignoring the sword. "You can tell your girlfriend to come out. I know she's there, so what does she hope to gain by stalking me?"

Evelar said nothing, but pressed the point harder against the spy's windpipe.

Kratis held up his hands. "Alright, I get the picture. Get that sword out of my face."

"I think not."

The spy shrugged. "Have it your way."

Lightning fast, the spy grabbed his own weapon and bashed Evelar's sword out of the way. Spinning as he stood, the spy engaged the former revealer in combat.

Evelar backed under the onslaught, but soon he rallied and leapt to the fight. He parried the spy's lightning strokes with a force that sent the man reeling back time and again. The spy was no longer the attacker.

Miyam watched from the bushes, waiting until she was needed before rushing into the fray. Evelar concerned her. He seemed to have forgotten all his training and was expending far too much energy. He could not keep up such a vicious assault.

Kratis was buckling under it, but Miyam wondered if Evelar could defeat him before his own strength began to falter. As she watched, Evelar began to slow, his swings losing some of their force. His breath was shallow and his hands were beginning to tremble with effort.

Then he stumbled and almost lost his footing. The spy leapt into the opening and thrust at Evelar's chest. The former revealer barely managed to block the spy's sword. The force of the impact pushed him back, and this time he did fall. Kratis stood over him and raised his weapon, ready to strike.

From the trees, Miyam dashed into the fight and caught the spy's blow on her own sword. Fighting left-handed, Miyam pushed the spy backward across the clearing.

Hearing Evelar recovering behind her, Miyam pressed the advantage, hoping to weaken their opponent. But the spy was incredibly strong, and his stamina was astounding. He seemed barely winded.

Evelar rejoined the fight, and Kratis defended desperately. Now he was outnumbered and he was tiring fast. Parrying wildly, he raised the fingers of his left hand to his mouth and gave a piercing whistle. Three men stepped out from the trees and rushed to the spy's aid.

Evelar and Miyam were surrounded and outnumbered. They fought frantically, hoping only to survive. Both were trained fighters, and normally they would be quite able to succeed at two to one odds. But both were tired and these three newcomers were fresh. They stood back to back and held on.

Suddenly, Miyam's sword was flung from her hand, and the man who had caused the loss swung his sword for the kill. Miyam activated the band on her right arm, and the mote knife in her sash leapt into life. Too swiftly to be seen, the knife slit the man's throat. The blood spurted from his jugular, and within moments the man collapsed at her feet.

Kratis gave a shout at the sudden death of his friend, and savagely renewed his attack on Evelar. Miyam calmly sent the mote knife toward another of the newcomers, lodging it in his windpipe. The man gasped, sucking the knife in further, and began to choke.

Miyam could hear the rasp in his lungs as he slowly drowned in his own blood. With a gurgle of expelled air that frothed red, the man fell. The odds were now even, and the spy fought grimly, his face set with hatred. The third newcomer pulled out of the fight with Evelar and rushed at Miyam.

But she was ready for him. With a jerk of her wrist, the mote knife pulled free of the second man's throat. She let it hover in front of her as the third man approached, making sure that he saw it. Then, savagely, she sent it straight into his left eye.

The man screamed and clutched at the knife, but Miyam pulled it free and he covered the eye with both hands. Then, with surgical precision, Miyam allowed the knife to slit his throat. She turned to watch the fight between Evelar and the spy. Kratis stared at the bodies of his fallen comrades and faltered.

He raised his eyes and stared at her in shock. Evelar lowered his attack and let the man see his imminent defeat. With a scream, the spy pulled a knife from his belt and threw. Miyam stepped aside and let the knife pass harmlessly by. At the same time, she sent the mote knife spinning toward the spy.

Evelar watched it come, and just before the knife hit the spy he reached out and caught it in his left hand. The spy's eyes widened, and he looked at Evelar in shock. The former revealer lifted his hand in front of the spy's face, the blood already beginning to seep between his fingers.

Kratis stared at it, realizing at last that he had taken one chance too many. As Kratis looked again at Evelar, the former revealer calmly ran him through. They locked eyes for a moment, then life drained away, and the dead spy slid off the sword to the ground.

Evelar held his bleeding fist gingerly away from his body.

"You dear, silly man," said Miyam. "Do you want to chop off your fingers?"

Evelar grimaced as she took his wrist in her hand.

"Can you open your fist?"

"I'd rather not," he replied.

She smiled grimly. "Sit down."

"Here?"

She looked around at the scattered bodies. "You're right."

She took his sword from his unresisting hand and sheathed it for him. Then she took his good hand and led him away from the scene of battle, with the horses trailing obediently behind.

After a short distance, Miyam halted and forced him to sit. She built a fire and set some water to boil. Then she began to tear strips of cloth from her underskirt to make bandages.

"Have you anything for the pain?" she asked.

Evelar nodded. "In my pack."

She found the herb and made a hot potion for him to drink. Then she dropped a silver needle into the pot of boiling water. She gently pried open his fingers. He grunted as each finger came away from the knife that was embedded in his palm. She whistled softly and he groaned in dismay.

"That bad?"

"Don't worry, dear," she said. "I didn't do too badly in field medicine!"

He gave a wry half smile. "You came first, if I recall."

"Can you feel anything?"

"Not really."

"Good, then you won't feel the needle."

"How comforting."

"I suppose I should remove the knife first."

"That's probably not a bad idea."

She made a patch from some of the cloth and took hold of the protruding edge of the knife. She locked eyes with him for a moment and he nodded. Swiftly she pulled the small blade free. Evelar grunted and gritted his teeth.

She pressed the patch against the wound and told him to press it firmly with his other hand. She wiped the knife clean on some cloth and clicked it into its sheath. Then she measured out a length of fine twine, which she placed in the water with the needle. She wrapped a bandage tightly about his wrist to slow the bleeding, then she fished out the needle and twine and set to work.

First she carefully stitched the gash on each finger, and then turned her attention to the long deep wound across his palm. When the job was done, she applied a healing salve and bandaged the hand carefully. Then she removed the tight bandage from about his wrist.

He had made no sound while she worked, but he was

trembling when she had finished. "It's funny," he said, shaken. "I've suffered much greater injury than this without nearly so much discomfort."

She smiled. "You forget a sword in the belly usually renders you unconscious, from the pain if not from the injury itself. This is small, not life threatening, and the hand is very sensitive."

He grinned. "I bow to thy greater wisdom, my beloved."

She blinked at the archaic phrase, then leant forward and kissed him.

"You did very well, dear."

The mid-afternoon sun blazed down as the two revealers struck out across the burning sand. Evelar once more wore his red bordered, midnight blue revealer's cloak. The horses had been well watered and the oilskins were full. Soon they would be deep in the desert and they hoped to find the nomads before the water ran out.

Evelar was not worried. For perhaps the first time since joining the College almost twenty years ago, Evelar was actively seeking out his people, instead of trying to avoid them. He expected to encounter their scouts within a day or two.

They travelled through the afternoon and long into the night, stopping only when the desert night grew cold, the sand finally giving up its heat. They set up the shelter and kept each other warm until dawn. Before noon the next day, Miyam saw riders approaching.

As they loped closer, their great desert beasts carrying them through the haze with ease, the leader seemed familiar. His mount knelt in the sand and the head scout dismounted quickly.

"Greetings, cousin," he said, giving the hand signal of welcome.

"Ontaro," said Evelar.

"Your visit is unexpected, coming so hard upon your last. What is afoot?"

"I must see Old One," said Evelar. He hesitated. "And my father."

"Is something amiss?"

"You could say that."

"Then we must make haste. Leave your horses with my scouts. We have a spare camel that will carry you both."

Evelar nodded, and he and Miyam followed Ontaro to where the spare animal stood chewing its cud. The scout who held its halter handed it over and went to collect the horses. Evelar made a clicking noise and the camel knelt obediently.

He helped Miyam to climb up and then swung up behind her. He showed her where to hold on, and took the reins in his good hand. The revealer kicked in with his heels and the camel lurched to its feet. Miyam clutched at the animal's neck in an attempt to keep her balance.

"I won't let you fall, my love," Evelar murmured.

"I know," she replied, and relaxed a little.

Then they were off, and she tensed again as the lurching speed of the animal caught her by surprise. Evelar chuckled. He wrapped his free arm about her waist, holding her close to his body. She sighed and let her own body relax, using the College training to calm herself. Then she opened her eyes and looked around.

"How fast are we travelling?" she asked.

He shrugged. "Fast enough. I've never bothered trying to judge the speed. There are no landmarks out here to give any indication of distance."

"I don't think I like it," she said softly.

He laughed. "You'll get used to it, my love."

*

An hour or so later they rode into camp. When they arrived at the tent of Old One, Evelar's father was talking quietly with his venerable uncle. Shevron looked up in surprise.

"My son, back so soon?" he said.

"Yes, Father," Evelar replied. He glanced at Old One and bowed with respect. "Would you excuse us, Sir?"

Old One nodded benignly.

Evelar took his father's arm and led him toward his own tent. Miyam gave a look to Old One and followed.

"What is it, Son?" asked Shevron.

"I'd rather wait until we're inside, Father."

"Has something happened?"

"Yes, Father."

"What?" The old man stopped outside the tent. "It's your sister, isn't it. What's wrong?"

"Just come inside, Father."

"No!" said Shevron harshly. "I want you to tell me now. What has happened to Seiliar?"

Evelar looked at Miyam, and she put a hand on his arm reassuringly. He looked back to his father. "She..." He dropped his eyes.

"Tell me," said Shevron in a dangerously quiet voice.

Evelar sighed. "She has... gone home. She is with Sky Father."

Shevron's face went ashen, and he clutched at Evelar for support. Miyam took his arm.

"Come inside, Sir," she said. Shevron nodded dazedly and allowed her to lead him into the tent.

After relating the events of Seiliar's death and their subsequent revenge, Miyam and Evelar left Shevron alone in his tent and returned to Old One. There, they tried to convince the old patriarch to mobilise his people against the kalkar.

"Tell me then," said Old One. "What is it you want me to do? We are safe here. Why must we help?"

"Because you are not safe here," Evelar replied.

"For countless generations we have wandered these sands, and never has an invader threatened our existence here. We alone know how to live in the sands."

"We are no longer alone here," said Evelar. "This enemy is at home here. They need only sunlight to survive. They neither want nor need water. The desert is the perfect place for them."

"Then we will fight them here."

"We cannot fight them here. Once they establish a presence here, we will never be able to defeat them."

"We will prevail."

"Not here. Practically the only thing that kills them is water, which we have very little of."

"We know where to get it," said Old One stubbornly.

"Not enough," said Evelar in frustration. "They come in the tens of thousands."

"I feel we are not needed in this fight. Our numbers are small. What help can we give?"

"Small though we are, the rest of Sharné needs our numbers. We need water to defeat them, which the rest of Sharné has in abundance. And they need us because we know how to use water efficiently. So the alliance would go both ways."

Old One grunted noncommittally.

"We cannot sit back and watch them come. If we do not help, there is a good chance that the rest of Sharné will fail."

"They are not our people. Let them fail."

"They are my people now, and I am of the sand. That makes them your people too, Great Uncle. If they fail, we will be alone. Then the kalkar will find us and destroy us.

We cannot fight them on our own."

There was a loud ululating cry. A scout loped into camp and slid quickly down from his beast. Shevron came out of his tent at the cry, and followed as the scout made his way to where Old One sat debating.

"Sir, we've received messages from all corners of the sands."

"Go on," said Old One.

"Invaders, travelling north in two great armies. They travel only at night and do not stop for water."

"How many?"

"Thousands. A great horde, larger even than the force that was destroyed by the rain some six or seven moons past. It stretches back into the deep sands, several groups following one after another."

"How quickly do they move?"

"Faster than we can ride. One force has already reached the northern borders near the sea. Some say the port of Tellemot has already fallen. The other column moves west toward Yerterma, and they will reach the mountains within a few days."

"You see, Sir," said Evelar. "They're like nothing we've seen in countless generations. They've already passed you by without you even noticing. They will take the sands and make them their own."

Old One turned to Shevron. "What do you think?"

"I think we should help, Uncle. If we do not, we will die."

Old One shrugged. "Death no longer matters to me. But I would not want to condemn my people." He looked at Evelar then. "Do what you will."

* * *

TWENTY ONE

Leaving his naval force at Tellemot, Ordel took his army west toward Yerterma. A week later, he rode ahead to greet Umbro.

"Welcome, Your Highness," the King of Yerterma called as he rode up to him. "I trust your journey was uneventful?"

Ordel shrugged. "The kalkar have not yet made an appearance, if that's what you mean. I have heard some disturbing rumours, though."

"You refer to the horde that marches north?" said Umbro. "I am told it is larger than we first anticipated."

Ordel nodded. "And it is not the entire force. Some already march toward Tellemot, straight across the desert. They may already be there."

"Oh my. We should perhaps send help to Tarnel."

Ordel smiled and shook his head. "Half my force is already with him."

"Half?" the King looked dubiously at the force pulling up ranks behind the Prince Consort of Shirall. "Yet you bring some ten thousand with you. I had no idea Shirall had command of such a force."

Ordel shrugged. "We called on our influence with Sar Let and Sar Sor. Their navy boosted our strength significantly. The naval crews are now joined with the rest of Tarnel's force at Tellemot."

"Nice to have powerful friends, Your Highness," said Umbro quietly.

"I just hope it was enough."

The Prince Consort of Shirall sat in the King's private sitting room at Yerterma, quietly plotting with Umbro. The new weaponry, designed with kalkar in mind, was developing slowly, and they worried that it would not be ready when the horde came.

"Your Majesty?" an uncertain voice said from the doorway.

"Yes?" Umbro said to the guard.

"Ah... there is a man down at the gate. He claims to be a king... someone from... Zel..."

"Lenent? From Zelona?"

"Yes, that's the one," said the man with relief.

"Well bring him in, man!"

Ordel breathed a sigh. "Now that is good news."

When Lenent entered, Umbro and Ordel rose quickly to greet him, full of eager questions. He raised his hands with a chuckle.

"Please, I have no time. I must be off for Mytar immediately."

"You look exhausted. Surely you can rest and eat," said Ordel. "And maybe wash?"

He shook his head. "When you hear my message you will agree. There is no time to waste. I must stay ahead of the horde."

"Then let me at least feed you while you talk," said Umbro moving to the door.

He said something to the guard, and returned to his seat.

"Now, Your Majesty, take a seat and tell us what is so important?"

Lenent began his story, telling of the presence of tribesmen in his city and the assassination attempt, then the similar events in Nella Fillenga that led to the death of the royal family.

When the food arrived, a simple plate of meat, cheese and fruit with a flagon of ale, he continued talking around mouthfuls, his obvious hunger lending urgency to his words. When he had finished, Umbro sat back and pondered.

"So, your experience tells us we are all in danger," he said quietly.

Ordel nodded. "A timely warning indeed."

"Have you any idea how widespread this is?"

Lenent shook his head. "All I can say is they were so well integrated into society that even the true locals were taken by surprise. This is a plot that is far reaching, and a long time in planning."

"In that case, you are right, the others must know. I will send a communication."

"No, I tried that. The kalkar stopped it. I still get headaches thinking about it!"

"Then a messenger."

"How will you know if your messenger is trustworthy? It could be a tribesman instead. That is why it must be me."

Ordel let out a sigh. "This plot is insidious."

"Forgive me, Your Majesty," said Umbro then. "But what has brought on this concern for your fellow kings?"

Lenent looked a question at him, brow furrowed. "I do not understand."

"I apologise, Sir, I am relatively new to my crown. Perhaps I have missed something, but when I first met you last year at the conference you seemed... distrustful, almost hostile. What has changed?"

Lenent shook his head, nonplussed.

"I think I understand," said Ordel with a smile. "Lenent has always been rather... protective where Shirall is concerned. Perhaps it came across as abrupt."

"I had no idea I had given that impression."

"I did not realise such an alliance existed," said Umbro. "I still have much to learn, I see."

"Oh, I would not call it an alliance," said Ordel with a smirk. "Not exactly..."

"Still, it is one reason why I must get to Shirall," Lenent replied with a pointed look at the Prince. "After Mytar," he added as an afterthought.

Ordel chuckled. "As I suspected, we are only a stop on the road..."

Lenent shrugged. "Naturally the Queen must be warned... as head of the council of kings."

"Is it my wife you wish to warn, or is there another more... important person you wish to see?"

Still confused, Umbro looked a question at the Prince. It was Lenent's turn to chuckle.

"You are a shrewd man, Your Highness, and a good friend. I wish you the best of luck in the coming battle. You are going to need it."

Ordel had heard Lenent's message with trepidation. His life was in danger, as was Umbro's. He had tried to clean the tribesmen out of the city, but they had hidden themselves too well. They had managed to blend in and even the residents could not tell them apart from the normal population.

All he could do was wait and be ready for the attack. When it came, he would have to hope that he was able to fend it off. He pushed the worry aside and set about organizing the defence of the city.

Prince Ordel looked out across the grassland to the south east of Yerterma. There lay the desert. From there the enemy would come. His force had been drilled in water combat, and wagon upon wagon of barrels stood ready inside the walls, the water brought down as snow from the highest peaks. The defence of the city would last only as long as the water.

As night fell, he knew that the battle would be joined. Within an hour after sunset, the lookout called from the tower.

"They come!"

There was a shadow over the moon, the black mass of winged enemy rolling in like a storm. But the defenders were ready. The use of water missiles was becoming more sophisticated. The men who had joined them from Nella Fillenga were already seasoned fighters against this enemy. The first barrage against the horde was so successful the enemy faltered and retreated. But it was a short-lived victory.

The next wave was on them and the catapults fired again. Once more the enemy was repelled. Then the battle changed, the kalkar landing and avoiding another airborne attack. Now it was the turn of the archers, firing down into the fray, behind the enemy lines. Hand to hand combat was fierce, the conventional metal weapons of the humans having little impact on the enemy.

Short of a direct hit to the internal organs or a decapitation, the kalkar shrugged off their injuries and kept up the attack. Umbro had been working on a new weapon, a small water filled missile thrown or fired from a sling at close range, but the damage was minimal. The heavier missiles and arrows were still most effective and the men on the walls kept up the barrage. Somehow, the armies held the kalkar at bay that first night.

Umbro woke suddenly from a deep sleep. Light streamed in from the edges of the heavy curtain over the window.

He glanced down at his young wife, sleeping with the baby cradled against her chest. Then he heard the noise again. Someone was trying to open the door.

The King shook his wife awake and silenced her with a finger to her lips. Quietly he led her, with the baby in her arms, to the dressing room, and closed the door.

The King retrieved his sword and stood by the door waiting. Finally, the door began to open slowly, and the assassin slinked into the room. Umbro held his breath as he passed, then struck from behind. The would-be assassin sank silently to the floor, killed by the one he would have killed.

The Prince Consort slept. He had been feeling increasingly more drained over the past weeks and he had found himself sleeping much more heavily. The battle of the night before had left him deeply fatigued, though he would never admit so to his generals. He did not hear the slight sounds as the assassin entered his room. The man stood over him and a knife flashed in the light from the edge of the window.

The sentry paused in his rounds. He had seen something down amongst the wagons. He called to his watch mate.

"Lorry, did you see that?"

"See what?"

"Look." He pointed down.

As they watched, a dark stain began to spread out from the base of one of the wagons. Lorry peered at the wagons. A dark figure flitted briefly between the wagons and another stain began to spread.

"What is that, Hilt?" said Lorry.

Hilt looked, his brow furrowed. Then he went cold and looked at his friend.

"The water!" he gasped. He raced for the ladder, Lorry close behind.

Lorry yelled to the world in general. "Awake! Look to the water!"

The assassin looked up, listening to the faint cry, and a smile of satisfaction lit on his face. He went to the window and pulled the curtain aside slightly, looking down into the courtyard. With a chuckle, he let the curtain fall and returned to the Prince's bedside.

Umbro raced down the corridor, and as he approached Ordel's rooms he noticed that the guards here were dead too. He heard the sentry's cry, but he was more worried about Ordel. He hoped he was not too late.

He knew the Prince Consort was not handling the nocturnal war as well as once he would have. He had seen the light slowly fading from the Prince's eyes as a deep fatigue set in. Finally he reached the door, paused and cautiously looked in. The assassin stood over the bed, knife raised triumphantly.

The King charged at the assassin, driving the sword into his back before he had a chance to react. The knife fell from his hand, but he turned and faced the King with a grimace of hatred. He swung a fist at the King, but Umbro stepped out of the way and picked up the knife.

The assassin stumbled, and looked at the sword point protruding from his stomach as if noticing it for the first time. With a gurgling growl, the assassin fell to his knees. Then he groaned and fell forward, twitched a little and lay still. Umbro breathed a sigh and turned to Ordel. The Prince lay quiet, and Umbro knelt beside him in dread. Was he too late after all? He put a hand on the Prince's chest and let his breath out in relief. He was breathing.

"Your Highness," Umbro said softly. "Wake, Ordel."

The Prince murmured something and settled again.

Umbro gave him a little shake. "Highness," he said, louder this time.

Ordel groaned as he woke. "What is it?"

"You've missed all the fun."

"What are you talking about, Umbro?" Ordel sat up slowly. Then he saw the assassin's body. "Oh my!"

Umbro grinned. "Your Highness has a gift for understatement."

Umbro and Ordel walked among the empty barrels, puddles of water at their feet. The alarm had come too late. Not one wagon was left full. With a heavy heart, Ordel suggested they sound a retreat. Umbro sent the civilians straight to Shirall, including his own young family, while the armies headed north. Perhaps they could offer their help to Atwin and Erris in Mytar.

* * *

The King halted his horse and looked out over the Plain of Drasmil. In the distance the River Farr shimmered in the early spring sunlight, but that was not what drew his eye. On the plain and about the walls of his city, an army was gathered. A big army.

The entire military force of Drasmil and its vassals stood awaiting him. Some eighteen and a half thousand soldiers and over six thousand cavalry were camped outside the walls of the city, called from the farthest corners of Drasmil. Almost twenty five thousand men were his to command.

Atwin dismounted and knelt in the dirt, head bowed in respect to the men gathered before him. Then he and his brother rode on to meet the legion commanders. They dismounted before the five generals who commanded the legions, and Atwin watched in surprise as the leaders of his army knelt before him.

"Oh get up," he said.

"Yes, Your Majesty," said one hurriedly as they stood.

"May I say welcome home, Your Majesty," said another.

"Thank you, General Tratska," the King replied.

"We are glad to see you finally in your rightful place, Your Majesty."

"Oh? I like not the inference, Tomkiss."

"He did not mean to imply disrespect for the late king, Your Majesty," said another graciously. "He merely meant to express gratitude. You are free from Gerard's shadow at last."

"If I were you, Grunzi, I would not speak of the late king in that manner."

"I apologise for my colleagues, Your Majesty," said the first General. "Shall we just say that we are happy to see you home safely, and freed of the shame that has plagued you in recent years."

"I thank you for the sentiment, Lisbon, but I warn you all to refrain from further denigrating the late king. My father was a good man."

"Forgive me, Your Majesty, but how can you say that, after the way he treated you?"

"I say again, Sydnay, my father was a good man. Which of you can say that he has ever heard me speak otherwise?"

The Generals shuffled their feet and looked at each other guiltily.

"I will not tolerate any disrespect toward the late king. My father was misguided. He was not a happy man. At the end, he knew his mistake and was haunted by it. I will not have his memory shamed by his lapse in judgment."

"Yes, Your Majesty," the Generals chorused.

"Now, Generals, report."

*

King Atwin of Drasmil separated out one fifth of his country's considerable army to remain as a home guard. These men he set to work preparing the defence of the city.

Taking the rest of the army he wasted no time marching directly for Mytar, where they would see their first combat in this war.

* * *

In Mytar, King Erris watched from the battlements as the army approached. Atwin and his generals rode in the lead, a force twenty thousand strong stretching forever behind them. Erris watched a moment, then strode from the battlements, heading for the stables. He rode out to meet them.

"Greetings, Your Majesty," said Atwin.

"Greetings, Your Majesty," Erris replied ironically.

"I request permission for my army to set up camp by your fine city."

"By all means," said Erris. "If I have your word that you will not use them to abuse my hospitality and take my city from me."

Atwin laughed. "I shall try to restrain myself."

Erris smiled. "I welcome you, Atwin and invite you and your generals to enter the city as my guests."

"I thank you, Erris."

"Well, that is the formalities seen to, I believe. Come. A meal awaits you."

TWENTY TWO

There was an army outside Mytar. The King of Zelona sat his horse on a hilltop to the south of the city, having just crossed the Heights through the western pass. The passage had been long and gruelling, but still it had taken less time than he had expected.

Alone, he was able to slip through where a group could not. But he had been surprised at the apparent lack of resistance. The tribesmen seemed to have disappeared.

Lenent made his way toward the city. He had no plan to get through the encamped army, but he hoped someone would believe that he was a king and let him through. He came as close as ten yards from the outskirts of camp before he was stopped.

"Halt, stranger," said the guard. "Come no closer."

Dismounting, Lenent held up his hands in supplication. "I bring news for your commander."

"You may give your news to me."

"Ah... I fear that will not do," Lenent replied. "Who is in command here?"

"Why the King, of course," the guard said.

"Erris?"

"No, Atwin, King of Drasmil."

"Atwin is king?"

"That's right."

"I must see him. This news concerns him most of all."

"I can't do that."

"Why do you not go and tell him that Lenent of Zelona is here, Hmmm?"

"I..."

"Just do it," Lenent said firmly.

The guard shrugged. He called to another soldier and sent him off.

Some twenty minutes later, the young soldier finally returned, followed by a self-important colonel.

"Who is this?" he said rudely.

"He claims he has a message for the King, Sir," said the guard.

"You can give your message to me, stranger."

"I am sorry, Colonel," said Lenent. "This is not for your ears."

The Colonel bristled. "I don't like your tone, stranger."

"Look, I do not have time to argue. Just go and find Atwin."

"Unfortunately, the King isn't in the camp right now. You'll have to tell me."

"Now hear this," said Lenent, angry now. "Take yourself, at once, to wherever it is that Atwin can be found, and tell him that Lenent, King of Zelona, is waiting outside the camp. Do this now and I might consider letting you keep your rank!"

The Colonel rose up to his full height. "Now listen here..."

"No! YOU listen here, CORPORAL! I will not stand for this insubordination. I have made a reasonable request. I expect it to be carried out. I am sure when Atwin discovers that you have refused me, he will make your demotion official!"

The ex-colonel spluttered. "Wait here," he barked. He turned on his heel and stormed off.

This time, Lenent had to wait almost an hour before the ex-colonel returned, and the King was beginning to think the self-important officer had run off without even attempting to inform Atwin that he was there. But finally the man did return, bringing with him a young man with an air of authority.

"Your Majesty," said the young man. "I apologise for the delay. I am terribly sorry you had to be put through this. I am Prince Calib."

"Your Highness. I have heard good report of you from your brother, the King."

Calib bowed from the shoulders briefly. "My brother has been concerned about you, Your Majesty. He heard in Shirall that you had disappeared. He is happy to know that you have finally reappeared safely."

"Where is he now?"

"In the palace, with Erris. Come, I will take you to him. But first he has ordered me to make sure you have a chance to refresh yourself after your journey."

Lenent smiled at the thought of a bath and a change of clothes, and nodded for Calib to lead the way. He was now several days ahead of the enemy, and he finally felt justified in taking a short break.

In the palace at Mytar, Lenent was given the royal treatment he had missed for so long. He bathed and was given a marvellous meal, and then he felt ready to face his fellow kings.

"Welcome, Your Majesty," said Erris with a smile.

"Thank you, Your Majesty," he replied.

"I trust you are well, Your Majesty," said Atwin.

"I am feeling much improved... Your Majesty," he said with a grin.

Atwin groaned. "I will never get used to that."

"Oh, you will," said Lenent. "Just do not let it go to your head. That is the secret of good ah... kingship, Your Majesty."

Atwin laughed. Then he turned serious. "What is the

news that so concerns you?"

"You know that Derrek was killed?"

Atwin nodded.

"He was assassinated."

"What?"

"Tribesmen had infiltrated the palace, and when the siege broke, they struck. They almost got me too, and not for the first time."

"What do you mean?"

"The same thing nearly happened to me in Zelona. It seems the tribesmen intend to remove the rulers of Sharné."

Atwin frowned. "We knew they were up to something, but we could not fathom what. It seems that Evelar's warning was a timely one."

"What are you talking about?" said Lenent.

"The revealer told us in Shirall that tribesmen had infiltrated the city, and possibly the palace as well."

"Well, the threat is real," said Lenent. "We have to get word to Shirall, before something happens to Delsi or the Princess."

"I will send a communication," said Atwin.

Lenent shook his head. "I tried that. The kalkar can hear every word. Damn near blew my head apart when they discovered what I was doing. They have a lot of power when it comes to the mind."

Atwin cursed. "I had forgotten that."

"Someone will have to go personally," said Erris quietly.

"I will go," said Lenent.

"You have done enough already, Your Majesty," said Atwin.

"Exactly. I have been out of the picture for weeks. I can stay that way much more easily than you could. You or Erris would be missed, and we cannot trust this to anyone else."

"What about Calib?"

Lenent shook his head. "You need him to keep that army of yours in line. I assume he does most of the command work?"

"He is right there, Atwin," said Erris. "Your brother is a link between you and the army. They follow you without question, but they know him. He is their friend."

Atwin nodded. "It looks like you are right, Lenent. I am sorry you cannot rest here for a few days."

"I will leave tonight."

As Lenent set out across the Farreechedd Plain, following the River Ree north-east to Shirall, King Atwin of Drasmil and King Erris of Mytar gathered their forces for a siege.

The people had been called in from the surrounding towns, and were sheltered within the walls of the city. There was not the access to water here that Tarnel had been able to make use of in Tellemot. The closest major water course was the River Ree to the north of Mytar. Atwin had left part of his force on the northern shore to build a defensive position in case he was forced to order a retreat.

The tribesmen were taking an unexpected hand in the conflict, and the new King of Drasmil could not begin to understand why they had sided with the kalkar. Atwin avoided making known the presence of the tribesmen in the city. The population was already unstable, and a possible threat from within would only push them over the edge of panic.

Though he tried to hide it from his generals, Atwin was not confident of success. His army was well trained and ready to fight, but conventional warfare would not work on the kalkar. Unless they could gain access to more water, there was no way they could defeat the horde. Deep within himself, the young king knew that retreat was inevitable.

Atwin watched the horde approach. They had come

from the west, across the mountains. King Lenent had mentioned this force making its way north to the south west of the Dragon Mountains. He had not mentioned how large it was.

Four's prediction of two forces moving at once seemed to be correct. Atwin's men were ready. The water brought from the river was stacked in barrels against the inside wall. The King hoped they could cause some damage before they had to abandon the city.

The army had managed to keep the kalkar at bay for one night, but hope was not high. Atwin slept fitfully. The assassin had been careful to make no noise, but the young king seemed to jump at every move the assassin made.

The man had begun to wonder if it was worth all the effort. He finally decided to throw caution aside and strike, to hell with the consequences. He raised the knife above his head. Outside, from the battlements, the sound of a horn broke the silence. Atwin was awake in an instant.

He saw the assassin standing over him. He grabbed the knife that he kept at his side and struck a glancing blow as the assassin drove his own knife toward the King's chest. Atwin rolled aside and slashed again at the assassin, but the man had lost his courage. He did not want to die. He turned and ran.

Atwin gave chase, but when he came to the courtyard he stopped, letting the assassin go. Soldiers were milling about, and the flagstones were wet. Erris was already there, and there was blood on his hands and shirt. He signalled to Atwin.

"I fear we must leave," said the King of Mytar dejectedly. "The water is lost. Come nightfall, we will have no defence against the horde."

*

Atwin's army marched north, bearing its wounded stoically. Mytar had been overrun at nightfall, and the half-completed evacuation had become a battle for survival. Everything the kalkar touched turned to flame, including people.

When the last of the survivors quit the town, the kalkar stood at the gates and on the wall, and watched them go. They had not pursued. But Atwin felt sure that they were now following. Naali burned almost constantly now. He had felt it since before the battle at Mytar.

The King knew that the kalkar were slowly gaining control of Sharné. He hoped that Ordel and Umbro had survived the fall of Yerterma. After what he had seen, he was deeply convinced that Yerterma had indeed fallen. If so, then Ordel was in a precarious situation. His small army would be trapped between two huge forces, each equally indestructible.

Finally, Atwin led his army across the River Ree, and they pitched camp on the north bank of Lake Mytar. The advance force had fortified the town of Selon on the south bank and dug a moat around the campsite.

They had rigged a pump into the lake and filled hundreds of barrels. They had dug channels radiating out from the lake to prevent the horde from circling around to attack from the sides, forcing them to advance on wing across the lake.

They had done well. When the horde finally arrived, the army was well fortified and ready for battle. First, the horde sat and created wings. Then, they rose and crossed the lake in waves, only to be shot from the sky by sprays of deadly water. The supply of water was endless, and the horde could be held off for weeks if necessary.

The kalkar force was diminished steadily. On the fourth day, Ordel's army approached the horde from behind. They had collected a good supply of water as they crossed the

Heights, and now they put it to use.

Trapped between the two forces, the kalkar horde was decimated, and Ordel and Umbro pushed through to join Atwin and Erris. The two armies became one and the Kings ordered a celebration. It was the first victory of the war.

The victory was short lived. The armies had barely finished celebrating when the force which had decimated Yerterma could be seen approaching the lake. The Kings readied their troops and awaited the attack.

Once again, it seemed to go well. The abundance of water made defence possible, and indeed the humans were even able to return the attack. However, this force was persistent.

The armies held out. But before a week was gone, the lookout gave warning. Another force approached from the south east. The horde which had destroyed Tellemot was about to join in the battle. The kalkar numbers were swelled to three times their previous size.

The dark ones spent the rest of that night organising their force. The human armies were ordered to rest and come nightfall they were ready for another attack. But this time the numbers were overwhelming.

The catapults could not be loaded fast enough and finally some of the horde made landfall on the north shore. Once they had gained land, the catapults could not be effective. The armies fought desperately, but it soon became clear that they could not prevail.

Finally, Atwin ordered the retreat. They fought the last hour before daybreak, then fell back as the kalkar froze in the sunlight. Before heading north, Atwin ordered the army to move amongst the kalkar and douse as many as possible. Then, with regret, they quit the battlefield.

* * *

TWENTY THREE

Averil hated not knowing how the war progressed. Now that communication was not possible, she felt isolated and completely at a loss. The few messengers that did make it through had very little to say except that things were going badly.

She worried about Atwin and Ordel. She worried about all the Kings, who had become friends over the years. She worried most particularly about the one who was still missing.

The Princess Regent paced while the Queen sat by the fire, listening to her nervous footsteps.

"Please sit, sister dear," said the Queen. "I am sure all will be well."

Averil shook her head. "It has been so long, Delsi. No news for weeks."

"We had news just yesterday from Ordel, and Atwin's messenger arrived this morning."

"That is not what I meant, sister."

"Ah, I see. Are you finally admitting you still care for him then?"

"Who?" said Kandi from the chaise in the corner.

"I am just worried, Delsi," said Averil with a snort.

"If you say so."

"Who are we talking about, Mother?" said Netta, sitting near the Queen.

"Someone your aunt almost married, a long time ago."

"Mother?" said Kandi.

"Delsi!" Averil protested.

The Queen chuckled. "Why hide it?" she said. "Your husband is long dead, I am surprised you did not take him back years ago."

"You know why not, Delsi. It would never have worked. I had to stay here, and he had his own country to run."

"I am sure you could have worked something out."

Lenent approached the gate with relief. Shirall city was kalkar free as yet, but he knew it would not stay so for long. As he rode under the arch, the guardsman halted him with a word.

"Please tell the Regent that Lenent of Zelona is here," he said to the man.

He sat the horse and waited for a reply. Thankfully he did not have to wait long, and the guardsman passed him through. King Tarnel of Tellemot was there in the outer courtyard waiting to meet him.

"Welcome, Your Majesty."

"Greetings, Tarnel. I am glad to see you alive and unharmed."

"You refer to the assassin I presume. It is a good thing I sleep lightly," he laughed. "You are the one who disappeared. You have had us all worried."

"It was important to get the warning to the others," he shrugged. "Let us join the Queen."

"I have been trying to convince Her Majesty that she should take the Princess and go," said Tarnel. "But she will not leave us."

"I was hoping to convince her of just such an action myself," Lenent replied. "The force that comes is invincible."

"I had feared as much."

Leaving the horse at the stable with a page, Lenent

hurried down below with Tarnel. They made their way directly to Averil's drawing room, Lenent feeling both nervous and happy.

At the door, the guard offered to announce him, but he stopped him with a wave of his hand.

"I will announce myself, if you please," he said.

With just the briefest hesitation he placed his hand on the door and pushed, bursting unceremoniously into the room. He noted the Queen sitting by the fire with her daughter beside her. Out of the corner of his eye he saw Kandina on the chaise in the corner, but his gaze was caught by Averil, hurrying toward him.

She was smiling, taking his hands, kissing his cheeks, murmuring in his ear.

"I was so worried, Len," she whispered. "I am glad to see you."

He smiled and kissed both her hands, then dropped them in embarrassment and brushed past her to greet the Queen.

Averil sat in her private chambers, slowly brushing her long brown hair, trying to shut out the worry. Delsi would be leaving soon with Netta and Kandi, if she could be convinced, but Averil intended to stay no matter what the Kings decided. She would not desert her city now.

The door opened, and the Regent spun in surprise. Who was barging into her private room unannounced? Visions of a masked assassin filled her mind, but then she relaxed as the real intruder entered. Averil sighed.

"You should not be here, Len," she said.

"Why?"

"The guard will talk. The last thing we need is a scandal."

He shrugged. "He is asleep."

"What?" her eyes widened as the image of the assassin

came back to frighten her.

"Relax," he said as he locked the door. "I will protect you."

"You will? And who will protect me from you?"

"Now, Avvy, I would never hurt you."

"No? You just disappear for weeks without a word."

He groaned. "You know it was necessary."

"I know," she sighed. "But I was so worried."

He stood behind her, hands on her shoulders. She leant back against him, wanting to give in. It always started this way, and somehow he always won even when she knew the risks, even when it had been years between visits and she should be over him. All the hiding and being discreet was not worth the pain when he left again.

"You should go. Someone will come."

"You always say that," he chuckled.

"This time I mean it, Len," she said slipping away from him to pace the floor. "I cannot keep doing this."

He frowned. "That is not what you said last year at the conference."

"No, but I should have said it a long time ago. I cannot keep seeing you a few weeks at a time with years in between."

"What are you saying?"

"I am saying I have had enough! I want my life back!"

He looked like he had been slapped. "Are you saying you no longer want me?"

A sob escaped her and tears welled in her eyes, but she swallowed it down. "No Len, you know I love you, but I am sick of waiting."

He crossed the floor in two strides, pulled her into his arms and kissed her. He had won again, she thought as she gave in in spite of herself.

The King of Drasmil strode into the audience chamber

at Shirall. He had ridden day and night from Lake Mytar, and arrived worn and unwashed and deeply sad. He was greeted by a small gathering, who waited anxiously for news of the war.

He had hoped that Lenent had been able to persuade Delsi to travel north out of harm's way, but he was concerned to see her still there, sitting amongst her advisers. She was a strong willed woman, and she was determined not to desert her people for a second time. Still, it was dangerous for her and Netta to stay at Shirall, especially with the army so close and a battle imminent.

Atwin had ridden ahead of the army, left under Ordel's command. It would not be long before the long line of soldiers began to arrive, and once they joined with Tarnel's army and the home guard they would fill the plain below Shirall. The kalkar would be less than a day behind.

He did not wait for the Queen to speak. "Your Majesty, you should not be here."

"I am glad to see you too, Atwin!"

"I am sorry, Your Majesty, but it is not safe here."

"Are you worried about me, or is it my daughter's safety that concerns you?"

"That goes without saying, Your Majesty. And of course we should not endanger the child."

Delsi smiled. "We will leave when the time comes, Atwin. But first, tell me of the war."

"Your Majesty, things bode not well. Everything south of the river is lost. The armies have joined, at less than half their original number. Soon they will be here, where we plan pitched battle for control of Shirall. As I have said, you should leave now. I see very little hope of victory here."

"Atwin, where is your optimism? Surely things are not so bad?"

"Your Majesty, I cannot stress this strongly enough.

There is no way we can win this war with our current numbers or mode of defence. Whenever victory is in sight, the horde doubles in size and we are forced to retreat. Their numbers are endless and no conventional weapon makes more than a minor impact. I strongly advise you to take yourself and your family out of here. We will hold them as long as we can and then we will follow."

"Your advice is duly noted. I will wait for Ordel."

"As you wish."

"Now, dearest Atwin, must we be so formal?"

"I am sorry, Delsi. This endless war has me anxious."

"As are we all," she replied. "Why do you not go clean yourself up. Rest until the army arrives," she smiled. "Netta awaits you in my garden."

The King bowed. "Thank you, Delsi."

She came to him, eager for news. "Atwin, this war worries me. Leena tells me things go not well."

Atwin lowered his head. "We have lost many good men."

"Where is my father?"

"He follows with the army. He will be here soon."

"I like this not. We cannot win, Atwin."

"Do not say that. We must not give up hope."

"It seems to me you already have. You forget I hear your thoughts. You cannot ignore the amulets."

He bowed his head. "Sometimes I do forget that you are there. I am sorry. It is this damned war."

"You are so tense, Atwin," she said, placing a hand gently on his chest. "You should rest." She wrinkled her nose then. "And wash!"

He sighed and took her in his arms. "Just being here with you is rest enough." He held her tenderly. "I have missed you, Dayna," he murmured.

She smiled. "I had forgotten that name."

"I had not."

She pulled away slightly, a thoughtful look in her eyes. "Atwin," she said softly.

"Hmmm?" he brushed the hair from her eyes gently and stroked her face with the back of his hand.

"How many men have we lost?"

"Too many," he said softly. He began to play with her hair, unbraiding it carefully and with great concentration.

"How many?" she insisted.

"Perhaps half, maybe more," he said. Her hair was loose now and he buried his face in it, breathing in its sweet fragrance.

"What about the women?"

"Women?" he murmured, brushing the hair aside. Lowering his face to the nape of her neck, he brushed his cheek gently against the soft skin.

She tried to ignore him. "We need to boost our numbers somehow. The women could help."

He paused in his nuzzling. "What do you mean?" He kissed her neck below the ear.

"We could join the men on the walls. It cannot take much strength or skill to fire a catapult."

He groaned. "Must we discuss this now?"

"Think about it," she said, carried away by her idea. "The army needs help. You have thousands of people standing idle because they are women. Why not use them?"

"Netta, do you realise what you are suggesting? Why the idea is impractical. Just organizing the women into any usable force would take more time and resources than we can spare."

"So you would risk a horrible defeat just to save a little time and effort?" she pulled away from him. "I expected better of you."

"Netta, please. I would rather not think about it right

now."

"Well I would like to talk about it. Nobody will discuss anything with me. I am supposed to be taking Mother's place as soon as all this is over, and I am told nothing about what is going on. I carry Leena, but she gives me no influence over the council. I am an invisible person, Atwin and it is starting to irk me."

"You are not invisible to me," he said softly, drawing her closer again.

She hesitated, drawn by his loving gaze. Then she quickly turned away. "It is not fair," she said. She walked away from him, her back stiff. "I had hoped at least you would want to listen."

He groaned and followed her. "Netta, I will listen. But please, not now." He wrapped his arms about her waist from behind. "Later. I have had enough of war," he said as he began to nuzzle at her neck again. "That is the last thing I want to think about," he murmured.

She began to relax into his arms, but her mind was racing. "You know, I think..."

"Shhh."

"But do you not..."

With a groan of impatience, he spun her to face him and planted his mouth firmly on hers. She stood still for a moment, then finally melted against him, her idea forgotten.

The Princess Kandina stepped out from behind a shrub and stood watching. Her heart ached, but she had begun to heal in the long weeks of his absence. She avoided Netta, mainly because she was always so damned friendly, as if Kandi's defection had never happened. The young princess wanted to scream at the injustice of it all. But perhaps she had learned something. She did not disturb them. She quietly walked from the garden.

*

Atop the battlements, high above the courtyard, Delsi stood alone. She was listening to the soldiers milling about on the plain below. She strained to hear one man in particular. The last of the army was finally trailing into camp, and the commander was busy marshalling his troops. He was a figure of presence and he demanded attention.

He had always been her strength, and these weeks without him near had been difficult. She needed to know he was alright. So she listened from afar. But Delsi was concerned. Something in his demeanour seemed wrong.

Down in the camp, as he marshalled his troops, Ordel was acutely aware of the woman who waited. He smiled to himself. Once the tedious business of inspection was over, he would join her. He had missed her terribly.

They had not been apart in thirteen years. She stood tall, outwardly unaffected, but if the man had been standing beside her he would have seen the tears in her blind eyes. They would be together soon enough.

Finally, the commander dismissed his army. He watched them turn and head for the cook fire, where a large pot was boiling and a pig was roasting on a spit. Then the Prince turned and looked up at the woman on the battlements. He held her gaze for a long moment, as if she could actually see him standing there. Then he placed a hand on his heart and inclined his head to her. She repeated the gesture.

Then she turned and felt her way to the stairs leading into the courtyard, and he headed for the gate. He was waiting for her when she neared the bottom of the stairs. He stood looking up at her and she smiled. Then she descended the last few steps to meet him. They stood together, hands clasped between them.

"Welcome home," she said finally. Then she moved close and rested her head gently against his chest and he closed his arms about her.

* * *

The nomad force was growing. More clans joined the march every day from every corner of the desert. By the time they saw the end of the Barren Wastes their company was several thousand strong.

Evelar and Miyam rode at the head of the column, leading the nomads toward Tellemot. At the edge of the desert, a small group was left behind with the camel herd and the rest of the nomad force continued on foot. The two revealers rode ahead on horseback, scouting the land for danger.

When they came to Tellemot, the sight that greeted them was bleak. The town was charred and blackened, the smoke still rising like steam from the ruined houses. The city was deserted, only the kalkar stink left behind to tell of what had happened.

"We're too late," Miyam whispered.

Evelar could only nod, eyes flashing.

"What now?" she asked.

"We follow the trail and attack the kalkar while they stand during the day. We will use all we know of water to destroy those that did this."

Miyam nodded. "It's as good a plan as any. For this they deserve to die."

The passage through the mountains was long-ranging and productive. The days were spent dousing kalkar. Some units spent many nights stalking tribesmen and disposing of them face to face.

Their efforts were not enough to return the mountains to human control, but they kept the enemy on edge, and it made the nomads feel a little better after the destruction they had seen. Evelar and Miyam knew that they were a long way behind the dark march, but that only made them more willing to wreak as much havoc on the enemy forces as possible.

Finally, when it appeared that they could do no more real good on their own, they decided it was time to head north to join up with the armies. They joined the highway north of Rusae and from there were able to travel at double speed.

The nomad life made healthy warriors and, though on foot, they moved at a steady pace, in a ground eating jog. They travelled that way for many hours at a time. Then, on a dark day some five days after leaving the Heights, Evelar and Miyam rode back to the column. They had finally met the horde's trail. Soon they were moving through the now burnt fields of northern Mytar. They would be in Shirall within a few days.

* * *

TWENTY FOUR

Kandina stormed down the hallway toward her room. She had the sense not to disturb her cousin and Prince Atwin, but she could not help being angry. She had lived so long in the hope of winning him that she could not stand to see him with another, especially her cousin, even if they were married.

She was totally absorbed in her hurt. The Princess did not notice the young man approaching. Her head was bowed. He strode toward her, intent on some business of his own. When they collided, it was a shock to them both. They pulled back from each other in surprise.

"Kandi," said Calib quickly.

"Calib?" she said hesitantly.

The few times she had met him her preoccupation with Atwin had kept her from actually noticing him. Now, she studied him with interest, remembering that impromptu kiss that had so angered her, finally admitting to herself that she had actually liked it.

Looking at him now she realised, with a jolt of recognition, how much he resembled his brother. An idea began to form in her mind. If she could not have Atwin, perhaps his brother would be more amiable.

She took his arm. "Can I talk to you, Cal?"

"Certainly," he replied.

She led him down the hall to her chambers and invited him inside.

"What did you wish to talk about, Kandi?" he asked as he followed her into the room. She turned and closed the door, pushing the bolt home.

"You," she said quietly.

He gave her a bewildered look. "Me? I do not understand."

"Us," she murmured, moving closer.

"Us?" He shook his head. "There is no 'us', Kandi."

She placed a hand on his chest, as Netta had done to Atwin.

"But there could be," she said quietly. "Could there not?"

He took her hand and removed it from his chest. "No Kandi, please."

He sounded so like his brother. Kandina was glad that she had made this choice. She knew that he was right for her. She replaced her hand and touched his face with the other. He shivered.

"Kandi..."

"Oh do not be such a prude, Cal," she said.

She ran her fingers through his hair. "I have been such a fool. I am sorry I was so blind."

She moved even closer. Calib stood stiffly, holding himself in tight control.

"Kandi..."

"What?" she whispered.

"Stop..." he said. "Please."

"Why?"

She wrapped her arms about his neck and looked up into his face. He groaned. His hands clenched at his sides and he breathed heavily. He wanted her, even after all that she had done. He fought with himself, wanting to hold her, even now. She touched his mouth with the fingers of one hand.

"Fight it not, Cal," she said softly.

She stood on tip-toe and touched her lips softly to his. He pulled back, but she persisted and he found himself returning the kiss. He could not help himself. He had loved her for so long. Involuntarily, his arms went about her.

He lingered over the kiss, all thought of her duplicity forgotten in the softness of her form. But then he realised what he was doing and his eyes opened wide. He stiffened and pulled away from her.

"No," he said in a strangled voice.

"What is wrong?" she said, moving closer again.

He pushed her away. "I cannot."

"Why not, Cal. You like me, do you not?"

A moan escaped him.

"Oh, Cal," she said happily. "I knew it!"

She reached toward him again but, before she could cling to his neck, he grabbed her arms firmly at the wrists and held them away from him.

"You are too late, Kandina," he said flatly. "I cannot love you now."

He strode to the door and slid the bolt. She followed after him.

"But Cal, why ever not?" she cried.

He looked at her. "After what you did to Atwin and Netta? How can you expect me to forget that, let alone forgive?"

"But I am sorry, Cal. Can you not try?"

"No Kandina," he replied. "I think not."

He flung the door wide and slammed it behind him, leaving her alone with mouth agape. He stood against the door for a long moment. He placed one hand against the wood and rested his head next to it, eyes downcast. Then he heaved himself away and hurried off. Kandina stood still, a look of pained surprise on her face. Then she made another decision.

"Calib!" she cried.

She flung the door open and raced after him. But the Prince was already gone. A sob escaped her. She rushed down the hallway, looking for him. There was no hope. Too late she realised the full extent of her foolishness.

She knew now that Atwin was only ever a fantasy for her. Now she had lost Calib too, and suddenly he really meant something to her. He was right, she was too late. Sobbing bitterly, she ran.

She paid no heed to where she went. Finally, she found herself outside, in the open air. It was dusk. The sun had sunk below the horizon and the pale light was fading from the sky. There was a strange, warm smell to the air, and the sound of the soldiers outside the city drifted to her. A movement caught her eye and she turned to see a small, strangely cloaked figure approaching.

"You are the daughter of Averil?" said a soft voice.

"Yes," said the Princess.

"I am Four Zjobock Dhort," said the voice. "I have been expecting you."

"What do you want?" Kandi asked.

Four shrugged. "What do you want?"

"I know not what you mean."

"Oh?" Four said. "Do you not?"

"I... Of course not."

"I think you do, Kandina. Why did you betray your family?"

"I..."

"By the way, the Leader gives Its thanks."

Kandina gasped. "I did not know," she wailed. "I swear, I thought Gerard was just going to send her away somewhere."

"Do you really think that is an excuse?"

"Well..."

"Do you hate your cousin that much?"

"Of course not!"

"Then why would you want to cause her so much pain?"

"Pain? I never..."

"Did you not think that you might be hurting her?"

"I..."

"I take that as a no. You thought only of yourself. You were jealous of her and you thought that by getting rid of her everything would be alright. Did you even consider how you might hurt Atwin?"

"I would never hurt Atwin."

"But you did. You took Netta from him."

"I thought if she was gone he would like me again."

"But he never liked you in the way you wanted him to. You know that."

"I thought I could make him love me."

"That is no excuse."

"Look, what is this? How dare you accost me like this! You have no right. What is it to you what I did? It was a mistake, that is all. It is none of your business!"

"Oh, but it is my business. You see, I happen to like your family. Do you even know why I am here?"

"How could I? Nobody tells me anything."

"I helped Atwin find her. I told him how to get her out of the caverns where my people live. I am a traitor to my own kind and the Leader knows this. I cannot go back. I would like to think I have friends among your kind. None of your family will condemn you openly, but you have hurt them all, and I have no qualms in telling you so."

"But I did not mean to hurt anyone."

"Do you really think that will make it go away?"

"Well I..."

"They know not how to forgive you. You have been selfish and thoughtless, and they cannot get over what you have done. You should not expect them to."

"I do not expect it."

"Do you not?"

"No..."

"Forgiveness will be a long time coming, Kandina, and when it finally does, you had better be ready to accept it gratefully. You should think long and hard on what you have done. You are no longer a child, as you are so fond of saying. Why not prove it?"

"But I said I was sorry!"

Four sighed. "I think you do not realise exactly what my people did to her. Shall I tell you?"

Kandi nodded, though she thought perhaps she did not want to know.

"When Gerard handed her over, she was beaten, repeatedly. She was given no food or water. When she started to weaken from lack of food she caught small animals captured on the plains. They were not cleaned or skinned. She had to pull them apart with her bare hands, rip them open with her teeth and eat them raw."

Kandi gagged at the thought.

"Netta did this. Not because she was hungry, though that helped, but because she needed to feed her child."

"Child?" Kandi gasped.

"You did not know? Perhaps that is just as well. Maybe you would have been even more cruel if you had known."

"No!"

"If you say so. Do you want to hear more?"

Kandi shook her head, but said "Yes."

"When my people found out that she was carrying a child, they beat her even more, and even aimed blows at her stomach. It is a miracle that she did not lose the child. When they carried her over the sea, her flesh was burnt by their hands. She still bears the scars, though you have probably never seen them."

Kandina covered her mouth with her hand.

"When they took her into the caverns she was left untended and alone, for days on end. They gave her enough raw meat to keep her alive. They did not give her water. I suppose they were too afraid to carry it to her. They left her in darkness on a cold stone floor. Such things are no discomfort to us, but others of my people do not understand humans as I do.

"When Atwin brought her out, she was a shadow of her former self. She did not speak for many days. She would allow only Atwin and her mother near her. Even her father, who she loves dearly, was afraid to approach her unasked."

Kandina sobbed, and tears fell unheeded.

"So you see, Kandina, your actions caused greater suffering than any human has ever known. Your whole family is effected by it. You have even lost the one who truly loved you, all because of jealousy. Was it worth it?"

Kandina shook her head. She could not speak, and she could barely see through the tears.

"You may go," said Four then. "I have nothing more to say to you."

The Princess lurched to her feet and stumbled away. She had no idea where to go, and she did not care. She just wanted to get away. She ran for a long time. Vaguely, she was aware of the army to her left and kept clear. Finally, she collapsed in a field outside town and wept bitterly.

TWENTY FIVE

The Queen and her advisers gathered in the council chambers to discuss strategy. Ordel had finally convinced her that it was time for her to go, but she wanted to see everything organised before she left.

"Does anyone know where the nomads are?" said Tarnel quietly.

"If they have agreed to help, they should be here soon," Ordel replied.

"And have they agreed to help?" asked Lenent.

"I know not," said Ordel.

"Then we cannot rely on their help," said Erris. "We must assume they are not coming."

"They will come," said Atwin from the doorway.

He entered the room, dragging Netta behind him.

Delsi rose from her chair, sensing her daughter's presence. "Netta, you should not be here."

"Why not?" said Atwin. "She has as much right to be here as anyone else."

"But she has had a hard time. We should not expose her to these things," said Ordel. "It is for your own good, Netta," he said apologetically.

"I am alright, Father," she said. "I can handle it."

"We are just concerned about you," said Delsi.

"Please do not leave me out, Mother," said Netta.

Delsi gave in reluctantly. "Come sit by me, then."

Netta joined her mother, and the conference continued.

"Tonight we will begin evacuating the women and children," Ordel began.

"No!" said Netta. "The women can help."

"What?" said Tarnel.

"You need their numbers. It is suicide to send them away when they can help."

"Are you serious?" said Tarnel.

"The idea has merit," said Atwin defensively.

"But it is unorthodox," said Tarnel dubiously.

"Are we worried about tradition or survival?" asked Atwin pointedly.

"What do you suggest we do?" asked Lenent quietly.

"Select a female regiment, teach them how to use the catapults and send the rest to Eeasto with Delsi and the others," said Atwin. "Netta is right. We do need the numbers."

Ordel nodded. "We shall do as you say. Without the nomads, we need all the numbers we can get."

Atwin stood and rang the bell, telling the soldier that entered to find Calib and send him into the council. When he arrived, Ordel apprised him of the plan and set him to work organizing the women. As he was leaving, he stopped at the door.

"By the way," said Calib with a worried frown. "Has anyone seen Kandina today?"

Averil looked at him uncertainly. "She was not in her room this morning," she frowned. "Why?"

"I... think someone should look for her."

"You think something may have happened to her?"

"I know not. It is possible."

"I will arrange a search party," said Ordel then.

"No," said Calib. "I will go."

He smiled at her lovingly and brought her to him, holding

her gently. Then something touched her hand. The horse was cropping the grass at her feet, his bridle jingling. She smiled. The horse moved and the bridle scraped against her hand.

Kandi woke with a start. A bug was crawling across her hand.

"Cal?" she said softly.

She lifted herself up on one arm and looked at the man beside her. She reached out and stroked his hair. Then she stopped. She pulled the hair back from his face. She groaned, remembering.

The hair was the same and he had the same build, but this was not Calib. Kandi sat up, thinking back to the night before. He had come across her in the field. He had comforted her in her distress. He had been kind to her and when he had made his intentions known she had not resisted. Now she felt cold.

What had she done? Silent tears fell and she looked down at the stranger. She could not stay here. She had allowed herself to be used and she felt mortified.She dressed hurriedly and left him sleeping there.

She wandered aimlessly. She came across a stream and bathed, washing away the smell of him. Then she wandered some more. Eventually, she found herself on a beach to the west of Shirall, looking out over the Gulf of Shira. Kandi walked across the sand and into the waves.

The tide was rising, and the surf was rough. When she was toppled by a large wave, she stayed where she landed, not caring that she might drown. That was where Calib finally found her. He saw her lying in the wet sand unmoving and his breath caught in his throat.

He hurried across the sand and knelt beside her still form. Her eyes were open but unseeing.

"Kandi?" he said carefully.

She let out a sob and he sighed with relief.

"Can you move?" he whispered.

She shook her head. "Why should I?" she replied.

"You will catch your death of cold," he said.

"I care not."

"But I care," he murmured.

He made her sit up. Then he picked her up and carried her out of the surf. She was shivering now, the world coming back to her.

Kandi moaned. "Let me die," she said brokenly.

"Why?" he said, setting her down.

"I have done a terrible thing, Cal," she whimpered. "How can you ever forgive me?"

He did not reply. She clutched at him.

"I am so sorry, Cal," she sobbed, burying her face against him.

He held her gently for a long moment. Then he pulled away.

"Come on, Kandi," he said. "Let us get you home."

She resisted. "I cannot go home," she wailed.

"Why ever not?"

"They all hate me..."

"You know they do not," he replied.

"Cal?" she whispered. "Do you hate me?"

"Of course not."

"But you said..."

"I said a harsh thing, Kandi. It does not mean I hate you."

"You should," she sobbed.

"No, Kandi. I know not what to do with you."

In her private rooms, Averil lay curled in the arms of her secret lover, denying the whispering voice that told her to seal up her heart. For thirteen years she had lived for his visits, the loneliness of ruling Shirall made bearable by those few moments of happiness.

"I still think you should go with Delsi," he murmured. "I need to know you are safe."

"I will not leave you," she replied. "Not now we finally have a chance."

He pulled her closer and she smiled. Now that Delsi was back and Netta was soon to be crowned, now that Atwin would be king, she was no longer tied here by her duties as regent. She could seek her own life at last, maybe with Lenent in Zelona, once this war was over. She felt him take a breath.

"There is something I need to know."

"Hmmm?"

"Why did you marry him?"

She stiffened. "That was a long time ago. Why ask now?"

"I have always wondered. I know you were already promised, but I thought you would turn him down. I thought we would be together."

She heard the hurt in his voice and felt a lump in her throat. "I am so sorry, Len. I had to go through with it, I had no choice."

"Of course you had a choice."

"No, Len, I did not. My father was making an alliance with Tellemot, a joining between his younger daughter and the King's younger son. It was politics."

"You could have waited for me."

"You were gone, Len! You were dealing with your father's death, and the first invasion was just begun, your own kingdom was under threat. I was young and frightened and alone."

"I was coming back!"

"I could not be sure. You could have been gone for years. I had no time to waste, I needed to be married before..." she caught her breath, she had said too much. She had never intended for him to know.

His eyes narrowed. "Before what?"

"Before..." she shook her head, but the look in his eyes sent a shiver down her spine. "Before I showed..." she whispered.

"Showed? What do you mean?"

"Oh, Len," she blurted, sobbing now. "I was with child..."

He sat up straight, eyes wide. "Are you telling me... Are you saying Kandina is..."

Her tears flowed unheeded and she nodded, unable to speak.

"My daughter!" he gasped. Then he chuckled and lay back on the pillows, pulling her back into his arms.

"That settles it then," he said. "You are definitely going north with Delsi, both of you."

"But..."

"I will not have my family put in danger. I will see that you are safe."

"Your family?"

"That is what you are."

"She must never know, she would not understand!"

"I know, I see that. But I will do everything I can to protect her none the less."

The Kings were saying their last farewells to their families. Tarnel stood with his wife and ten year old son, Erris waved to his twin daughters and their maid as they hurried aboard, and Umbro embraced his young wife and baby son.

Averil stood close by Lenent, watching the others embark. Neither gave any hint of their relationship, knowing it was not the right time to reveal their secret, but she took comfort in his presence and the feather light touch of one surreptitious hand at the small of her back.

Delsi and Ordel stood to one side of the Princess and her prince. They had already said their goodbyes and they stood waiting for Delsi's turn to board the ship.

Netta smiled wanly. "I do not want to go," she sighed.

"I know," Atwin replied. "But you must."

"I could help. Leena wants to be involved."

"Yes." He placed a hand on her stomach. "But what about her?"

Netta smiled again. "I know. I will not risk her life by staying. But I will miss you."

"And I you," he replied.

She snuggled into his arms. "I wish I did not have to go. You will be careful, will you not?"

"Worry not. I will join you soon."

Listening to her daughter, Delsi felt a pang of sympathy. She too wanted to stay in Shirall. She turned to her husband and slipped her arms about his waist. He kissed the top of her head.

"It is time to go, love," he murmured.

"I know."

She accepted his kiss and turned to go. As she walked toward the ramp ahead of her daughter, her steps dragged and she resisted the urge to run back to Ordel's side. Then, when she placed a foot on the wood of the ramp, a chill swept over her. She stopped short with a gasp.

"Mother?" said Netta behind her. "Are you alright?"

Delsi turned to her daughter and her face was stricken. She was trembling. Seeing her distress, Ordel moved toward her. Netta took her arm.

"Come, Mother. We must go."

Delsi shook her arm free. "No!"

"Delsi, love?" said Ordel softly.

She let out a cry and ran to him, sobbing brokenly.

"Delsi, what is wrong?" he asked.

"Oh, Ordel," she cried. "I am afraid!"

He felt himself go cold. But he tried to reassure her. "Everything will be fine, love."

She pulled back. "No," she whimpered. She held his face between her hands. "Something terrible is going to happen," she said.

He held her. "Do not say that, Delsi."

"I know it," she cried. She pulled him down to her level and pressed her cheek against his. "You have to come with us!"

"You know I cannot do that, love. The army needs me."

"Let Atwin take them. He is well able."

"Delsi, I cannot desert them." The coldness of fear gripped him. "What have you seen?"

She lowered her voice, so that only he could hear. "I am afraid, Ordel," she whispered. "If you do not come now, I may never see you again!"

"Of course you will," he replied, though her statement had sent a shock through his soul. "I will see you in a few days."

She shook her head, the tears streaming down her face. "I will not go without you," she whimpered.

He held her by the shoulders to steady her. "Delsi, love," he said. "Listen to me."

She sobbed, but quietened.

"You must be strong," said Ordel then.

She nodded.

"Be strong, love, for me. You must take Netta to Eeasto for me. Promise me you will look after her until Atwin can join her."

Delsi nodded again, her voice caught in her throat.

"Now give me a smile to remember."

She tried to smile through the tears.

He pulled her to him. "Good enough," he murmured.

"Now go, love." He kissed her lingeringly and she clung to him. "Come, now," he murmured.

She sobbed quietly. Then she kissed him again and turned away, leading the way straight-backed onto the ship. Averil moved forward and gave Ordel a quick hug.

"Look after her for me," he said quietly.

Averil nodded and followed Delsi onto the ship, where she stood at the rail, eyes catching Lenent's where he stood with the other kings. Almost imperceptibly, he nodded reassurance.

The Princess Kandina trailed after her mother. She looked back time and again, hoping to catch Calib's eye, but he kept his head bowed, refusing to let her see his face. Finally, she turned her back to the shore and climbed the ramp to the deck. Only then did Calib look up, following her wistfully with his eyes.

Atwin joined his brother and Ordel, and they watched as the ship pulled out of port. Once the ship had turned and was sailing out of the harbour, Atwin and Ordel made their way back to the ruined palace with the rest of the Kings. But Calib stayed where he was. Seeing the young prince, Lenent hung back and went to stand beside him.

"She will be alright," he said quietly, almost to himself.

Calib looked at the King in surprise and gave a small smile. Lenent placed a reassuring hand on his shoulder and stood watching for a moment. Then he followed the other kings back to the palace.

Calib stood there on the dock, watching the ship as it slowly shrank into the distance. He was still there long after the curve of the shore hid the ship from view.

TWENTY SIX

The Kings gathered once more in the conference room beneath the ruined palace at Shirall.

"Now that our families are safely removed from danger," said Atwin. "We must make some drastic decisions."

Ordel nodded. "We all know this war goes badly for us. The kalkar are everywhere and seemingly unstoppable."

"What do you propose we do?" said Lenent.

"We need to decide what our next step will be," said Erris. "If Shirall falls, where do we go?"

"Surely, we take the battle to Drasmil," said Calib.

"Yes, I would have suggested that," said Atwin.

"But we all know we are losing this war," Umbro said. "Do we really want to lose yet another battle?"

Erris nodded. "That is something to consider."

"What are you suggesting?" said Atwin.

"That we make Shirall our last stand, and if we fail head straight to Eeasto to gather our forces and regroup," said Umbro.

"You mean to desert Drasmil?" cried Calib.

"No, Your Highness," said Umbro. "I mean evacuate and save your people."

Atwin sighed. "Umbro, you suggest a bitter act. In my heart I cannot like it."

Tarnel raised a hand. "Your Majesty, I understand your concern, and believe me I feel your pain at this suggestion. But perhaps we can examine it on its merits."

Calib frowned. "Your Majesty, what merit could there be in such an act? You are asking us to abandon our home without a fight."

"I know my suggestion strikes a nerve," said Umbro. "Atwin, I know you have a loyalty to your kingdom, and I would never expect you to betray your heart. But it must be examined from both sides."

Atwin nodded and sat back in his chair, arms crossed. "In that case, Umbro, give me both sides."

The young king of Yerterma gathered his thoughts. "First, if we stay and fight, we lose more men here at Shirall, and let us face facts there is a high chance we will lose the city and beat a battered retreat."

Erris nodded. "Then we go on to Drasmil. Fight another battle, lose another army of men, possibly to be defeated once again. We face another retreat, another uncountable loss of life, sending us north to regroup."

"Go on," said Atwin with a scowl.

"If we choose to make Shirall our last stand, we give your people the chance to get away without injury, and we save the armies from yet more heavy losses," Umbro concluded.

"In addition," said Tarnel. "Shirall will act as a diversion. We keep the enemy firmly occupied here while the refugees of the world can be ferried to safety in the north, where they can melt into the mountains of Martose and await the final outcome."

Atwin nodded. "I see your logic, but... forgive me if I still need something more. Convince me that this is right for Drasmil."

"If I may, Your Majesty," said Lenent.

Atwin nodded.

"I have witnessed this war from its beginning. I saw my home destroyed, my people decimated and destitute, crying for help from our allies. I saw Nella Fillenga overrun and its royal family completely destroyed. I saw more destruction, more refugees, more death.

"I travelled the length of this land on my own, seeing the devastation the kalkar left in their wake, people displaced and without hope. I have no idea how many are dead, but I do know if I could have saved my people by escaping ahead of the horde, I would have done so. You have that chance now."

Atwin considered. "Calib?"

The Prince frowned. "I like it not," he said. "But Lenent is right."

Atwin nodded. "Then we are agreed. It is abundantly clear we cannot win the war at this point in time. Hopefully a new strategy can be developed once we are all together at Eeasto."

Calib sighed. "Agreed."

"Calib, you will take a small force to Drasmil to begin the evacuation. Gather as many refugees as you can and meet the ships at Sar Sor to begin sending them across the Sea of Skies. The rest of us will prepare Shirall for a protracted siege."

The commanders of the armies gathered the refugees already at Shirall. All able-bodied men were recruited into the army, and all of the women without children were selected to be trained in the use of catapults.

All remaining people were distributed onto the ships and sailed north to join Delsi in Eeasto. With those people gone, the army set about preparing the fortification of Shirall.

Ordel set Shirall's engineers to work creating a mechanism for pumping water continuously from the sea. Those who had been involved with the creation of the underground palace were well suited to the task, and the work progressed well. By the time the scouts returned with news of the approaching horde, the city below the palace was literally filled with water and surrounded by a moat.

Much to the consternation of the men, the women had decided to play soldier and were now dressed the part, trousers and all. One young woman moved among them, long dark hair twisted up under a page boy's practice helmet, fine features smeared with mud.

She had journeyed far with the refugees, her quiet confidence boosting their spirits and keeping them focused. Moving along the battlements, passing from one group of women to the next, giving encouragement and helping prepare catapults and ballistae, she generalled the women like a trained soldier.

Standing at the ready, she looked out over the city and the plain beyond, seeing the men milling around preparing in their own way. Seeing a commotion, the woman peered closer. A group of soldiers were gathered around one unpromising man, who appeared to be wearing armour cobbled together from whatever mismatched pieces he could find.

The men around him were arguing amongst themselves and deferring to his every gesture. She knew who that was. Leaving a last word of encouragement, the woman hurried down off the battlements and out the gate, determined to meet the man. When she caught him, the soldiers parted unwillingly. With a raised voice and an air of authority the young woman made her way through the throng.

"Are you Freakles the farmer?" she said to the man.

He groaned, stress showing in his frazzled face.

"You should not be here."

He frowned. "Who're you?"

"That matters not. You need to be protected. If you really are the last male kin of King Derrek, you should be inside talking strategy with the others."

"I don't want to be inside with them, I don't belong there."

"Until a closer heir steps forward you do, and I intend to get you there."

"What's your name?"

"I am Mirta, the late king's cousin. And you are coming with me."

The kalkar seemed aware that this was the end of the current phase of the war. When the horde arrived at Shirall, the dark ones were content to surround the city and wait. They had learned the limitations of their prey, and with that understanding they had discovered that humans could not live for long without food and water.

The Leader had ordered his force to stand ground outside Shirall and starve them out. Thus the siege began. Ordel was sure they could last at least a few days, but there were a lot of people within the city and supplies were not endless. The armies, trapped between the walls and the horde, were nervous and the generals sat long in conference with the commanders.

Atwin waged a day-light offensive against the horde, sending his men out amongst them with plentiful supplies of water. It would not be long before the men were exhausted from the effort. After four days, with no reaction from the standing kalkar, the nomads arrived behind them.

This seemed to be the signal the enemy had been waiting for, and the night attacks came in earnest. The women put the catapults to good use, sending sprays of water into the advancing horde with devastating effect.

The nomads used water sparingly, but with surprisingly good results and it seemed the horde would break. When daylight came on the fifth day, Evelar and Miyam made their way through the sizzling force to the city, joining the Kings in the palace.

"Your Majesties, I'm sorry we were so long in coming," said Evelar with a bow.

"What kept you?" asked Atwin.

"We thought it might be useful to cause a little damage along the way," the revealer replied. "The tribesmen seem to be losing heart. I suspect they'll break the alliance before too long."

"That is good to know," said Ordel. "Their little attempts on our lives are becoming irritating."

"I wouldn't lower my guard just yet, Your Highness. We have no way of knowing how many are still among us."

"I agree," said Atwin softly.

"If I may make a suggestion?" said Miyam then.

"Of course," Ordel replied.

"It may be necessary to absent Your Majesties from danger. Without a target, the assassins will leave of their own accord."

"You mean retreat?" said Tarnel. "I am not sure I like that idea."

"I know it sounds like running away," said Miyam. "But Your Majesties aren't dispensable. If you're dead we have no council, and without a council we have no hope at all."

"I hate to say it," said Umbro quietly, "but I think she may be right."

"Who will lead the armies if we go?" said Erris.

"I will stay," Ordel replied.

"And I," said Atwin in a firm voice.

"I'm not certain we should put both of you in danger," said Evelar then.

"At least it will only be two of us," Atwin replied. "We can watch out for each other without having to worry about everyone else."

Ordel nodded in agreement. "This is one time when numbers do not ensure safety."

"Then, we will go," said Lenent. "If we are all in agreement?"

There was a general murmur of assent.

That very day, the Kings of Sharné prepared to sail on the evening tide. Miyam and Evelar sailed with them, leaving the nomad force under Shevron's control. They felt they needed to be present in Eeasto when the Kings arrived, to ensure that meetings began at once.

Taking one ship from the small fleet that had remained in Shirall, they slipped away at dusk. At the same time, Ordel sent the rest of the fleet around the cape to Sar Sor to meet up with those returning from Eeasto. It would not be long before retreat was inevitable.

As night fell, the attack came anew, and within a few hours the defenders had forced the enemy back. A new feeling of hope grew among the soldiers, and they fought with vigour. But Atwin felt uneasy. Naali warned him of impending danger, and he knew that the kalkar were not defeated. He felt sure that another force was on its way.

As the moon rose over Shirall, dark shapes could be seen winging in from the east. Most of the city had been evacuated, the long line of people heading north. A small force remained behind to stall for time, and the kalkar about the city were still sustaining heavy losses.

News of the reinforcements had come late that day and the decision had been made to quit the city. Atwin was overseeing the retreat, while Ordel took command of the last regiment.

The new force attempted to land in the city, but the streets had been flooded and they could not risk the deadly water. Some half of the enemy landed outside the city and engaged Ordel's small force. The rest remained aloft and dove on the frightened soldiers from above.

Atwin ordered catapults fired into the air and many fell, but the attack continued. Ordel began the retreat, and Atwin brought the last of his men to help. But before he could reach Ordel's side, the kalkar unleashed a new and deadly power.

There was a blinding flash of green, and the front ranks of Ordel's force reeled back. The ground smoked and the men stood frozen in shock, the dead lying blackened before them. After each wave of green fire, the kalkar who shot it froze, their daily energy used up. Atwin pushed his way through the ranks, searching for the Prince Consort. He was nowhere to be found.

Fear giving way to anger, the young king reacted instinctively, drawing on the power of Naali. Previously he had only used the power with Netta in tandem, now he took independent action for the first time. The amulet about Atwin's neck glowed blue, the fire growing rapidly to engulf him.

Reaching out with both hands, he countered the kalkar attack, his blue flame leaping forward to meet the green power of the kalkar, snuffing it instantly. The icy glow spread out over the enemy causing rank upon rank to melt into the ground.

His men stopped and stared at their king in awe. There was a reverberating guttural cry from thousands of kalkar mouths. Then more green bolts of fire followed from above and more soldiers fell. The men ran from the onslaught, fear gripping them.

A concentrated beam shot forward from the enemy lines, hitting Naali full force where he rested on Atwin's chest, throwing the King backward to land with a thud, winded and smouldering.

Gasping for breath, he struggled to a sitting position as General Tratska rushed to his aid. Searching for Naali in his mind, he found no reply. The presence in the amulet was silenced. Atwin hoped it was only temporary.

The kalkar halted in their advance and watched as the human army fell apart. By the end of the night, the army was in full retreat and the kalkar horde had halted the chase. Some miles from Shirall, Atwin called a halt. He called two soldiers to him and ordered them to accompany him back to the city.

Ordel was still missing and the young king was determined to find him. Or his body, he thought with a shudder. The horde stood sizzling around the edges of the battlefield. The three men picked their way through the mingled bodies and gooey puddles that covered the battlefield. Some of the corpses were still warm, suggesting they had not been dead long. Perhaps Ordel was lying somewhere, injured but not yet dead.

Atwin fervently hoped he would find him before it was too late. Finally, they reached the point where the green fire had struck. The dead lay in piles, some so burnt that they were unrecognisable. Atwin swallowed hard. This was where he had last seen the Prince, standing tall at the head of his army.

Atwin and the two soldiers began the unpleasant task of searching among the bodies. They removed those from the top of the piles to reveal the corpses beneath. Ordel did not seem to be there. At last, they turned to the foremost pile. The bodies were thick on the ground and, at the very bottom of the pile, they found Ordel's limp form.

Atwin knelt beside him. Miraculously, he seemed to have been shielded from the full force of the fire bolt, though he was burnt terribly. It was as if his men had unanimously jumped in front of him, to take the blow themselves. His breathing was shallow and at first Atwin could not feel it.

The Prince was near death, but his heart was still beating in his chest. The soldiers lifted his body and laid it across the saddle of the spare horse they had brought. Then they slowly made their way back to the army.

Later in the day, the Prince awoke. He called weakly for Atwin and clutched at his arm when he came to his side. He said something, and Atwin had to lean down close to hear him. The Prince whispered, his voice almost inaudible, and his hand gripped Atwin's arm.

"Tell Delsi," he whispered painfully. "Tell her that... I love her..."

Then he sank quietly into oblivion.

The army boarded the fleet at Sar Sor with the horde close behind. As they sailed out of the harbour on the early morning tide, the horde took wing and swooped down on the ships. Where they landed, the sails and the decks caught alight. The sailors frantically tried to douse the flames, but some ships were lost. At last, dawn turned the sky a rosy hue and the kalkar retreated, leaving the fleet as it headed north to safety.

Four Zjobock Dhort watched as the fleet escaped. She had fled the flooding of the city, and she had seen her people die, but still she could not return to them. So she hid, avoiding both sides, her confusion driving her to remain alone. When next night fell, she spread her wings and flew north.

* * *

TWENTY SEVEN

The Maestro stood atop a tower high above the College, watching as the ship hove majestically into port. He had no idea exactly who was aboard, but he thought he knew. He hoped fervently that Ordel was with her, but something told him that his hope was futile.

Perhaps he would follow after. The old Maestro sighed. Ordel had always been a little too independent. It just might be the death of him one day. He went cold. Then he shook himself and descended from the tower.

A young apprentice was waiting to meet them when the ship pulled in at the dock. Bowing to the Queen and her party, the boy led them up the hill to the College. Once inside the great iron gate, the Apprentice offered to lead them to the hastily prepared guest quarters. It was not his place to question why the Maestro was allowing so many strangers into the College.

Delsi smiled at the boy. "When can we see the Maestro?" she asked.

"I'll see if he's available," said the Apprentice with a bow.

When they had reached their rooms, the boy ran off to find the Maestro while Delsi and her family washed away the rigors of travel. The Apprentice soon returned, and Delsi took her daughter with her to see the Maestro.

"My dear Delsi," he said, embracing her fondly.

Delsi smiled. "Hello, Thoy," she said. "It is nice to see you again."

"Is this Netta?" he said. "You've grown into a beautiful young lady."

Netta smiled shyly.

"How is my son?" he asked then.

"He is well," Delsi replied. "Or he was when I left him," she said fearfully.

"You felt it too?" he said then. "I'd hoped I only imagined it."

"I am so very worried, Thoy," said Delsi.

"I hope there's no need," he replied.

A week later, the Kings arrived in Eeasto. Leading their horses through the gate, Miyam and Evelar looked at each other and smiled. Entering the College after so long away was more than a home coming, it was a giving up of worldly identity and assuming of their anonymous names. Names which became like treasured secrets known only to their fellow revealers, welcoming them into a close and loving family.

'Hello, my Sand,' Miyam whispered silently.

'Hello, my lovely Mist,' he whispered in return.

She smiled, savouring his first official use of her new name, the name which had been her mother's before her. The Maestro welcomed the Kings personally, for the first time in many years opening the doors of the College to a large group of outsiders. Desli scanned the group but did not feel her husband's presence.

"Is Ordel not with you?" she said, her worry plain in her voice.

"No, Your Majesty," said Lenent. "He and Atwin stayed behind to lead the defence of Shirall. Calib is coordinating the evacuation of Drasmil, and we should see refugees begin to arrive here soon."

"I am glad to see you all safe," said Averil quietly,

including them all, though her eyes rested on only one.

The assembled kings set up talks in the impromptu conference room, usually used as a meeting place for the counsellors and the Maestro when dealing with College matters. Freakles, the farmer representative of Nella Fillenga, sat silently in his chair, totally out of his depth.

This was not what Freakles would call a normal day on the farm. The Kings all knew each other, and besides they were kings! He had no idea how to talk to these men. Hell, he had not even met a king before a week ago!

He fervently wished he was back on his little farm in the south of Fillenga, happily tilling his fields. The Princess Mirta had stayed with him, proving to be an excellent adviser, and he knew he would never have managed this far without her. He was not cut out for politics and military strategy.

"It is clear we cannot win," said the King of Tellemot. "The horde is just too great. Their numbers grow every day. The armies cannot hold the shore forever, and if the kalkar keep coming our forces will be overrun by sheer force of numbers."

"Tarnel is right," said Erris, the King of Mytar. "I have seen what they can do. Just when you think you have them under control, a relief force comes winging across the sea to join them, and there is nothing to do but run."

"And even that is futile, unless the dawn catches them," said Umbro of Yerterma.

"There has to be some hope," said Lenent. "We cannot give up."

"I understand now why the dark ones were able to enslave our ancestors before Rexa came. Their numbers are just too great, and almost nothing kills them, except water."

"Which we have in abundance, Erris," said Umbro. "I

know how you feel, but I am not planning to sit back and let them take over again. That would be unthinkable."

"Then what do you suggest?"

"I know not," he said in exasperation.

"Gentlemen, please," said Delsi then. "This bickering is getting us nowhere. I know things look bleak, but we must think of something. None of us want to be slaves of those creatures."

There was a knock at the door, and a flustered apprentice entered and kneeled before the assembled monarchs and advisers.

"Report," said Delsi.

"Your Majesties, the fleet comes."

The assembly looked at each other.

"Have you any news?"

"No your Majesty," the girl replied. "But one sails ahead of the others. Perhaps a messenger is aboard."

The Kings and their advisers stood tensely on the battlements of the castle which was the central building of the College at Eeasto, and watched the fleet on the horizon. One small ship sped its way to shore, hopefully carrying news.

Within an hour, it had made its way into port. At Delsi's suggestion, they returned to the conference room to await the messenger. Within a few moments, the door was flung open and Atwin strode in. Netta rose from her chair, but he stopped her with a look.

His face was tense, and his eyes held a deeply buried grief. He looked around the room and ran a hand through his short hair nervously.

"Welcome, Atwin," said Delsi. "What is the news?"

Atwin hesitated. "Your Majesties," he said slowly, "the news is not good. The horde has doubled in strength, and the army is in full retreat." He turned to Delsi. "I am sorry, Your Majesty. Shirall has fallen."

Delsi sat in silence. From beside her, Averil put a comforting hand on her shoulder. "How many men did we lose?"

"Too many. You do not want the numbers."

The Maestro was looking at Atwin with a peculiar expression. "The army follows on the ships we saw out there?"

Atwin nodded. "Yes, sir."

"Who commands them?"

"My brother, Calib."

The Maestro looked to Delsi and back again and slowly rose from his chair. The Queen, sensing his discomfort, turned her head in Atwin's direction.

"There is something you have not told us," she accused.

Atwin sighed. "Yes, Your Majesty. We lost some important people, including... one of our high commanders."

The change in her face was terrible as the coldness of fear gripped her. "Where is Ordel?" Her voice was tight.

Atwin looked about, not wanting to see her reaction. "He..."

"Where is he?" she nearly screamed.

"I... I am sorry, Your Majesty," he said softly.

She took a step backward and raised a hand to her mouth. "No..." she murmured.

The Maestro sat down slowly, shock evident on his face. He bowed his head and a small groan escaped him. Sand and Mist exchanged a look, and the Journeyer went to the old Maestro in concern.

"Sir, are you alright?" she asked.

The Maestro shook his head slowly. "It cannot be..."

Delsi let out a little cry and stumbled toward where Atwin watched. She took his face in her trembling hands.

"Tell me it is not true! He will stroll in here any moment, will he not?"

Atwin did not reply.

She shook him. "Atwin? Please say he is alright!"

The King of Drasmil hung his head.

"No!" she cried.

The Maestro looked up at her. Mist could see the tears standing in his eyes. As the Queen's grief gripped at her, the Maestro rose and turned away from the assembly. Delsi heard him and stumbled toward him. She clutched at his arm.

"It cannot be true," she whispered. "Tell me it is not true." Her voice rose in panic. "Thoy, please," she cried.

The Maestro pulled her roughly to him, giving in to his own grief. Sand and Mist exchanged another look, surprised at the Maestro's reaction to the news.

Netta had been staring at Atwin in shock, her face stricken. Tears fell unheeded. Atwin went to her and wrapped her in his arms. She buried her face in his shoulder and wept.

Averil paced. This was becoming a habit. Too much worry. Now, Ordel was dead. Her heart ached for her sister. Ordel had been a good friend. But the years of ruling her country, putting on a brave face and hiding her heart, made her grieve in private.

In her small apartment the Princess Regent fretted. She did not notice the door open and the man enter, so it was with a jolt of surprise that she found herself clasped in his arms.

"Calm down, Avvy!"

She was not used to having him there to comfort her. She had dealt with so many crises on her own over the years, this was a new experience. At first she could not give in, her back stiff and her hands pressed against his chest. Then he began to stroke her hair. Averil shivered, the tender touch a complete surprise.

"You need not be so strong, Avvy. I am here now and I am not going away."

She stared at him, eyes flickering as she studied his face. A small sob escaped her and she melted against him, but a part of her still held back.

"When this is all over," she whispered. "You will be gone again, and I will have to pick up the pieces."

"I promise you now, I will not leave you again."

She shook her head. "This is war, Len. You know what happened the last time. My husband was killed, Delsi was sent into exile, and I was left to rule Shirall on my own with a small child. You were not there then, and you will not be there this time. You will have a kingdom to heal, and I will still be needed in Shirall. Delsi needs me now more than ever!"

"That is why I love you," he murmured. "You have a heart that never stops giving. It is time you took something for yourself. Delsi will be alright. She has Netta and Atwin, she will not have to cope on her own."

"But what if something happens to them too?"

"Everything will be alright. I am not leaving until I can take you with me."

She sobbed again, weakening in spite of herself.

"What about Kandi? I will not drag her away from her home, and I cannot leave her."

"I would never ask you to do so. But I have a feeling she will soon be making her own plans."

"What do you mean?"

He touched a finger to the side of his nose and gave a wink. "Let me just say I see a match in her near future."

Her eyes narrowed. "What have you been up to?"

"Absolutely nothing, I swear. They are doing it all on their own."

"Who?"

He winked again. "Wait and see."

He pulled her firmly into his embrace. "As for you, my beautiful love, I have waited thirteen years for my turn, and I will not go home without you."

"Four has said they will keep coming," said the revealer.

"Therefore," said Mist, "we must find a way to stop them from coming."

"The army is holding them back with their water bombs for now."

"Which gives us a little time."

"Let's use that time to come up with a plan."

"Let's get over our pessimism and think," Mist finished.

"They are right," said Lenent. "Something has to be done."

Freakles said nothing. Two more kings had arrived during the night, and he felt somewhat intimidated.

"What is their usual strategy?" asked Axellandr, the young king of Martose.

"They really do not have one," Lenent replied. "They like to overwhelm us with numbers."

"Then how do they keep themselves together? How do they communicate across such a large force?"

"We think they have some sort of telepathic ability," Erris replied. "But I know not how true that is."

"Oh, it's true, Your Majesty," said Mist quietly. "We did manage to infiltrate their home base, and Sand developed a temporary link with their group mind. They're being controlled by a strange being they know only as 'the Leader.' But they don't normally have such a comprehensive link. The Leader has joined them together."

"Perhaps we should seek out this 'Leader' then," said Lenent. "If he is gone, their force might fall apart."

"Not possible, I'm afraid," said Sand. "Even the kalkar themselves do not know who the Leader is."

"How can you be sure this 'Leader' even exists?" said Selwyn, the outspoken king of Lenel. "He seems rather insubstantial to me."

"Not 'he'," said Sand. "'It.' And believe me It is real. I have spoken with It. There is no doubt that Its control over the kalkar is iron fast."

Axellandr rose from his chair and went to the large map on the wall. "Any force, no matter how large, can be defeated with the right strategy. Now, what if we were to take the seventh battalion through the village of Sun Lay," he pointed at the map. "We could lay a trap on the other side of the river Lenel, here, and take out a good half of their force."

"You forget, they do not die from conventional wounds," said Atwin. "And when they are cornered they come up with the most annoying ways of killing us."

"Like what?"

"Well," said Atwin, "if we ambush them outside Sun Lay, they will probably fire those green rays at us again, like they did at Shirall. There is a lot of sun in that area and not a lot of water. They will be at the height of their power, and we will have limited defence."

"Wait a minute," said Selwyn then. "Go back a bit. Green rays? What the hell are you talking about?"

"Yes," said Sand, sitting up straight. "What green rays?"

"You remember the sun shot?" said Atwin.

Sand nodded.

"This was very like that, but instead of a ball of light and heat, this was a ray, like..." He shrugged. "It was a highly concentrated beam. It cut through everything."

"I wish you'd mentioned it before," Sand said.

Atwin shrugged ruefully. "Sorry, my friend. I guess I forgot."

"You forgot something like that?" said Selwyn incredulously.

"I have had a lot on my mind, alright?"

Selwyn raised his hands in mock defeat.

"So what do we do?" said Tarnel. "It seems they not only outnumber us, but out weapon us too."

"It is hopeless," said Umbro mournfully.

"Perhaps not," said Sand.

"What had you in mind?" asked Atwin.

There was a quiet laugh. "You are in the College now," said an old man's voice. "Anything is possible."

"Be quiet, Father," said Axellandr dismissively.

The old man leant over to Freakles and winked. "Youth, eh?" he chuckled. "The old man is senile, eh? Knows not what he is saying."

Freakles smiled nervously. The old man laughed again.

"Go ahead, young man," he said to Sand. "Tell them what you can do."

The revealer looked about at the assembled monarchs and cleared his throat. "Your Majesties, what I am about to tell you is something of a College secret. We have... certain abilities, which we like to utilise when seeking out information. We may be able to help in this matter."

"What do you mean?" said Umbro.

The revealer took his wife's hand and both stood, moving away from the table while the others watched. Miyam closed her eyes and Sand raised his free hand level with his shoulder. He concentrated. Atwin covered his ears as a deep hum resonated through the room.

The old man, too, flinched from the noise, but the others seemed not to hear. Sand pointed at the fireplace and, when the hum became unbearable, released the energy in a tightly controlled beam, lighting the pile of timber set in the grate. He lowered his hand, breathing heavily, and Mist led him back to his chair.

"Well done, my boy," said the Maestro from the doorway.

Mist went to him. "How are you feeling, Sir?"

He smiled. "I'm fine, dear. Delsi is not, but she will recover in time. Thankfully, it's not often one loses a loved one so suddenly."

"May I ask you something, Sir?"

"Of course, dear."

"How well did you know Prince Ordel?"

"Not well enough," he replied. "Something I deeply regret."

When the revealer had regained his breath, he looked up at Atwin. "Was that something like what you saw?"

"Quite," the King replied. "How did you do it?"

"Basic College training gives members a small measure of control over the hidden powers of the mind," said Mist.

"This is how I was able to gain access to the group mind of the kalkar," said Sand. "But the beam is harder."

"Many of us can't contain such power," said Mist, "and those who can, can't always control it."

"The beam is used only in the gravest of emergencies."

"I always assumed you revealers were left alone because of the service you provide," said Axellandr. "The College has always given out the impression that it had no power of any consequence."

"Well…" said Sand with a shrug. "We lied."

TWENTY EIGHT

The armies of the world were camped on the northern shore of the Sea of Skies. Civilian refugees from all parts of the southern continent were filtering into Eeasto and were being quartered in the city and in the tunnels beneath the College.

The kalkar horde sent the occasional flight across the sea, but the army had so far managed to repel them with a barrage of water bombs. They could not hold out much longer, however. It seemed that the enemy force literally doubled every day.

Delsi had locked herself away, unable to function with her beloved husband gone. Netta sat with her, her own grief held tightly under control. The Princess was torn between the need to attend the meetings, and her mother's need of her company and support.

The Queen needed her daughter to be strong for her now. So Netta stayed with her. In the conference room, the Kings of Sharné and their advisers continued to discuss strategy. Atwin stood at the map that was pinned to the wall, planning troop deployments with Axellandr, the young king of Martose.

"It is clear we cannot defeat them with our current force," Atwin was saying. "We need to enhance our strength somehow."

"I will agree that we are outnumbered. And compared to the kalkar, we humans are relatively easy to kill. Water is not the easiest weapon to utilise, I fear."

"The kalkar have the strength of numbers," Sand said, joining them at the map. "Physically we can never win."

"They also have the mental power to coordinate their numbers," Mist added from her seat.

"We need to match that with something of our own," Sand stated.

"Yes, but what?" said Axellandr wearily.

Sand thought for a moment. "We of the College have some small ability, which could be tapped somehow."

"Small?" said Atwin incredulously. "Those rays of yours are anything but small."

Sand shook his head. "That's not what I meant. The rays are still primarily physical."

"I do not follow," said Axellandr.

"The energy that forms the ray is a measurable physical force," said Mist. "It therefore has its limitations."

Sand nodded. "The power of the ray comes from the strength of the person controlling it."

"What are you getting at?" said Atwin.

"To defeat the black horde, we need to cripple their psychic network," said Sand. "To do this, we need to create a similar psychic charge of our own."

"How?" said Erris quietly.

"The revealers can all utilise the brain's psychic ability," said Mist. "If we could channel it somehow, so that we are all linked..."

"We might just be able to send a non-physical charge that will break the kalkar net wide open," Sand explained.

"Without it, their physical coherence will fall apart," said Mist.

"Then we can send in the army to finish the job," said Atwin in comprehension.

"A good plan," said Axellandr. "But how do you propose

we do it?"

Sand shrugged. "I have no idea."

Atwin returned his attention to the map, and Sand watched as he pointed out the current deployment of troops along the coast. Axellandr looked on impassively.

"What about the Awakener?" asked the old retired king of Martose. "Has there been any sign yet?"

Those at the table looked at him in surprise.

"What?" said Selwyn, the King of Lenel.

Mist sat bolt upright with a strangled grunt. All attention turned to her and she managed to control herself.

"Ah... nothing," she said, trying to cover.

The others turned back to the old man, but the Maestro stared at Mist strangely.

"What are you talking about?" said Selwyn.

"The Awakener is a legend," said the old man. "He is supposed to appear in a time of crisis, and lead the world to a new understanding."

The Maestro looked a question at Mist, asking for an explanation. She tried to ignore his gaze, but he refused to look away. She tried not to meet his eyes.

"An understanding of what?" said Tarnel of Tellemot.

"Why life, the universe and everything," said the funny old king of Martose.

"You cannot be serious," said Selwyn incredulously.

Exasperated, Mist finally gave in and locked eyes with the Maestro. She raised an eyebrow and looked pointedly toward the three men gathered, oblivious now to the conversation, in front of the map.

The Maestro followed her gaze. He looked first at Axellandr and sent a careful mental probe. Nothing caught his mind. He turned his attention to Sand, but did not probe his mind, knowing that the Artisan would feel it instantly.

The Maestro went on to look at Atwin. His mental

probe turned up nothing of interest. He turned back to Sand and tried to send a minute mental finger probing into the Artisan's mind. Sand turned from the map, a look of annoyance on his face.

"Would you please stop that?" he said.

Then he returned his attention to the map on the wall. The Maestro's eyes opened wide and he looked back at Mist. She nodded at him almost imperceptibly.

"Oh my," he mouthed.

The old king noted the exchange and chuckled. "What about you, Sand," he said. "Have you seen any?"

"Any what, Your Majesty?" the revealer replied absently.

"Signs of the coming of the Awakener," the old man replied.

"Father, what are you talking about?" said Axellandr. "We do not have time for this."

"Well?" said the old king, ignoring his son.

"The Awakener?" said Sand. "I don't recall seeing anything that would point to..." he stopped.

The pointer he had been using slipped from his grasp and clattered on the floor. Selwyn threw up his hands in disgust. The Maestro watched Sand with bated breath. Mist stood up and sat on the table to get a better view, placing one foot on her chair and folding the other leg in front on the table. She rested her hands on her knees, eyes twinkling. Sand's mind was racing.

He suddenly remembered several incidents where he had surprised himself. He went through them mentally, his hands moving unconsciously in illustration. He remembered the search for Naali in the Sacred Halls.

With Mist's help he had travelled mentally over half a continent before losing the clairvoyant link to the King's amulet. He stretched out one hand, grasping at the air in front of himself. Even with Mist's help, he should never have been able to see so far, unless the first sign was being fulfilled.

"Clairvoyance," said Mist quietly.

He closed his eyes, one hand pressed to his forehead as he remembered his unexpected ability to communicate with the wild stallion, Windfoot. All the signs had to have an unusual or powerful element to them. He knew with certainty that the second sign had occurred then.

"Telepathy," said Mist softly.

He tried to remember what had happened next. At the end of the trail they had headed for Zelona, where he had found the image on the old oak table. His finger again traced the pattern. He realised with a jolt that the third sign was...

Mist nodded. "Divination."

The next he knew instantly. His hand grasped at an imaginary pile of sand as he remembered creating a diamond. He pushed the hand away from himself, recalling how, with Mist's help and with the diamond as focus, he had broken the crystalline casing about Naali.

"Channelling," said his wife with a smile.

He opened his eyes and looked at Mist. She grinned and gave a wink, and he realised with a sinking feeling that she had worked this out long ago.

"Does anyone here know what is going on?" said Umbro then.

"I certainly do not," said Selwyn.

"Nor I," said Erris.

"I do!" said the funny old king of Martose.

"Be quiet, Father," said Axellandr impatiently.

Sand looked away and closed his eyes again, shutting out his audience. He searched his mind for the next sign, hoping that he would not find it. But there it was.

He pressed one hand to his forehead and the other he reached out in front, closing the fist firmly. He had quite deliberately created a permanent mind link with Mist when he left her behind at the College. A link that was still in place.

"Mind Link," she said.

Of course, that led him immediately to the sixth sign. He brought his balled fist quickly back to his chest. He had mentally transported Mist from the College to the kalkar homeland, on the other side of the world. He swallowed hard.

"Translocation," whispered Mist.

Compelled, Sand thought on. He was at first relieved to see no seventh sign. But then, with a groan, he saw what he had missed. He clutched at the badge that held his cloak in place about his neck. He had declared himself outside College law so that he could avenge his sister's murder.

Mist sighed. "Rebellion."

This brought him face to face with the eighth sign. He spread out his hands in front of his body and raised them slightly as he remembered his conversation with Zayus and the twelve councillor spirits.

"Divine Contact!" said Mist triumphantly.

His eyes snapped open and he looked again at Mist, shaking his head in denial. The final sign: the Awakener realizing his own identity.

"Revelation?" he whispered. His eyes glazed over and he reached blindly for support. "Atwin...?" he murmured. "Could I have a chair...?"

"Certainly," said the King of Drasmil.

With a worried look at the revealer, he retrieved a chair from at the table. But Atwin was too slow. Sand clutched at the wall but missed and his legs gave way underneath him. The revealer found himself on the floor, his clutching hand ripping the map off the wall and pulling it down on top of himself.

"Oh boy," said Atwin, putting the chair down nearby. "First Father, now you."

He hauled Sand into the chair. Mist, still seated on the table, threw her arms triumphantly into the air.

"Yes!" she cried gleefully.

She jumped off the table and ran around to the Maestro, throwing her arms about him from behind.

"Yes!" she cried again.

She ran to where the old king of Martose sat and took his face between her hands, kissing him full on the lips. Young Axellandr gasped in shock. Then she grabbed Atwin in a huge hug and spun him around.

"Yes, yes, yes, yes, yes!"

She released Atwin and he fell against the table, the air knocked out of him. Mist stopped and looked at Sand.

"Finally!" she said happily.

Then she strutted over to where he sat and calmly slapped him on the side of the head.

"It's about bloody time," she stated.

Then, humming, she returned to her seat on the table.

"Sorry," she said to the room in general, without a trace of sincerity.

Sand sat in utter shock. The slap had brought him out of a daze, and now the world seemed incredibly cold. He searched about for something, but he did not know what. Finally, he looked to the Maestro for help.

"Well, my boy," said the Maestro with a look of extreme pride.

Sand, totally terrified, held the Maestro's gaze. He began to shake, and then a tear slid down his face. Seeing that, Mist stood in concern.

"He is crying!" said Umbro.

"I do not believe it," said Selwyn.

"What could cause Evelar to break?" said Erris in shock.

"It is simple," said the funny old king. "He is the Awakener."

Sand was trembling violently now, silent tears streaming down his face. Atwin placed a comforting hand on his shoulder, but Sand shook it off harshly.

"Don't touch me," he mumbled.

Mist took two hesitant steps toward him. "Umm..."

Sand looked vaguely in her direction, but refused to meet her eyes. She went to him and, without touching him, knelt by his side. He began to sniff a little.

Slowly, Miyam looked up at his face and used the mind link to force him to look at her. He stared at her brokenly, and her own tear filled eyes overflowed. He reached out and brushed a tear away in amazement. She leant her face into his hand and they stayed that way for a moment. Then he staggered to his feet.

He looked around, without meeting anyone's eyes. He walked slowly toward the door. He reached for the door handle and paused. Then he opened the door and stepped out of the room.

He walked down the corridor, slowly at first. As he increased his speed, wanting only escape, an ill-timed apprentice stopped him.

"Sir Artisan, thank goodness I've found you. General Ashtad asked me to tell you..."

Sand pushed him away roughly and began to run. The Apprentice lost his balance and fell against a suit of armour, pulling it to the ground on top of himself. Sobbing uncontrollably, Sand raced down the corridor.

People rushed from the room at the noise, in time to catch sight of Sand's cloak disappearing around a corner. Atwin and Erris saw the Apprentice entangled in the armour, and helped the shaken young man to his feet.

"Well," said Selwyn. "That was fun."

TWENTY NINE

Sometime after midnight, Sand found Mist in the Maestro's study. The old man had stayed up with her and now dozed in his armchair. On the table, folded neatly, was a cloak the Maestro had triumphantly produced after Sand was revealed as the Awakener.

He said its location in a hidden vault beneath the College had been passed down through the centuries, known only to the Maestro, sealed in and miraculously preserved. The cloak was made of thick silk in the traditional blue of the College, but it had a black border. No other rank had ever been given that colour, so it had to belong to the Awakener.

When Sand entered, the Maestro awoke. The Awakener was ragged in appearance and tattered in spirit. His eyes darted to and fro and his body shook, but his eyes were dry. Without hesitation, Miyam went to him and slipped an arm about his waist, leading him to a chair. Before she could get a chair for herself, he grabbed at her and pulled her close, burying his face against her body.

She wrapped her arms about his head and shoulders and gently stroked his hair. The Maestro silently left the room. Mist held Sand lovingly as he trembled in her arms. Finally, he dragged himself into a semblance of control and pulled back so that he could look into her eyes. He smiled wanly. She returned the smile and bent down to kiss him tenderly.

"I need your help," he blurted.

"Of course you do," she said. "That's what I'm here for." She brushed the straggly hair from his face and kissed him again. "I have the potion ready."

He breathed a sigh of relief. He could use the link that was already there, and the potion would make the channel easier to secure. Then he could transfer some of his own emotional upheaval to her so that he could think.

He drank half the potion without ceremony and gave the rest to her. She drained the goblet. He took her hand in his and began the mental probe. Sand would need his wits in the days ahead. He could not cope with the conflict within and still be an effective leader. So she willingly took the burden onto her own shoulders.

They would need to remain in close contact, so she could keep the tide under control for him, so that he might concentrate on his job. It did not take long. When it was finished, Sand straightened. Mist trembled, but held steady. Without speaking, they curled up together on the hearth before the embers of the fire and slept.

Early the next morning, Sand led Mist by the hand toward the conference chamber. All was ominously quiet. The corridors were empty and the flagstone floor was cold. The sudden appearance of another revealer approaching caused Mist to jump in response to Sand's surprise. The Adept nodded as he passed.

"Sand," he said in greeting.

"Reep," Sand replied.

The Adept walked on and Sand continued on his way. Then Reep turned and looked back.

"Sand?" he said.

Sand turned. "Yes?"

"Why do you wear black? I have never heard of a rank that carries that colour."

"I doubt it not. There is only one."

"Which?" Then his eyes widened as he realised what the black meant. "The Awakener?" he said in awe.

Sand did not reply.

"When did that happen?"

Sand stood impassively.

"Well, congratulations!"

"I'm terribly sorry Reep," said Sand then. "But I have a very important meeting to attend."

"Yes, of course, Sir," said Reep. "I'm sorry I kept you." He hurried off.

The council proceeded with Sand now taking the lead. To all outward appearances, he was his old self. His strength was indomitable and his great mind swept all others before it. His status as the Awakener put him above everyone else in the room, his black bordered cloak emphasizing the point.

Mist sat at the head of the table, saying nothing. The struggle within kept her vague to the world around her. Her own personality was submerged beneath Sand's emotional struggle. Her very essence belonged to the Awakener, and they were as one person. There was no verbal interaction between them, but they were linked inseparably.

Their usual habit of completing each other's sentences was gone, which made those who knew them rather nervous. She trembled constantly and twitched occasionally. Any comments directed at her took some moments to sink in, and her answers were short and inconsequential. The Maestro watched her in concern.

"The first thing we need to realise is that physical war is no longer an option," said Sand.

"So what do we do?" said Lenent of Zelona.

"We must surrender the shore to the enemy."

"What?" said Tarnel in shock. "You must be joking!"

Mist's body gave a jolt, but Sand stood firm.

"I'm deadly serious," Sand defended himself. "The Leader is playing with us. It knows we can't win, and each person we lose in defence makes Its final victory more inevitable. It's our move."

"But how can we even think of retreat?" said Selwyn. "That would be certain failure!"

Mist twitched.

"Our failure is certain if we don't retreat," said Sand calmly. "A good commander has to know the value of strategic withdrawal. Why waste lives?"

"So we retreat," said Erris of Mytar. "Then what?"

"The army will camp outside Eeasto, where they will wait."

"Wait for what?" said Axellandr.

"For the signal, of course," Sand replied. "We'll give the Leader a surprise."

"What sort of surprise?" said Lenent suspiciously.

"The Leader expects physical attack. Or defence, as the case may be. We will not give It what It expects."

"I see," said Atwin. "We strike mentally?"

"Precisely."

"But how?"

"That's where you and the Princess come in," Sand stated. "I need Naali and Leena to hold the mind link together. I'll take the focus, first joining the revealers together, then through you I'll join with the rest of the people."

Atwin frowned. "I thought it was not safe for Netta to use Leena's power right now."

"I'm sorry, my friend, but we'll have to take that risk. There's no other way to do this."

Atwin nodded dubiously. "What do we do once we are all joined?"

"The revealers will know what to do and they'll be under my control. Your link will include the army and other non-College personnel. The minds will be untrained and untested, so I won't be asking them to do any of the real work. The revealers can handle that. Your link will provide the muscle. Then we'll give the Leader something to think about."

"Sounds good to me," said Axellandr. "How do we call the people together?"

"Chain of command," Atwin replied.

Sand nodded. "Representatives will come to me to learn the basics, and they'll teach the rest."

"I cannot believe you are pinning all our hopes on some... nebulous power, which I am not even sure exists," said Selwyn harshly.

Mist twitched again and Selwyn slammed a fist down on the table. "Must she stay here in that condition? She is not helping and she makes me nervous."

The woman gave a little jolt.

"Can we not send her away?"

"That would not be a good idea," said the Maestro from his unobtrusive corner. "It's vital that she stay."

"Why? What good is she doing?"

"Suffice it to say that her and Sand can't be separated at this time."

"Why?"

"Because it could kill him," said the Maestro.

"I cannot believe this..." Selwyn mumbled under his breath.

The army gathered outside Eeasto. Behind them, just outside the city wall, stood four small figures. Evelar and Miyam stood silently, alongside Netta and Atwin. The kalkar horde stood motionless on the south bank of Lake Asto. The two forces awaited sunset.

The sun sank lower and the sky on the horizon began to glow orange. Evelar gathered himself for the link. Every living human mind would soon be his to control.

He gave the signal and Atwin began to gather the army. Netta followed his lead and gathered the civilian minds to her. With the two amulets augmenting the power, the two joined minds, and the non-College half of the link was secured. Glowing blue, they stood firm.

Then Evelar called the revealers to him. For them it was easier, their well trained minds familiar with the technique. When the link was established, Evelar reached out and joined with the Atwin/Netta link. He felt the force of the minds within him and smiled. The Leader had no idea that humans could control such power.

The sky darkened. Evelar waited. Finally, with an ominous reverberating crack, the kalkar army came to life. They milled around for a moment. Evelar waited. Within minutes, order was established and the dark horde stared across the lake at the human force on the other side.

Still Evelar waited. Eventually, it became clear that the horde mind was in action, and the kalkar army began to prepare to cross the lake. They squatted and after several tense moments the wings began to spread.

Still Evelar waited. As one, the kalkar horde rose from its collective crouch and spread wings wide. Each individual now sported a wing span of three yards. With a push, they rose from the ground in their thousands.

And still Evelar waited. He had gathered a huge amount of energy within, and he wanted the right moment to release it. Finally, as the front ranks approached the near side of the lake, Evelar sent the energy at them in a concentrated wave.

The front ranks reeled back. A good many kalkar

plummeted into the deadly water below. Those that were able to stay aloft battled their way back to the far shore. The enemy ranks were in disarray.

Evelar searched for the group mind. It had all but disintegrated. One more strike and the enemy would be crippled irreparably. Evelar gathered the energy and sent several short bursts. The group mind of the kalkar fell apart.

The dark horde milled about aimlessly, but Evelar did not dissolve the human link. He wanted to make sure the horde was really broken. Individual kalkar stumbled and fell. Some toppled into the lake. Some even threw themselves into the water, rather than endure the pain that the attack had caused. The water boiled.

Finally, Evelar allowed the human minds to slowly separate. It would be a long time before the Leader could gather Its horde together into a semblance of order. Atwin sent a force across the lake and into the enemy lines to wreak what havoc they could while the horde was out of action. Then the four made their way back to the council chamber.

As a precaution, Sand had asked the revealers to be ready to re-establish the link. On occasion, he checked the enemy's progress, monitoring the state of their group mind. The Leader was attempting to bring them back together, but the kalkar were not cooperating.

Some were simply too weak or in too much pain to join the group. Others had thrown up a mental shield and huddled within their own protective shell, totally inaccessible to outside influence. Some individuals sensed that the Leader wanted to use them again and chose not to cooperate through fear.

The Leader exerted Its will, but to no avail. Its anger was dangerous, but there was no way It could pull Its force together to send it on another strike. The Leader was becoming desperate and the Awakener knew something was going to happen.

Still he was unprepared when it did happen. In the council chamber, a shock wave swept over all in the room, and the Kings and their advisers clutched at their heads in pain.

Netta and Atwin felt the darkness arrive as did, of all people, the funny old king of Martose. The Maestro groaned. Mist gave one massive convulsion and collapsed on the table. Sand sagged against a chair as the tide of his emotions came flooding back into his own mind and body from the severed link.

With a curse, the Maestro jumped up and rushed to the Awakener, dragging him closer to Mist's limp form. The old revealer put one hand on the girl's head and the other on Sand's forehead. He concentrated. Then he brought his hands together in a thunderous clap, mending the channel. Mist snapped upright, once more trembling with the struggle. Sand straightened and took a deep breath.

"Thank you, Sir," he said. He led the weary old man back to his seat.

"What was that?" asked Selwyn.

"Something very bad has come into our world," Sand replied.

Lenent rose slowly and went to the window to look out over the battle field. "Ah... I think you should see this," he said.

Axellandr joined him. "What is that?" he said in a hushed tone.

The others followed.

"There is nothing there," said Selwyn.

"Correction," said Atwin. "It is something made of nothing!"

Sand and the Maestro stared at it, and the Leader's identity was suddenly and startlingly revealed.

"What is it?" said Erris nervously.

"I have no idea," said Tarnel. "But I like it not."

Then the funny old king tottered over and peaked over his son Axellandr's shoulder.

"It is Kayus..." he said in fearful wonder.

THIRTY

Sand shared a look with the Maestro. Then he took Mist by the hand and both disappeared. The Maestro and the others looked out over the field to see the two revealers appear before the lines outside the walls of the College. The council made its way outside, onto the battlements, to watch.

There was an evil laugh from the one called Kayus, and the Lord of Nothingness rushed to meet the Awakener. The revealer stood tall, supported invisibly by the girl at his side. His mind was ready, the combined minds of the College once again under his control. This was the first battle for the Awakener. This would prove his identity beyond all doubt.

"I greet thee, empty one," he said to the one called Kayus.

"Well met, Awakener," said Kayus gleefully. "Thy presence doth refresh my spirit. Come, who is the small one on whom you lean so heavy?"

"That is not important."

But it was important. Evelar knew that he could not be the Awakener without her, and Kayus knew that she was his strength.

"We shall see, Awakener. Let us not waste any more time."

Kayus did not simply strike. It invaded. The blow threatened to send Evelar reeling backwards, but the collected minds of the College of the Art held strong in the Awakener's grasp.

From somewhere in the depths of his soul, where his link to the revealers was still in place, Evelar found the power to return the attack. Kayus screamed, but the scream became a laugh.

"Thou shalt not thwart me so quickly, Awakener!"

As the human race watched in awe a battle raged, between a mortal man and a terrible spirit. For a long time they were evenly matched, the Awakener strengthened by the well trained minds under his control.

The two great powers traded titanic blows in rapid succession, but slowly cracks began to appear in the human collective. Several revealers dropped away from the link with the Awakener, either dead or unconscious. With each successive blow from the enemy, more of the weaker minds were blasted away.

The Awakener returned the assault but his blows had less impact than before. He felt the power weakening, and desperately held tight to the stronger minds, but the pure muscle power of those lesser minds was gone now. The loyal minds of his collective clutched to the link but it was becoming clear as more and more were cast off that the enemy was now the stronger power.

Blow after blow rained down on their valiant mind link, and soon the last few strongest minds began to fail. In the end, the last of the revealers disappeared from his mind, and the Awakener was left alone with only Miyam holding tight. Kayus was intrigued.

"So, the small one hath power after all!"

Kayus struck again, this time straight at her. The girl flinched and fell to her knees, but did not break. Evelar clutched at his temples. Before they could recover Kayus struck yet again, but deviously this time. A tendril of power slipped through the Awakener's defences and deep into his mind.

The toughest shield could not withstand the probity of nothing. How can you fight nothing? He pushed against the force entering him, but his power slipped through it, not even slowing it.

Only then, while fighting for possession of his own mind, did Evelar learn the true nature of Kayus' power. And then his mind was not his own. His consciousness watched powerless as his own hand swung back and struck the woman across the side of the head.

The watchers on the walls gasped. Miyam reeled from the blow, clutching at her head, ejected cruelly from Evelar's mind. Deep within, the man's soul recognised her, and for the briefest moment struggled for dominance. He saw her huddled on the ground, hands over her ears, moaning softly. She looked up at him pleadingly, tears streaming.

The part that was still Evelar reached out to her in concern. He placed a hand gently on her head and, before Kayus could prevent it, sent her out of danger, placing her in the midst of the Kings and their advisers on the walls of the College. Kayus struck then and the Awakener fell screaming to the ground.

Suddenly, the screaming stopped. Despite her throbbing head, Mist stood up, helped by Atwin and the Maestro, and looked. The Awakener stood, but the man was a puppet. His body moved jerkily as Kayus took full possession. It made him raise one hand. Mist felt the bolt of energy, and cried out as a large section of the gathered army was blasted away.

"We have to help him!" said Mist then.

"Help him?" said Selwyn incredulously. "He just attacked you!"

"It wasn't his fault!"

Another burst came. More defenders fell away.

"We have to stop it!" said the Maestro then.

"How?" said Mist shakily. "The Awakener is lost."

"Lost?" said Axellandr. "What do you mean?"

"Kayus has control," Mist explained.

"You mean that is Kayus doing that?" said Atwin.

The Maestro nodded. "It's picking off our people one by one. It's systematically destroying our defence."

"Then the battle is lost..." said Lenent.

"And the war," said Erris despondently.

Out on the field, the Awakener finally stopped fighting. He could not succeed. He gave in to the Leader. A laugh escaped his lips. It was the cold, maniacal laugh of Kayus.

Then, quite suddenly, the laugh died and a growl filled its place. The observers looked in awe at the spirit that had appeared. Shining purest white, the spirit stood silently, daring Kayus to accept the challenge.

Mist watched the scene, knuckles white as her hands clenched helplessly by her sides. Her head still throbbed, but she ignored it. From within Evelar's pliant, doll-like body, Kayus laughed.

"Comest thou here to join me, Brother?"

"No, Kayus."

"Thinkest thou perhaps to fight me, Brother?"

"If thou wouldst deem it necessary," the spirit answered.

"Thy confidence will be thine undoing, Brother. Give up this pretence of power."

"Thou shalt know whose power is pretence, Kayus."

Behind the great spirit another appeared, and others, all glowing their own special colour. The twelve forgotten councillors ranked behind their leader.

"So," said Kayus. "Still the mighty Zayus dost others need, to fight his battles for him."

Zayus did not answer. The spirit shimmered and joined

Kayus within the Awakener's body. A great battle followed.

The two mighty spirits waged war within the body of the man. The body was tossed about. Light exploded about it and strange cries issued from its lips. Mist clutched at the parapet, watching in fear.

One of the twelve separated itself from the others, and streaked toward her in a rainbow of colours. It joined the Kings on the wall.

"I am Herm," it said. "I am come to inform thee that we are here..."

"I am so glad you told us," said Selwyn.

"To help," said Herm, with a stern look at Selwyn.

The spirit turned to look at Mist. He placed a hand on her head in benediction, and her pain disappeared. She looked at him in wonder.

"Fear not for thy beloved, faithful one," he said gently. "The future of thy world doth rest on his shoulders, but behind him we do stand."

Mist nodded uncertainly.

"I am Herm, reader of the signs," the spirit said then. "Know that what I say will come to pass. Mighty Zayus will prevail."

With that enigmatic statement, Herm streaked back to rejoin the divine council. One by one, the twelve high councillors joined Zayus within the Awakener's frail human body, and it began to glow. Finally, Kayus was expelled.

"Why wilt thou not face me alone, Zayus?" the spirit of nothing cried.

"Thou knowest my nature is not such, Kayus. It is what differs between thee and me. These others are all part of me, and I am not whole without them. Thou art always alone, Kayus, and that is why thou wilt fail."

"Enough. Face me, Brother!"

But more spirits appeared. Countless souls ranged

themselves on the field, a great multitude of lesser spirits. These, one by one, joined their council within the body of the Awakener.

Faster and faster they entered the body, in a stream of light. The glow about the man's body increased, until it became too painful to watch directly. Finally, all became one in the Awakener. The spiritual conglomerate faced its age-old enemy.

The first strike was titanic. The sky overhead rolled, and ozone crackled in the air. Mist flinched. The second strike sent sparks flying between the two combatants, and the smell of burning sulphur filled the air. Kayus screamed in hurt and frustration. Zayus spoke from within the conglomerate.

"Now dost thou know, Kayus? Thou art Nothingness. I am All Things. Thou canst defeat me not."

Kayus screamed. "We shall see!"

The Lord of Nothingness struck again. The skies crashed. The night was banished. The very stars seemed to explode overhead. The gods within the man reeled back and the doll-like body flipped over backwards.

Kayus laughed and struck again. The body rolled, tumbling helplessly, as if pushed by a great wind. Mist groaned and put a fist in her mouth to stop herself from crying out.

"Thy vessel doth fail thee, Zayus."

There was no reply. But the body picked itself up and rose to its full height. It stood tall and straight. It waited. Zayus did not strike. Kayus laughed again and struck.

The blow reached its target. It hit the edge of the glow. It bent. It reflected. And it rebounded. Kayus was thrown back under the force of Its own power. Then the gods sent out a bolt of lightning and the Nothingness was thrown backward. Kayus screamed.

The gods struck again and sulphur burned in the air. Kayus reeled even further back. It tried to return the attack and was blocked again, Its power sent back onto Itself. Kayus screamed again.

Zayus struck again and again. And Kayus fled.

With a despairing wail, the spirit of Nothingness was sent back to Its eternal exile. But, just as the wailing faded into the distance and was lost in time, the echo of a laugh came floating back.

Slowly, the divine host began to break away from its link within Evelar's body. The multitude of lesser spirits assembled on the field, jointly rising and returning to their home in the otherworld.

The twelve councillor spirits then separated from the link. The glow about the Awakener's body subsided, and only Zayus remained within. The twelve waited in silence, glowing.

Then Zayus slipped out of the man and joined his brethren. The body, relieved of its divine visitor, collapsed sack-like to the ground.

Mist gasped. She reached out with her mind to see if he was alright. She found nothing. Frantically, she focused her mind on the lifeless form, desperate to find some spark of life. He did not respond.

The Maestro placed a hand on her shoulder, and she looked at him, stricken. She shook her head and searched again, not wanting to believe it, but Zayus stood by the empty body, head bowed in sorrow. The god bent and picked him up. Mist looked on in horror as realisation set in. She cried out in agony.

"NOOOOOOOO!" she screamed, a long drawn out cry of anguish.

Heedless of the deadly drop, the woman tried to jump over the parapet, desperate to reach him. The Maestro and

Atwin held her back and she struggled frantically against them, sobbing hysterically.

The god rose up, taking the body with him. She screamed again and fought against the two that held her. The two men tried to calm her, but still she struggled.

"Let me go!" she sobbed.

Then, a spirit separated himself from the others and raced toward her, shining golden. The spirit stood in front of her on the parapet and smiled. All fight seemed to drain from her, and the men fell back to gaze on the face of Pollon. The spirit spread his arms to her.

"Come, beloved," he said gently.

She went to him and he enclosed her in his divine embrace. He rose up, taking her with him, and in a streak of golden light they followed after Zayus and the body of the Awakener. The rest of the twelve fell in behind and were gone.

When the divine light finally faded from the sky, the silence was deafening. The Maestro looked up, to where his two best pupils had disappeared into the ether. He bowed his head in the profoundest grief.

* * *

THIRTY ONE

Light illuminated the world. It was a light that came from nothing and everything. There was no sun, but everything gave off a soft blue glow. Cool, pure, blue. The woman and the spirit drank in the beauty of the place.

On entry into this dimension of blueness, the spirit had assumed his true form. He shimmered next to the woman, a being of pure golden light. The being of light extended what might have been a hand. The woman took it in hers, and he led her into the glowing blue space.

They walked together in a corridor of light. She knew the meaning of ultimate peace. Even the grief that raged in her heart could be forgotten here. After an eternity that took no time at all, the spirit raised his head.

"Come," he said in his golden voice. "They await thee."

The spirit led the woman by the hand, showing her the blue light in all its glory. He did not hurry. Time seemed to have no meaning in the blue. Forever and a second blurred into one and could not be distinguished. But in her anguished heart she fretted.

Eventually, they came to a wondrous light. They paused, and the woman gazed in awe. It was a small room, made entirely of blue light but solid, with floor, walls, seats and windows.

The spirit bade her sit and they began to move, leaving the bright light behind. Through the windows she could now see blackness and stars, as if she were floating in a bubble in the night sky.

At last they approached a structure, an unearthly building of turrets and long stretching limbs. It looked like a great academy in the grand old style, but that was merely her human interpretation of what could not be explained by any previous experience. Atop the structure, was a huge glowing blue dome, the focus of the blue light. The moving room attached itself to the side of the building and the door opened.

"Come," said the spirit and he led her inside.

The woman followed the spirit into the great entrance hall of the blue building. He led her down a corridor and up an impossibly long flight of stairs. Logic told her that they had broken free of the dimensions of what her mind told her was a building. But the stairs rose ever upward.

Finally, they entered a long corridor, at the end of which was a door. They entered the room. Inside the door, the woman stopped in awe. The hall was huge and it had no walls. Outside was starry blackness, inside was glowing blue. She knew her mind was doing its best to show her what she thought should be there, but she could not accept it.

A very human-sounding cough brought her attention back to the hall and its occupants. Seated on the floor, cross-legged, was a being of utter whiteness. It shone with all the energy of life itself.

"Come forward, Child," said Zayus in his softly booming voice.

The woman moved forward, unable to resist that divine call.

"Be thou not afraid, Child. I welcome thee."

The woman came closer, her eyes lowered in the great spirit's presence.

"What dost thou fear, Child?"

The woman looked up timidly.

"Speak, my child."

"I don't fear for myself, Lord Zayus."

"Thou fearest for thy beloved, my child?"

The woman lowered her head and nodded.

"Knowest thou that he was not intended to come here?"

She looked up again. "What do you mean?"

"The one called Awakener hast not completed his predestined task. He should not be here."

"Then why did he die?"

The spirit sighed. "It was a mistake."

"A mistake?"

"We... knew not that such energies would be unleashed."

She shook her head. "I don't understand."

"To defeat my brother Kayus, we of the blue had to combine our energies in one vessel. Of those on offer, the Awakener was the only one capable of withstanding such a linkage. His mind is admirable. But his body..."

"What of it?"

"Flesh and blood, my child. Thou who art still confined in the physical realm are weak in body. Only a being of energy such as I could contain the forces of light."

"Then why did you use him?"

The spirit hesitated. "We forgot the frailty of flesh and blood."

"So it was your fault!" she said, angry now. "You killed him because of your arrogance and stupidity! How could you be so foolish? I don't care if you smite me down by raising your hand. I don't care!"

The spirit raised his hand. She kept going.

"You didn't even stop to think. You just dove right in, dragging every other spirit in with you, without even considering what it might do to him. You are a fool, Zayus! The Awakener was human, like me. He may have had the mental powers of a god, but he was still human. Can't you see that?"

"I am sorry, Child."

"Sorry? What good is that? How can I go back down there without him? Pollon once told me that without me the Awakener is nothing. But what am I without the Awakener?" She was crying now. "I hate you, Zayus. I hate all of you!"

"Enough," he said.

The voice was not harsh, nor angry. But in its calmness was a warning. The woman sank to the floor and buried her head in her arms.

"Before thou rend me with thy power, child," said the spirit. "Thou shouldst know that we of the blue are not the great divine beings thou believe us to be. We are human souls like thee, we make mistakes like thee. This image is but a projection, that I might speak with thee."

She said nothing.

"Thy beloved was brought here before his time. His task in thy world is not complete. Therefore he will not remain here."

She raised her head.

"Because the fault for his death is ours, we shall return him to thee."

She gave a little sob.

"Mine own energy already begins to heal the Awakener's spirit. Embrosia at this moment doth heal his body."

"But... Embrosia is death to a human body. How can it heal?"

"His body is already dead, child."

"I don't understand."

"Is it not sufficient to know that he will live?"

"I want to see him."

"That is not advisable, child. He is not of either world now. His body and his spirit are separated."

"Then show me his body."

Zayus hesitated. "Ask not, Child. It would only distress thee further."

"I want to see him," she said firmly.

The spirit sighed.

Pollon appeared. "Come, my beloved."

"Hate me not, my child," said Zayus gently as she followed the golden spirit from the hall.

After the long climb to find Zayus, the walk to where the man was housed was relatively short. Leaving what her mind tried to tell her was a hall, Pollon led the woman down a corridor and one flight of stairs, which were open to the night sky.

They entered another room filled with blue light like the rest. In the centre of the room was a strange round table, glowing blue with a great many tiny lights flickering on its top, breaking its sleek surface with spots of glowing colour.

On the far wall, several windows glowed blue. One held the shadowy shape of a human body, appearing to float in the light. She reached out to touch the glowing surface. It was hard like glass, and the glow intensified at the touch of her hand, but the body did not respond.

Pollon was watching her. "It is only a shell," he said.

She longed to touch the body, feel the hair that floated about his head like a halo.

"But I thought Zayus had healed him."

"It is not easy to leave this place."

"I don't understand."

"The body is ready to accept the spirit. It lives, but has no consciousness. His soul must want to re-enter the body."

"Does he not want to?"

"It is difficult to leave this place," the spirit replied.

She looked around. She felt the serenity of the place, but felt somehow removed from it.

"What is this place?"

"It is the place of healing, the place of life."

"What does that mean?"

"This place... is the centre of life. Here is the heart of the soul ship. The energy of our consciousness is centred on this point. All our souls are connected to this place and here we always return, to be stored until needed."

She shook her head, the strange words meaning little and the confusion only made greater by the spirit's explanation.

"Wouldst thou speak with him?"

She nodded. Pollon indicated a round light on the wall beside one of the windows, and told her to press it. The window opened and the spirit bade her step inside. She felt the light take hold of her body as the door closed her in. Then there was a slight shimmer about her and she found herself in a garden.

It was a garden without colour. Still it was beautiful. She walked down a white path, lined with white trees, under a white sky. The white pebbles on the white ground crunched under her white feet. She looked at Pollon beside her and he too shone white.

He smiled and spoke in her mind. *'Look, my beloved.'*

She looked to where Pollon indicated. On the ground by a white stream, a white spirit sat cross-legged. She walked slowly to where the spirit sat.

'Hello?' she said.

'Thou art welcome,' said the spirit.

'Who are you?'

The spirit looked at her blankly. *'I am... I was...'*

Her eyes opened wide. *'Evelar?'* She looked from the spirit to Pollon and back again. *'Is that you?'*

'I...' the spirit hesitated. *'I... cannot remember.'*

*

The woman sat with the spirit for a long time. Or was it a moment? At some point, Pollon left. At another point, a female spirit appeared. She shone a rosy white, her ethereal features a mask of purest love. The woman felt drawn to her.

'*Are you Aphris?*' she said.

'*Yes, dear one,*' the joiner of hearts replied.

'*Why have you come?*'

'*Because I am needed.*'

The woman smiled. '*Yes,*' she said.

'*What concerns thee, dear one?*'

The woman looked at the spirit. '*He's so lost,*' she said. '*He doesn't know how to return to his body.*'

'*He doth know,*' said the spirit.

'*Then why does he stay like this?*'

'*It is this place. He remembereth not why he should return.*'

'*I thought the soul could remember when it left the body...*'

'*It can. But not in this place.*'

'*I don't understand.*'

'*This is the place of light and life and love. It is the centre of all things. But it is also the place of cleansing, which doth include forgetting. It is the place through which souls pass before returning to thy world in a new body.*'

'*Will he remember?*'

'*Perhaps, when he doth return, he will remember this place. We have never sent a spirit back to the physical world in the same body from whence it came.*'

'*But will he remember, now, what his life was, so that he can go back?*'

'*He doth need reminding, which it seemest thou hast done admirably.*'

'*Then why doesn't he go back?*'

'*Because memory is not enough. He doth need a reason.*'

He doth need something for which he will go back.'

'Won't he go back for me?' she said in a small voice.

'I doubt it not. But thou art here with him. Why goeth back should he?'

'What should I do?'

'Thou must return to thy world without him...'

'I can't!' she cried.

'...and callest thou him from there,' the goddess finished. *'Be thou not afraid, dear one. He doth know that his destiny as the Awakener is incomplete. And there is another task yet to be fulfilled.'*

'What task is that?'

The goddess smiled knowingly, and indicated with a nod to something behind the woman. She looked around. Standing some distance away was another glowing spirit. It shone the same white as the scenery, and it was the size of a small child.

'Who is that?' asked the woman.

'That is one who doth wait.'

'For what?'

'It doth wait for a body in which it may return to thy world.'

'How long must it wait?'

'Until thee and the Awakener hath created it.'

'Oh!'

'That is why back the Awakener must go. And the child will have a destiny greater even than that of his father.'

* * *

THIRTY TWO

The counsellor raised a hand for silence. The gathered members of the College hushed.

"We are here today," she began, "to celebrate a passing. The passing of many, but also the passing of one who was the Awakener. We have lost a great many members in the recent conflict, a loss that is felt by all. But the loss of the Awakener is an even greater blow.

"He was a light, destined to lead the way to a new and greater understanding. But that light was snuffed out before it had a chance to burn. His destiny has taken him from us. Yet we should not mourn. Sand has gone home. We should not deny him his rest because we are selfish. In his passing see instead the higher good."

There was a murmur as the Maestro stood and stopped the counsellor with an upraised hand.

"My friends, I am finding it difficult to accept this loss," the Maestro began. "Our prophets were very clear on the Awakener's future. It is my opinion that he was not supposed to die. I know that we cannot deny him his rest, but I cannot do anything less than mourn. Perhaps not for him, but for us and the future we will now never see.

"The Awakener is gone before his time. The future is no longer certain. We have lost so many. I call on you now to give all you can for the future. We must rebuild our strength, and go on without the Awakener to guide us."

He stopped. All of the gathering looked up, to where

a glowing figure had appeared. Slowly, another form materialised beside the spirit. The second figure slowly descended and took solid form. It was a young woman in the green-bordered cloak of a journeyer. Gently, fluidly, the woman began to dance.

She spun slowly, and the gathered members recognised the opening movement of the Qarama, the dance of marriage. Though she danced alone, the woman moved as if she were not alone. It seemed an invisible partner danced with her.

As the Maestro watched, he thought his eyes must be playing tricks on him. The invisible partner was almost solid. He could have sworn that there was someone there.

The dance continued, and a shimmering light, faint at first, slowly grew where a partner would have been. The light began to solidify, and now it seemed a ghost danced with her. The Maestro closed his eyes to clear his vision then opened them again. The light was even stronger.

In the awed silence of the hall, a miracle was occurring. The light appeared to be solid. The figure was insubstantial, barely distinguishable as a figure, but it was becoming clear that a man danced with her. His features were a blur.

The Maestro watched transfixed as the figure grew yet more real. Soon it became apparent that the man wore a cloak. The cloak became recognisable as a blue revealer's cloak. With a jolt, the Maestro realised that the border was black. The man was solid now and seemed very much alive.

The dance was coming to an end. The couple whirled into the final movement and stopped. She raised her eyes to his and a small sob escaped her.

"It worked?" she whispered.

He touched her face and smiled. Then they were in each other's arms. The audience breathed a collective sigh. The Maestro came out of his trance and went to them. He coughed to get their attention.

"Sand?" he said, very quietly.

The man nodded once.

"Are you really here?"

The man nodded again.

"Are you alive?"

The man grinned, a flash of gold in his brown eyes. The woman snuggled closer and the man held her tightly. He looked down at her lovingly.

"Wouldst thou excuse us, Sir?" he whispered.

"Of course," he said, bemused by the archaic phrase.

The man bent to kiss the woman and together they vanished. The Maestro followed them with his mind. Then, embarrassed, he quickly broke the contact. He turned to the gathered Members.

"My friends," he said to the congregation in general. "We have witnessed a miracle. Let us rejoice."

Without the Leader to hold the dark army together, the kalkar lost interest in fighting. Then one evening, quite soon after the great battle, the horde quietly left. The war was over.

Four Zjobock Dhort stood watching as her people rose above the battle field and flew south. Even though there was no Leader threatening her existence, she was still afraid to rejoin them. All kalkar knew of her traitorous actions and they would never welcome her back. Ahead, a long life of exile awaited her.

When a male landed on the hill where she watched, Four cowered away. She was terrified that her time of punishment had begun. But the familiar touch of the male's beautiful mind reassured her.

"Four Zjobock Dhort," he rasped. "Why do you abandon your people?"

"I do so unwillingly," she replied.

"Then why?"

"I am no longer welcome."

"The Leader is no more," the male stated. "You will not be turned away."

"But I will be shunned. I do not wish to live in disgrace."

"Is self-imposed exile any better?"

"Alone, I will never hear their words. There will be no whispered condemnation. They will forget me."

"To be forgotten is worse than death," he replied.

"No," said Four. "To be forgotten is to be at peace."

"I do not wish you to be forgotten."

"What is it to you if I do not return?"

"The memories I have would be the last. I would like more."

"What can you offer me if I do return?"

"I offer protection. I will allow no words to be spoken against you. I will praise you for your courage and your wisdom."

"Twelve Suppreck Asfar, what you offer would require a mating. Is this your intention?"

"It is. Will you accept?"

Four looked out over the plain. She gazed toward where the retreating force could still be seen in the distance, heading for the island crossing far to the south.

"Yes," she replied.

The human armies broke up into their separate units and, gathering up the civilian refugees, headed home to restore their cities and repair their homes. The first to leave was the farmer, Freakles. In the conference hall at the College he took his leave of the Kings of Sharné.

"We wish you all the best in your new title, Freakles," said Atwin with a smile.

"Thanks, Sir, but I won't be accepting it."

"I am sorry to hear that. You know you had the support of the army, and that is very important to a king. From what I hear your country needs you. There is no other heir."

"Beggin' your pardon, Sir, but there's someone with a better claim, and much more suited to the job than me."

"There is?"

Freakles gestured to the young woman standing beside him. She exuded an air of grace and poise with a quiet confidence as she met the King's gaze with a strength that belied her youth.

Atwin had hardly noticed the girl's silent presence in the conference hall over the past weeks, and now he stopped to look for the first time. Who was this intriguing young woman? She gave a low bow and a smile.

"I am Mirta, Your Majesty. I am Derrek's cousin."

Atwin's eyes widened. "Why did you not introduce yourself before?"

"Everyone was so focused on poor Freakles, I felt I could do more good helping him. But now he insists that I come forward."

"Quite right too," said Lenent from his seat beside the Regent. "There is no law that says the heir must be male."

"No, Sir. But it was clear that he was the choice of the people. I hope they will accept me."

"I assure you, Mirta, they will love you," said Averil with a smile. "It has worked in Shirall for centuries. It will be good to see another ruling queen."

The other kings took their decimated armies, gathered their scattered peoples, and one by one departed Eeasto for their shattered homes. Finally, only the survivors of Zelona still waited for their king's word, along with the armies of Shirall and Drasmil.

The Queen and Princess of Shirall sat talking together

with the Regent and her daughter, letting the military men deal with business. Captain Poppel stood before his king in the presence of the others. King Atwin of Drasmil and his brother Prince Calib watched. Both had witnessed this humble captain in control of his rag-tag army with appreciation. He was a skilled officer.

"Sir, the soldiers are getting restless. They miss their families, exhiled in the west so many months ago. They want to know when we will head for home."

"As soon as you are ready, Poppel," said the King of Zelona. "But first I have some business to attend to."

The King rose and approached the Captain.

"For excellence in the field, accept this honour, General Poppel," he said with a grin as he pinned something to the man's collar.

As the King returned to his seat, Poppel glowed with pride, the gold stars of his promotion gleaming on his lapel.

"Thank you, Sir!" he breathed.

"Now, Poppel, I have a very important task for you. I need you to lead the people home."

"Yes, Sir! Of course, Sir! But... aren't you coming with us?"

"No, Poppel, not just now."

"Sir?"

"As I said, Poppel, I have some business to attend to first."

Atwin looked askance at the King of Zelona. "What are you up to, Lenent?"

The King winked. "I made a promise and I intend to keep it."

From where the women sat, Averil looked up with a smile, and the conversation hushed.

"What is this, Mother?" Netta whispered.

"I think I know," said the Queen.

"But, Sir," said Poppel. "The people need you. They need to know you are alive and well and ready to help them rebuild. What will I tell them?"

"Poppel, you will tell them I am coming home as soon as I may. And when I do, I will be bringing them a queen!"

"Oh!" Poppel gasped.

Averil let out an uncharacteristic little giggle and Delsi grinned, pulling her sister into a hug.

"I am so happy for you, sister dear!"

"Mother?" said Kandi with a frown. "What is going on?"

Poppel smiled at his king. "Congratulations, Your Majesty," he said, eyes twinkling. "And might I say, Sir, it's about time!"

"Yes, Poppel, it is," said Lenent with a grin.

Taking leave of their revealer friends, the royal families of Shirall and Drasmil took ship across the Sea of Skies. At the port in Sar Sor, Calib took the remaining legions on to Drasmil.

"I will get started on the clean up," he said to his brother. "And get everything ready for your coronation."

"Thank you, Cal. I will see you in a few weeks."

Heading on to Shirall, the full extent of the kalkar occupation soon became apparent. The Queen could not see the devastation, but she wrinkled her nose at the smell of smoke. Fields were burned, crops ruined, farms destroyed.

Approaching the city, the true cost of the siege became abundantly clear. The flooded streets had started to dry out, but the buildings were damaged beyond repair. The dual terrors of fire and flood saw to that. Rooves were burned away while floors and walls were rotten. Riding through the streets, Netta could not quite block the sense of loss.

Atwin wasted no time setting the army to work, clearing the streets of debris and rethatching the less damaged buildings. They set up a tent city to house the people while the repairs were under way.

The palace on the hill had escaped the flooding, but there were signs of kalkar everywhere. Even the underground palace had not escaped their fury. A small cohort was diverted from the city to clean out the royal apartments so the family could settle in.

* * *

In the College, a private memorial service was held for all the minds lost in the battle with Kayus, including Opal and her husband Dock, the first College casualties of the war. Sand and the Maestro began to construct a new management policy for the College, to incorporate the new teachings to be introduced by the Awakener.

"I'd like to set up classes in the mental Art for the general public, or at least the nobility," said Sand.

The Maestro frowned. "I'm not sure that's a good idea, my boy. The College is successful because of its secrets. If civilians were to learn some of the trade it might damage our reputation and make us less useful to the world at large."

"Perhaps," said Sand. "But maybe it would give them just enough of a taste to draw in more supplicants. It might just be a good thing."

"True," the Maestro replied. "But what of the danger that some less reputable characters would use such knowledge to their own advantage, or that such people would not respect the complex system of etiquette involved. It is important to prevent violations of privacy."

"Perhaps a compromise, then, whereby people could be taught to use the basic skills inherent within, but the deeper powers would be kept secret. Perhaps people will be more interested in joining the College if they have already tasted some of what a trained revealer can do."

When Mist found them, they were deep in debate over

the issue. Both men looked up when she entered. She said not a word, but looked straight at Sand. His jaw dropped. He stood, rounded the table and went to her.

"Did I miss something?" said the Maestro.

They ignored him. Sand grinned at his wife. That golden gleam was there again behind his eyes. She smiled back.

"What?" said the Maestro.

Sand put a gentle hand on Mist's stomach, and she covered it with her own.

"Oh!" said the Maestro.

Sand and Mist planned to make the journey south for Atwin's coronation, then stay on in Shirall for the birth of the new princess. To their surprise, the Maestro decided to go along.

To the best of their knowledge, the Maestro had not left the College in twenty years. He did not share his motives and they did not press. Welcoming them at Shirall, Netta embraced the Maestro fondly.

"Grandfather," she said. "I am so glad you could come."

"Grandfather?" said Evelar.

The Maestro smiled. "Didn't you know?" he said. "Ordel was my son."

The Princess Kandina had finally come to a realisation. Not only had she made a fool of herself over Atwin, but she had also lost all hope of forming a meaningful relationship with Calib. She felt it was time to apologise to Atwin. His reaction surprised her.

"Kandi, I do not want to talk about it. It is over."

"I just want you to know how sorry I am, about everything."

"You know that changes not what you did."

"I know. But I feel bad."

"And you thought to relieve your conscience?"

"I..."

"Look, Kandi. If you are looking for forgiveness, you will not get it from me, it is too soon for that. I know not when, if ever, I could forgive you. It seems to me you want someone to help you feel better, and that will change nothing."

"No, that is not it," she said. "I do understand and I really am sorry for what I did. Can you not accept that?"

"No, Kandi, I cannot. I will not heal your soul for you. And do not go running to Netta, trying to ease your own conscience, because she knows not what you did. I would like it to stay that way."

Princess Nettayna climbed the stairs to the courtyard above the underground palace. In the time since the war ended the space between the two gates had been transformed. What was once an overgrown ruin was now a lush garden, the first flush of new life heralding the repairs to the old above ground palace that had already begun.

The fountain in the centre of the courtyard had finally been repaired, the stonework cleaned and the pipes cleared. Now the water flowed in beautiful arcs from the statue of Aphris at its centre, the pool filled once more with water reeds, lilies and fish.

The gardens about the fountain had been repaired too, and the new plantings of flowers, herbs and medicinal plants were thriving. In the south west corner was a small garden room, entered by a rose arbour with new plants starting to climb the arch.

In the centre was a circular garden bed with a white stone in the middle and flowers all around. Beyond the garden was a semi-circular seat where the Queen sat. The Princess approached her mother with a smile.

"The garden looks wonderful, Mother."

Delsi smiled. "It smells wonderful too. Just how I remember it before it was ruined. We used to play here as children. Then as young lovers we would sit on this very seat for hours."

"I am sure he would be happy it is restored."

"Yes. I think he likes it here."

"Mother, it is time to go. The others are waiting."

"Yes, angel. We must not keep young Atwin waiting. It is not every day one is crowned king."

* * *

THIRTY THREE

The great plain of Drasmil was a moving sea of people, come to celebrate the new king. A long dark time of doubt was over, and a new light shone on the palace. A king, his new queen, and an heir on the way. The coronation was set to be a glorious affair.

The day dawned bright and clear, the dust of years settled, and the fog of war lifted. In the great audience hall the dignitaries of the world gathered to witness the ceremony. Atwin sat his late father's throne for the first time.

His wife sat at his side, and his brother stood nearby. The congregation held its collective breath as the priest of Zayus, standing in all his pomp and grandeur behind the King, held the crown aloft.

"I bring the blessing of the spirits upon you,

That you may know peace and rule well.

The heart of a king is strong and true,

The people rejoice in song with stories to tell.

Be thou wise, be thou fair, be thou honest too,

I bless this noble king, at the calling of the bell."

The priest lowered the crown to rest on the King's brow. As he did so a lone soldier at the window rang the ceremonial bell, and outside on the walls a thousand bells replied.

The people cheered and the army called his name in acclamation. The priest moved on to stand behind Netta, another crown now in his hands, lifted above for all to see.

"I bring the blessing of the spirits upon you,
That you may know peace and rule well.
The heart of a queen is loyal and true,
The people rejoice in song with stories to tell.
Be thou wise, be thou fair, be thou honest too,
I bless this queen, at the calling of the bell."

The crown was lowered and the bell was rung, the cheering floating in from the massed people outside.

* * *

In the palace garden at Shirall, returned home from the celebrations at Drasmil, Kandina paced as she mumbled under her breath. Why oh why did her mother have to agree to this joining? What was she to do now, when she needed her more than ever, now that she had lost Calib because of her own stupidity?

Now that Atwin was crowned and the formalities were over, and everyone had gone home, her mother would take her away, down to far off forsaken Zelona, where her chance of winning Calib back was next to nothing. Kandi fumed and paced, oblivious to the one who had followed her.

"Kandina, I wish I could say something to help you understand," the King said.

She spun, an angry retort flying easily from her lips. "This is all your fault! Why would I want to hear anything you have to say?"

"I care about you, whether you chose to believe that or not. I want you to be glad that your mother will finally be happy."

"What about me? How can I be glad that my life is about to be ripped apart?"

"I will not let that happen. It is part of the promise I made to your mother, that I would not take her away from you."

"So you would drag me away from my home and the

people I love?"

"No, Kandina. That is precisely what I will not do. We plan to stay in Shirall until you are settled."

"Settled?" she fumed. "You say that as if you have already planned my joining! Who is it? Some far off minor princeling I have never met before?"

"No, Kandina, he will be of your choosing, in your own time."

She shook her head. "Are you trying to tell me you will sit here and wait for me to join with someone before you take my mother away? I do not believe you. Your own country needs you more than that."

"My people have waited a long time. They can wait a little longer."

"But it could be years before I find someone!"

He shook his head. "I think you have already found him."

She sobbed. "He hates me for what I have done. It will never happen."

"Kandina, you are young and beautiful, and he loves you. If he is half the man I think he is, he will not let you wait for long."

She sniffed, wiping at the bothersome tears. "How can you know that?"

"I waited thirteen years too long. I made your mother wait, and I will not sit by and watch you wait. I know he will see reason, sooner than you think."

Some two months later, the new princess was born. The child was small but healthy, with fine golden locks and deep blue eyes that seemed to look right into the soul. Atwin survived the anxiety attack brought on by Netta's labour and they named the child Shedissa.

Shortly after the birth of the little princess, Miyam and

Evelar returned with the Maestro to the College. Miyam's own pregnancy was progressing, and she wanted to be home for the birth. Netta and Atwin promised to travel to Eeasto in a few months' time, when Netta and Shedissa were stronger.

The entire residency of the palaces at Shirall and Drasmil held their breath for Leena's announcement that a boy had been chosen to be the next bearer of Naali. The announcement did not come. The months of joy that preceded the birth were followed by an equal time of worry.

"Why did she not choose?" said Netta in concern.

"I know not," Delsi replied.

"I like this not," said Averil. "Never before has there been no mate chosen for the new princess. What shall we do?"

Delsi shrugged. "We can only wait. Perhaps the boy will come later?"

"Perhaps. Perhaps not."

"Perhaps," said Netta then, "Leena does not wish to choose."

"What do you mean?" said Averil.

"We are at the beginning of a new era," Netta replied. "Perhaps it is no longer necessary for Leena to choose. Perhaps Naali plans to choose for himself?"

"Perhaps," said Delsi dubiously.

The royal family tried to put aside their concern over Leena's failure to choose. The child grew well, soon taking her place at the centre of her family's world. The entire court doted on her, and her bubbling giggle filled the palace with light and laughter.

Kandi came to see the baby several times in the first few weeks, but Atwin would not let her take hold of the child. The young princess was hurt by this, and she found herself pleading with Atwin to let her hold the baby. The situation soon came to a head.

At one point, the room was filled with family visitors, including Calib who was in Shirall reporting to his brother, when Kandina arrived. She moved toward the cot, and looked in at the lovely child. Atwin stood behind her, watching distrustfully.

Kandi reached a hand into the cot to touch the child, and Atwin brushed her aside, picking up the baby and taking her to her mother. Netta looked at him strangely.

"Atwin, what is it? Why will you not let my cousin touch Dissa?"

Atwin did not answer. The room fell quiet. Averil shot a look at Delsi, and the Queen went to her daughter's side. Calib stood quietly by the door, watching as Kandina lowered her head, eyes glimmering with unshed tears.

"What is going on?" said Netta then. "There is something you have not told me."

"It is nothing," Atwin said softly.

"No, it is not. What has Kandi done to deserve this?"

The younger princess let out a sob, quickly stifled. Involuntarily, Calib took a concerned step toward her. Then he stopped, his eyes haunted. Netta looked from one closed face to another.

"Dearest Kandi," said Netta then, "Tell me what this is all about."

The younger princess looked up, tears falling unheeded. She looked about the room at her family. She saw the hurt in their eyes and the conflict. They still loved her, she realised suddenly. But they could not trust her.

She could not let this continue. With a deep, racking sob, she collapsed to her knees by Netta's side and buried her face in the cushions, weeping uncontrollably.

"I am so sorry, Netta," she wailed. "It is alright if you hate me."

"Hate you?" said Netta, surprised. "How could I hate you?"

"It is all my fault!"

"What is?"

"Everything. I told King Gerard to take you away. But I never intended him to give you to the kalkar. I am a horrid person."

Netta looked at those around her. "Is this true?"

They did not reply.

"Atwin?"

He looked about uncertainly. Then he looked at Kandi and back to Netta, and nodded sharply. Netta looked at her weeping cousin.

"Why did you do that, Kandi?" she said gently.

"I... I thought I was in love with Atwin. I thought if you were gone, he would love me too. I am so sorry! I was stupid and selfish. I have hurt you all and I deserve not your kindness. Send me off somewhere, I mind not. If you never want to see me again, I will understand." She broke down, unable to continue.

Netta put a hand on her cousin's bent head and stroked her hair gently. "Why would I want to send you away, Kandi? I love you like a sister."

Kandi shook her head. "How can you? I am horrible!"

Netta smiled. "No you are not. You made a mistake."

"But do you not see? I caused it all. All the pain and horror you went through was because of me!"

"I survived. No permanent harm came of it."

"But you could have died and it would have been my fault!"

"No. What you did was rash, yes, but you did it for love, not out of malice. You do not hate me, do you?"

"Oh no!" said Kandi effusively. "I love you, Netta. I never had a real friend before you."

"Then I forgive you."

Kandi sobbed brokenly, head buried in the cushions. "No one else will..." she mumbled into the cushions.

Netta looked up at the stony faces around her. "I hope you all realise what I just said," she stated pointedly. "The harm was done to me and I forgive. I expect you all to stop this senseless persecution. Kandi is a member of our family. Averil, she is your daughter. Let not one childish mistake destroy that. I will not allow it."

Tears shimmered in the Regent's eyes. Lenent put a comforting hand on Averil's shoulder, and she gave him a small smile.

Calib stared at the Princess, his eyes wide, his heart flipping and dancing in his chest. He glanced at his brother and saw that he was smiling now, no sign of anger remained. Unable to contain his confusion, Calib turned to leave the room.

"Cal," said Netta. "Please hate not my cousin."

Calib turned to look at her, his gaze straying involuntarily to where Kandi had lifted her pleading eyes to watch him.

"I could never hate her," he said with a shuddering breath, his eyes lifting to meet his brother's.

Suddenly Atwin understood.

"It is alright, Cal," said Atwin with a smile. "I want you to be happy. You have my blessing!"

Finally Calib relaxed, his eyes betraying him as he looked again at Kandi. She met his gaze and smiled radiantly. With one hand, Netta lifted her cousin from where she sat and smiled at her reassuringly.

"Would you like to hold Shedissa?" she said softly.

Kandi nodded, eyes shining.

Less than a month later, Prince Calib of Drasmil announced to the world his intention of taking a wife.

Princess Kandina floated about the palace at Shirall in a cloud of happiness, all her teenage anger and angst a thing of the past. Even her disapproval of her mother's imminent joining was gone.

"Mother, I am so sorry I made you sad," she said in a private moment.

"You could never make me sad, Kandi."

"But I did. I objected to your plans, I fought you and I made you wait. I should have been happy for you."

"Oh, Kandi. Do you not know how important you are to me? Your happiness and security are so much more to me than my own future."

"But you waited for so long, I know that now. Why did you never tell me? You have been so alone for years, and you let me believe you were happy."

"We have to live with our fate, Kandi. My fate was to rule Shirall while the man I loved was king elsewhere."

"That makes me so sad for you, Mother. When you finally had the chance to go to him it was me that stopped you, and that makes me feel terrible. Now that I know what happiness you were giving up it makes me want to scream at the injustice of it. I would not blame you if you hated me for it."

"You are my daughter, Kandi, my one and only true love and best friend, and I would never hate you for needing me. Now we can both be happy."

* * *

Mist awoke with a start, a hand on her distended stomach. She stared at the ceiling. Sand sat up next to her, his concern evident.

"It's just a cramp, dear," said Mist. "Go back to sleep."

With an uncertain look, Sand sank back down and closed his eyes. When she was sure that he was asleep, Mist sent a cautious thought in Netta's direction, reaching out to where she slept with her husband and baby in the guest wing of the College. The Princess had been learning, with Leena's help, to communicate without the messy, time-consuming spell that had so long been used by the royal houses of Sharné.

'What is it, Mym?' she answered groggily.

'Shhh... I'd rather not disturb Sand.'

'Is it time?' she whispered.

'Soon. I'll sleep a bit more if I can. Could you start getting things ready?'

'Leave it to me.'

When the link was ended, Mist sank into a heavy doze. She woke with a little gasp some hours later.

"Are you sure you're alright?" said Sand.

"Yes, dear. Everything's under control."

"Should I do anything?"

"Netta's handling it. I just need to sleep, while I can."

He frowned.

"Don't worry, dear. Go back to sleep."

He did as he was told. But Mist slept little after that. As the dawn sent a rosy glow over the land, she sent a second call to the Princess. Then she struggled to a sitting position and woke Sand.

"You're not alright, are you?" he said in a tight voice.

"Just go and open the door, dear. Netta will be here shortly."

With a concerned glance, he left the room to unlock the outer door. When he came back, she was struggling to rise from the bed. He ordered her to lie down.

"Don't be silly," she replied. "Help me up."

"You should be resting."

"Don't argue, damn it!" she said roughly. He blinked in surprise. "I know what I'm doing," she finished.

"Alright," he said dubiously, and helped her to her feet.

With a little moan, she leant against him, breathing heavily. Then she pulled away.

"Help me walk."

"But..."

"Just do it."

Sand paced. He had been evicted from the bedroom when Netta had arrived with the midwife some six hours ago. His link with her mind told him some of what was going on, and he did not like it.

Atwin watched him from an armchair. Even as he paced, Sand's eyes never left the closed bedroom door. The groans had been bad enough, but now he heard the first of the screams, and it rent his heart. He raced to the door, ready to burst in, but Atwin was quicker.

"I would not go in there, my friend," he said, blocking the doorway. "They will only kick you out again."

Sand returned to his pacing, cursing under his breath. The second scream left him staring in horror at the closed door. As before, he sent a worried thought to her, but she ignored him. The third scream brought a groan from his own lips, and Mist sent an angry thought.

'Why don't you go and find something useful to do...'

Atwin laughed. "Come, my friend. There is only one way to get away from this."

Sand looked at him.

"You forget I have already been through this. You need a diversion."

The revealer and the Prince sat at a table in the smoky common room of an inn just outside the College. The innkeeper brought two large pitchers of ale.

Evelar grimaced. "You know I hate alcohol," he said.

"That is only because you have never tried to like it,"

Atwin replied.

"I don't want to."

Atwin laughed. "Do you want to stop hearing those screams in your head?"

Evelar looked at him. "I doubt a drink will help."

"Oh, believe me, it does. Trust me."

Evelar looked at the drink dubiously.

"Just try it. See what happens."

Another scream filled the revealer's mind. He grabbed the jug and took a long drink. He grimaced at the taste, but he felt the warmth of it. He downed the entire pitcher.

Atwin gave him a shocked look. "You are desperate," he said, taking a sip of his own drink. "Have another."

Less than an hour later, both were quite happily drunk. Evelar gazed about him feeling slightly dizzy, wondering at the fog that dulled the screams and made the world appear fuzzy.

"My friend," said the Prince, "You are under the alfluence of incohol!"

Evelar shook his head, bringing on a wave of dizziness. "I'm not as thunk as some drinkle peep I am!"

Atwin blinked. "Wha..."

Evelar smiled beatifically and put his head on the table. Within moments he was snoring. Atwin ordered another drink for himself.

Some time later, Atwin felt a strange sensation from the amulet at his neck. Naali was jumping about against his chest, as if in great excitement. Then, with a huge gasp, Evelar lifted his head from the table, fully awake and suddenly very sober. He rose explosively from his chair and ran headlong from the room.

Atwin stared after him in astonishment. Then he peered drunkenly down at the amulet. Naali was singing.

In the bedroom at the College, Netta laughed happily.

The next king had been chosen.

Sand entered the bedroom cautiously, his eyes going to the bed where Mist lay. She had been cleaned up and dressed, but she looked exhausted. She was awake and feeding the baby. Netta motioned for him to come in. Mist looked up at him and smiled. Sand sat on the edge of the bed and bent down to kiss her lingeringly. The child grumbled a little and Sand pulled away.

"Would you like to hold your son?" said Mist softly.

He nodded. She passed the child across, and the Awakener studied him in wonderment, a golden glow in his eyes.

"Thou art welcome, little prince," he murmured, so softly that only Miyam heard.

At the doorway, Atwin coughed.

"What are you going to call him?" said Netta then.

"Zaviar," they said together. Then they smiled at each other.

"A fitting name for a king," said Atwin.

Sand gazed at his son, who would be king. He raised his eyes to look at his wife. She lay peacefully, eyes closed, a smile on her sleeping face.

THE END

Rekindling Truth
Ella Mortimer

Evelar, known as Sand, is the Awakener. Legend says the Awakener will bring truth to the world, but what is that truth and what is he supposed to do with it?

As Sand begins his predestined task the minds of those around him seem to fill his head. But underneath it all is another voice, carrying the long dead memories of a forgotten past.

Where are these memories coming from and what do they have to do with the strange amulet that belonged to his sister, an amulet so like those warn by the King and queen of Shirall?

As Sand's new memories bring to light the ancient history of the people who settled this world, our friends must embark on a new quest, to find and neutralise the great spirit who nearly destroyed them all.

Sand is about to discover that the truth is more amazing than he ever dreamed.

APPENDIX

CHARACTER SKETCHES

MIYAM

EVELAR

NETTA

ATWIN

DELSI

ORDEL

AVERIL

LENENT

KANDINA

KANDINA

CALIB

KING GERARD